CW01020052

Operation Sage

Colin Youngman

The Works of Colin Youngman:

Operation Sage (Ryan Jarrod Book 5)

High Level (Ryan Jarrod Book 4)

The Lighthouse Keeper (Ryan Jarrod Book 3)

The Girl On The Quay (Ryan Jarrod Book 2)

The Angel Falls (Ryan Jarrod Book 1)

**

Standalone Novels:

The Doom Brae Witch

Alley Rat

DEAD Heat

**

Anthology:

Twists*

*Incorporates the novelettes:DEAD Lines, Brittle Justice, The Refugee and A Fall Before Pride (all available separately), plus a BONUS READ: Vicious Circle.

Colin Youngman

This is a work of fiction.

All characters and events are products of the author's imagination.

Whilst the majority of locations are real, some liberties have been taken with architectural design, precise geographic features, and timelines.

A Seaward Partners Publication

Copyright 2021 © Colin Youngman

All rights reserved.

No part of this publication, paperback or e-book, may be reproduced, stored in a retrieval system, or transmitted, in any form or in any means – by written, electronic, mechanical, photocopying, recording or otherwise – without prior written permission of the author.

ISBN -13: 979-8-49101-980-9

DEDICATION

To Christine

*And the good folk of the town of Blyth whose spirit and reputation
I have taken untold liberties with whilst producing this work of
fiction.
Thank you for your forgiveness and understanding.*

v

PART ONE

'There exists a psychological phenomenon in which perfectly sane people find themselves atop a high place and experience a strong desire to leap.
The condition is so common the French have a name for it:
'l'appel du vide' -
the call of the void.'

April Smith

CHAPTER ONE

Geordie Amos shook his head. Of all the things his befuddled brain had forgotten, why had it chosen to remember the village's name was Merrivale?

His memory had taken him to a warm August day in 1976. A family holiday in Great Yarmouth. He was fourteen years old at the time, and his parents had brought him to visit a model village. Its title was Merrivale.

They were happy days, and they were long-gone.

Forty-five years later, he looked downriver at the real world, the real city of Newcastle spread out far below him, and realised it looked as make-believe as Merrivale.

Geordie raised his arms to shoulder height and rested them on a latticework of wrought iron. He peered through the barrier. The Tyne flowed beneath him, each ripple of its brown-grey surface contracting then expanding. Its movement reminded him of an earthworm wriggling through the city.

A pigeon strutted its way along the parapet towards him. It watched him curiously, head to one side, before it swooped down towards the Quayside in a flurry of beating wings.

It was a journey Geordie Amos would soon take.

The fence was higher than he'd thought from ground level. For a moment, he wondered if he could manage it. He braced his shoulders, put all his weight on his wrists and forearms, and muscled himself up until he perched on top of the barrier.

The wind was strong up here. His long lank hair whipped against his face and the muscles in his cheeks rippled like a skydiver's. Which, ironically, he realised he was, in a way.

All it needed was the voice in his head to tell him it was time.

When the voice came, it happened so suddenly, without warning, he almost toppled over, there and then. If he had fallen at that moment, it would all be for nothing.

He took one last look down before he lowered himself off the ledge onto the safety of grey shale and gravel.

With a heavy sigh, Geordie Amos pulled his mobile from a pocket and made the call.

**

They wore light coats but, for an early afternoon in autumn, the day remained pleasingly mild. Mild enough for the two men to take their coffee at an outdoor table near the kerb.

Habit and superstition dictated they sat there. The last twice they'd taken up this position on matchday, the Toon avoided defeat. If this is what it took to make it three in a row, it was the least they could do. Heaven knows where they'd sit once winter struck. The pub next door, probably, if there wasn't a fourth wave by then.

The elder man pored over the racing form while the younger studied his sourdough croque monsieur with approval.

A flash of sunlight from an approaching van caused the young man to shield his eyes. The van circled the car park and crawled to a halt. Inside, two men argued. They gesticulated at a map. One threw up his hands, grabbed a package, and slid the van door open.

Seconds later, his voice came from behind the van. 'Excuse me, do you know where this is?'

The man at the table put down his newspaper. 'You talkin' to me?' he asked in a feigned Travis Bickle accent.

'Yes. Please, where is this?'

'Where's where?' He pulled back his chair, its steel legs screeching on the pavement.

'This address. Where is it?'

With a sigh, the man left his son at the table and walked to the van where the lost driver held up a parcel wrapped in brown paper and bound by string.

'Howay, man. Me eyes aren't that good. Let's see.' He took the package and looked at the address. 'Nee idea, pal. Sorry.'

'Do you think your friend will know?' The driver wore a Gregory Porter style peaked balaclava.

'How, son – put your scran down a sec, will you? Any idea where this is?'

The young man idled towards them, cheeks bulging like a hamster's as he chewed his meal. He paid no attention to a car which had pulled up behind them, engine ticking over.

He looked over his father's shoulder. 'Never heard of it. Are you sure it's addressed right?'

The answer came in the form of a gun barrel's cold steel pressed against the back of his head.

'Into the van. Now!'

'What the fuck…'

The passenger had donned a motorcycle helmet and joined the driver. He held a knife against the throat of the older man. 'Don't say a word.'

The van's rear door slid open to reveal a third man. He struck a sniper's pose and pointed a pistol at head height.

'Get in!' the first man repeated.

'What do you want? We've got nowt worth having,' the older man asserted.

'I'm not asking again. In!'

'I'll get in, but let my lad go. He's done nothing.' The man didn't move. He wasn't going inside the van; not until his son was safe.

'In now, or I kill one of you and take the other.'

The older man reached a decision. He gripped the doorframe and levered himself inside. The third man grabbed him and thrust him against the wall of the cab.

His son stood paralysed, mouth agape, until the man in the balaclava poked the gun barrel against his cerebellum.

He joined his father in the rear of the van as the helmeted kidnapper jumped into the back with them.

The driver floored the accelerator. The van mounted the kerb and sped forward; one half of the rear door still ajar.

The table and chairs the men had been sitting at crumpled under the wheels like a Pepsi can.

A waitress hurried out on hearing the commotion. Patrons gathered in the doorway to watch. A couple in their mid-sixties occupied another outdoor table. They saw the events unfold before them in confusion.

Their granddaughter sat at the same table, her back to the incident. She remained oblivious to it all - until the elderly man stood and instantly sat back down again, a changed man.

Changed by the black hole in the centre of his chest.

The woman screamed. The sound died in her throat as another shot reverberated around the square - and left a bloody circle in her forehead.

From the wound-down window of the car, a burst of semi-automatic gunfire floored the waitress and three customers stood in the doorway.

By the time the vehicle set off after the van, the only witness left alive was a shocked and gore-soaked young girl.

**

Detective Sergeant Ryan Jarrod sat with his feet on his desk and hands behind his head. Life was so-so – much better than it had been - and work was a piece of piss.

He'd come to realise that, really, there was only one difference between his old career as a DC and his new role as a DS. The difference was about ten grand a year.

Yes, theoretically, he had more decision-making responsibility, but DCI Stephen Danskin always encouraged and empowered his squad to make their own decisions anyway.

Yes, Ryan also had more supervisory powers but, by nature, he already tended to take charge of situations.

And, yes, the rank required him to train in a speciality. Choosing which speciality had been the hardest part of the job to date.

Finally, after reflecting on his career and the situations he'd found himself in, he settled on Hostage and Crisis Negotiation and felt both relieved and fortunate he'd never encountered a situation where he'd been required to practice what he'd learnt.

So, for all those reasons and more, Ryan felt he was stealing a living. Not that he was complaining, mind, even though his colleagues took the mick out of him remorselessly since his promotion. None more so than DC Todd Robson.

'How's it going, *sir*?' Todd asked.

'Canny, man. Less of the sir, though.'

'Okay. Sir.'

Ryan balled up a sheet of paper and flung it at Todd. The big man dipped his head into it and volleyed the ball across the bullpen as it fell to his feet. He raised one arm in a Shearer-esque celebration.

'Much on, Todd?'

'Nah. No majors, anyway. What about you?'

'Much the same. Only difference with us highflyers is we have even more paperwork. That's about the sum of it.'

'Wouldn't know about that. I've never flown more than six inches off the ground in my life.'

Ryan chuckled as Todd continued.

'There's another difference. You Sergeant's get to mix with the hoy-palloy.'

'Superintendent Maynard, you mean?'

'Aye. Her.'

'In fairness, Todd, we all see more of her. She's much more hands-on than Connor ever was.'

Todd slipped a coin into the coffee machine. 'And Wilkinson before him.'

'I never knew him.'

'He was like Connor, more admin and politician than copper. Except, Wilko was a bastard with it.'

'Sam's alright, though.'

'Sam, is it? Bloody hell. You're on first name terms with the Super, now. Ouch!' He swapped the plastic cup into his left hand and shook off the hot liquid which had overflowed onto his other hand.

'Okay then, Superintendent Maynard is good to work with. Is that better?'

'Even after what she did to you and Hannah?'

Ryan shrugged. 'Not her fault, really. It was Danskin who promised Hannah and me we could still work together - providing we both passed the sergeant's exam – while he was Acting Super. It wasn't Maynard's decision. Once she came in, looked at the budgets, she made the call. Just the way it is, I guess.'

Todd Robson took time to study Ryan while he slurped his drink. 'And you're okay with that?'

'Have to be.'

'How's Hannah finding her new job?'

'I don't think she was sure about it to begin with. She reckons it was a bit of a mess at first. There were so many different agencies involved, nobody knew who was in charge. Hannah soon sorted that out.'

'I bet she did.'

Ryan snickered. 'Yep, that's Hannah for you.'

'And what about you and her? Things going okay, are they?'

Ryan looked as if he'd never considered the question before. 'I reckon '*okay*' is just about the right word to describe it,' he said at length. 'Different, but okay. We're taking it slowly I suppose you'd say.'

Suddenly feeling uncomfortable, he changed the subject. 'Anyway, how come you've stuck at DC all this time?'

Todd's battered face distorted in a crooked smile. 'You said it yourself. Paperwork. It's not my scene.'

'Do you never feel stuck in a rut?'

'Oh aye, sometimes. But you never know what's around the corner, do you? One day, it's boring as hell like today, the next we're out hunting some sod like that Lighthouse Keeper bastard, or The Mayan bloke.'

Ryan rubbed his eyes. Neither case held fond memories for him. 'Is that the sort of thing which gets you out of bed each morning?'

Todd thought for a while. 'No. Me bladder does that, usually.'

Ryan tossed back his head and laughed. 'Thank God I'm not at that stage yet.'

'Make the most of it, kidda. The day will come, mark my words.'

'So, it's '*kidda*' now, not '*sir*'', he said, playing Todd at his own game.

'Sorry, sir.'

Ryan screwed up another page from his notebook. 'Get outta here before I give you a shitload of reports to write up.'

Todd gave a mock salute. 'Yes, sir.' He scurried away before the paper ball reached him.

Ryan opened a file and began to read through it when his desk phone rang.

'DS Jarrod.'

'Call for you,' switchboard said.

Ryan waited for it to connect. When he heard noises coming through the handset, he repeated his introduction as he continued reading the file.

'DS Ryan Jarrod.'

He couldn't make out the voice.

'You're breaking up. Could you say that again? Sounds like you're in a wind tunnel.'

Ryan slammed the file shut.

'Say again?'

He sat bolt upright. Grabbed a handful of hair and twisted it.

For the first time as a Detective Sergeant, he knew he was facing something new. Something for which he was, as yet, ill-equipped.

It was the most frequent scenario all Hostage and Crisis Negotiators face.

A Suicide Intervention; known colloquially by a different term.

'Sad people on bridges.'

CHAPTER TWO

Pottery Lane ran behind the Forth Street City and County Police HQ. From there, it was a five-minute walk to reach the first truss of the King Edward Railway Bridge, but a fifteen-minute climb up rough and irregularly distanced foot holes chiselled into its blackened granite surface.

At the top, Ryan squeezed through a gap already cut in a chain-link wire fence and scrambled down towards the track on his backside, using his heels as rudder and brake.

Out on the bridge, the weather wasn't as calm as on the streets below. A gusty breeze swept Ryan's strawberry blond hair across to one side as he made his way towards Geordie Amos.

Amos was exactly where he said he would be. As he walked towards him, Ryan tried to look confident yet not overbearing, calm but not indifferent. Inside, his stomach churned more than a cement mixer.

Ryan's feet disappeared into a layer of gravel with each step he took. He walked like a toddler on a pebbled beach, which was as far removed as possible from the image he wanted to project.

Amos sat on the bridge facing westward, his back to the drop. Even from this distance, Ryan noticed the man's knuckles were white; his feet entwined in the cast iron latticework railing as if he feared he'd fall.

A good sign, Ryan thought. Also, most committed jumpers made for the Tyne Bridge. To his knowledge, no-one had thrown themselves from this bridge. Another good sign.

But it wasn't all good news. The King Edward Railway Bridge, the second most westerly of the bridges spanning the Tyne between Newcastle and Gateshead, was described as

Britain's last great railway bridge, and that's what it was: a railway bridge. Inaccessible by road and footpath, for Geordie Amos to make it here required planning and forethought.

Amos wasn't here on a whim.

Ryan remembered his training. All three sessions of it, to date. *Keep him calm.* He fiddled with the radio on his belt. Switched it off. He didn't want any interruptions.

Take your time. Ryan slowed his pace. Made sure the suicide risk saw his approach, slow and gentle.

And most important of all: *Take stock of the situation and your surroundings.*

The Tyne streamed forty metres below. Traffic flowed across bridges either side of them, and along the Newcastle quayside below. Yet, the only noise came from Ryan's feet crunching over the gravel, and a strengthening breeze which he feared would push Amos off the ledge before he had time to engage.

The bridge was wider than Ryan had thought, but the presence of four double railway tracks meant he had limited space in which to work. He cast a glance upwards. The overhead wiring gantries remained silent.

Ryan had pre-warned the Transport Police and was relieved to see they'd shut down the electrification. It was bad enough dealing with a man intent on jumping to his death without the added possibility that he'd climb upwards and fry himself.

Ryan waited until he was the length of a cricket pitch from Amos before he spoke.

'Are you warm enough up here?'

What a bloody stupid thing to say, he thought. Still, it was a neutral enough way to start a conversation.

Amos stared straight ahead. 'You came,' he said.

'Of course, I did. I'm worried about you.'

The man turned his head towards Jarrod. The man's eyes were empty and lifeless. There and then, Ryan feared whatever he said or did would be futile.

'And you came by yourself, yeah?'

'That's what you asked, so – yeah. You can trust me, you see.'

Ryan edged a little closer. Slowly, deliberately, he closed the gap between them to fifteen metres before holding his ground.

'I bet you think you can talk me down, don't you?'

'I'm not going to do anything but talk. Whether you come down or not has to be your decision.'

The wind whipped a strand of lanky hair into Geordie's mouth. He pulled it out with a grimy finger. 'But you think if I jump, I'll be making the wrong decision.'

Ryan squinted into the sun. 'I don't know enough about you. Tell me, and then I'll let you know what I think.'

The man shivered.

'See,' Ryan continued, 'You are cold. Have you got a coat in your bag?' He motioned towards a rucksack on the railway track next to the man.

Geordie barked a laugh. 'You really think I'm shivering 'cos I'm cold?' He shook his head. 'You've never done this sort of thing before, have you?'

'Of course,' Ryan lied. 'You aren't the only one with problems, you know. Even me: I've had my moments, I can tell you.'

Geordie Amos stared at Ryan with his empty eyes. 'You ain't seen nuthin' yet.'

'Look, I'm not going to come any closer, but why not come down off the ledge there? Just in case summat happens.'

The barking laugh again. 'Like falling off, you mean?'

'Well, yes.' Ryan struggled to pull something out from both his front pockets. 'Want a drink?' He held a bottle of spring water in each hand.

Geordie shook his head and wiped greasy hair away from his face.

'I'll just put it on the ground close to you. Look, I'll roll it, see? I'm not coming any nearer.'

The bottled curved a gentle arc through the shale and came to rest against the inner track.

'No, ta.'

'Okay. I'll just leave it there. We might be here a while. We've all night, if that's what it takes to get you down.' He saw the look on Amos's face. 'For your family's sake, that is. Like I say, everything else is your choice but, please, think of your family. You've got family, haven't you?'

'Aye. Not as many as I once had, but I've got a daughter and grandson. Maddi and Lance.'

'There you go, then. Think of them.' Ryan shifted his weight and the gravel crunched underfoot like virgin snow. There'd be no sneaking up to Geordie Amos.

'I am thinking of them. That's why I'm here.'

The comment threw Ryan. He unscrewed his water bottle and took a slug as he gave himself thinking time. He decided to change tack.

'Celtic, is it?' Ryan nodded towards the green and white scarf tied loosely around the man's neck.

Geordie glanced down. 'Nah. It's the Spartans, this. I'm Blyth through-and-through.'

'Bloody hell. Now I know why you're up here,' Ryan quipped.

'I've followed 'em ever since their cup run in '78. I was little more than a bairn back then. They were this close to the Quarters.' He released his grip on the rail and held thumb and index finger an inch apart.

The wind caught him, and he swayed. Grit and masonry tumbled through the air like acrobats, down to the dark waters below.

'Fuckin' hell.' Geordie swore as he grabbed the rail again, pallor whiter than before.

He doesn't want to do it, Ryan thought. *He's scared shitless, and he doesn't want to do it.* Encouraged, Ryan let the conversation flow. 'The good times will roll again, man. There'll be other cup runs. Just think if they got there again and you weren't around to see it.'

Geordie raised his face to the sunshine. Released a sigh. 'Whatever happens, I'm not going to see it. Not unless it happens this year.'

'Why's that?'

Amos risked another release and tapped a finger against his temple. 'Tumour. In here.'

So that's why we're here. It certainly helps explain things. 'They can operate, man.'

'Nah. It's terminal.'

Bollocks. 'Slow it down, then, at least. Give you more time, with your lass and grandson.'

Geordie cackled. 'Why'd I want it slowed down? If you were told you were going to die slowly, painfully, probably go blind; deaf an' all – would you ask to slow it down?'

Ryan began to wish he'd chosen Commercial Fraud as his specialism. 'Think of your Maddi and your grandson, then, if not yourself.'

'I am thinking of them, bonny lad.' He spat out a mouthful of hair. 'Them more than me. That's why I've got to go.'

'I don't think you want to, Geordie. Not really. I saw the way you panicked when you had that little wobble before. You also asked for help by the very fact you rang the station. You don't want to do it, do you?'

Geordie's head sagged towards the gravel and the tracks. 'I can't win this one.' He raised his eyes to meet Ryan's. 'I'm just sorry it had to be you.'

'Hey, if it wasn't me, it'd be someone else…'

'No. It had to be you.'

'I'm not following.'

'They told me it had to be you.'

'Who did?'

'The voices.'

Jeez. Geordie Amos doesn't need a Crisis Negotiator. He needs a shrink. I'm way out of my depth, here.

'Why don't you come down off there and tell me about it? We can go for a pint, grab a coffee, or even just have a swig from your bottle of water. It's still there. It hasn't moved, and I haven't come any closer.'

Amos shook his head like a carrion crow ripping apart roadkill. 'Can't do that. I'm sorry. I really can't.'

'You can, man. Listen, I can get you all sorts of help. Specialist surgeons, the works. Just, please, let me help you.'

Tears formed in Geordie's eyes. 'Why do you have to be so nice? Why couldn't you be an arrogant twat?'

'Thanks for the compliment, bud, but I'm serious. You never know what modern science can do. Look at the vaccine. Who'd have thought we'd ever get that developed and rolled out so quickly?'

'It's too late.'

'It's not…'

'It is. They know everything there is to know about you. That's why they chose you. Whatever happens now, it's too late. For both of us.'

Something stirred inside Ryan's stomach. 'What the hell are you talking about, Geordie?'

'The fucking voices, man. I swear I don't know who they are, but they've got them.'

'Got who?'

Geordie levelled his gaze at Ryan. Stared at him with eyes which, for the first time, showed life. Life, and something else. Compassion.

'They've got your dad and your brother, that's who.'

CHAPTER THREE

Ryan felt like he'd taken a kick to the nuts.

He breathed heavily until he'd composed himself sufficiently to ask, 'Who's got them? Why?'

Geordie Amos touched his ear then wrapped his hand back around the guard rail. 'I haven't the foggiest who they are, but they've got them. You're going to have to do a few things to get them back.'

Ryan gave his head a wobble. Hoped the movement would wake him from his nightmare. It didn't.

'I've got some instructions for you. No, orders; that's what they are. If you do what they tell you, your dad and brother will be fine.'

Ryan's mouth opened and closed, but no voice emerged. He had no words. His feet shuffled backwards. A heel hit the railway line and he landed in the gravel. Still his feet worked, shuffling his arse backwards through the stones, away from the man on the bridge.

He looked up at Geordie Amos, the sun silhouetting him as if he were a dark angel, and realised the man was talking to him again, but all Ryan heard was the singing of his pulse.

'No. This is nonsense. You're wrong.' Ryan's voice broke as he spoke.

'I'm sorry, son. It's not nonsense. It's hard to believe, I know. Trust me, I know. If you're not sure, make a couple of calls. Check it out. But careful what you say. The voices say you can't let anyone know, and you mustn't send anyone else up here. It's just you. You, and me.'

'If you're taking the piss, you won't need to jump. I'll push you off this sodding bridge myself.'

Calmly, evenly, Geordie said, 'That's the last thing you should do.'

He scratched his ear again. 'Go on – check it out. Not a word of what we've talked about, though. They'll know if you do.'

Geordie stared along the river. 'They always know everything.'

Ryan turned his back on Amos and crossed the tracks to the far side of the bridge. He lay his head against cold, blackened metal. Tried to clear the fog which enshrouded his brain.

He pulled his phone from his jacket. Called up James Jarrod's number. Put the phone to his ear. It rang and rang. Eventually, he heard his brother's voice.

Ryan stumbled back in relief, lightheaded with a lack of oxygen. He gulped down a lungful of air as his brother said, 'This is Jam Jar. I'm sorry I can't take your call right now…'

'Oh fuck. Fuck, fuck, fuck. Fuck.'

He rang his father's number. The call didn't connect. The phone was dead. Which is exactly how Ryan felt.

As he moved the phone from his ear, he glimpsed the time displayed on the screen.

14.55.

A dim light flickered amidst his brain fog. The time meant something. What? Think, man, think.

Ryan turned his head and, as soon as he saw it high above the city, realisation thundered into him like an Intercity 125.

Five-to-three on a Saturday afternoon meant only one thing. James and Norman Jarrod would be in their seats at the Cathedral on the Hill, St James' Park.

Local Hero would be belting from the PA system. James wouldn't hear his phone ring through the cacophony of noise as the teams emerged from the tunnel. Norman Jarrod, who had permanently 'borrowed' Ryan's season ticket, never took his phone to the match.

They were alive, and safe!

Geordie-sodding-Amos was talking bollocks. He was delusional, that's what it was. The tumour had addled his brain.

Triumphantly, Ryan turned to face Geordie, his face wreathed in smiles. The smile faded when he saw Geordie's tears.

'They didn't answer, did they?'

'No. But they're okay, Geordie. They're at the match. They're fine, and you will be, too, once we get you back to your family.'

Geordie stared ahead. His eyes narrowed, as if they were trying to see around the curve of the Tyne at Ouseburn and onwards to Wallsend, Shields, and the North Sea beyond.

'You sure they're okay, boy? Did they tell you that? I sure as hell didn't catch much conversation.'

'No, but…'

'Then you know fuck all.' Amos spat out the words. 'They've got them, sure as eggs are eggs. The voices are never wrong.' Geordie's demeanour had changed. He seemed agitated, angry. Then, his tone softened. In a whisper barely audible above the wind, he said, 'They can't be wrong.'

'I think they are wrong.' Ryan didn't know who he was trying to convince. 'Your voices aren't real, Geordie. It's the cancer. That's why we've got to get you seen to.'

Geordie didn't say anything. His mouth worked silently, but he didn't speak. Occasionally, his head dipped as if he was agreeing with someone. Finally, he raised his head to meet Ryan's eyes.

'Check with the station. See if it's been reported. You'll know for sure, that way. Use your phone, not the radio. Put it on speaker. Let me hear.'

Ryan obliged. 'Control from Charlie Two.' He licked his lips, his mouth and throat dry. He took a sip from the water bottle.

'Go ahead, Charlie Two.'

'I know this sounds weird, but have we any reports of an abduction occurring anywhere in the city? Within the last ninety minutes or so?' He looked at Geordie who nodded. 'Yeah, timescale confirmed. Check last couple of hours, to be sure.'

'Negative on abduction.'

Ryan closed his eyes. 'Thank you. That's all.'

'Charlie Two, are you away from the suicide risk?'

'No. I'm still here.'

'When you're done, check back in. We have a major ongoing incident, and the Super wants all available hands on deck.'

A queasiness filled Ryan's stomach. 'What sort of incident, Control?'

'A drive-by shooting.'

'Jesus. Up the West End somewhere?'

Control hesitated. 'Negative. It's somewhere called the Clavering Centre, in Whickham village.'

The phone slipped from Ryan's grasp as he slumped to the ground.

**

DCI Stephen Danskin stood outside the Co-Op looking across the square towards the Fellsider pub. Between the two buildings, a shield of pop-up screens, incident vans, SoC vehicles and forensic tents hid the incident scene from a gaggle of rubberneckers.

'You're trying to tell me, in broad daylight on a Saturday lunchtime, no-one saw a hit?' Danskin didn't try to hide the incredulity in his voice.

'That's about the size of it, sir,' DC Gavin O'Hara confirmed.

'There's a bloody supermarket one side and a pub the other. There's got to be somebody.'

'Just her.'

O'Hara tilted his head in the direction of a girl, about eleven or twelve years old, sitting in the rear of a marked car. A female family liaison officer sat alongside the girl, holding her hand. The girl stared straight ahead, locked in her own world.

'Who's she?'

'Michelle Eddison. She was at another table outside the coffee shop with her grandparents when it happened. Seems she was sitting with her back to the incident when it started. All we've got out of her so far is that she wants to go home.'

Danskin vibrated his lips. 'Okay. Let her go. We can chat with her when she calms down. Doesn't look like we'll get much from her for a while. She should be with her parents.'

'It's not that simple. She's holidaying with her grandparents. Her folks live in Chepstow.' O'Hara looked at the girl in the car. 'Her grandparents were among the victims.'

'Bugger.'

'Social Services say they'll care for her 'til her folks get here.'

Danskin massaged his forehead. 'Has Lyall not got owt for us?'

'He's with the pub landlord now. He's checked with the café proprietor. The only ones who saw anything are that lot.'

Gavin pointed towards four chalked outlines at the café's entrance, and two more on a bloodstained patio.

Numbered markers had been set out on the pavement around them, a posse of white-suited forensic officer knelt by each marker, and a photographer took shots.

'Fat lot of good they'll be to us now, poor bastards,' Danskin said grimly.

He shielded his eyes from the sun as he looked between the three units which made up the Clavering Centre. 'CCTV?'

'Only inside, sir.'

'What? All of 'em?'

'Aye.'

'Bloody typical.'

'You ought to know, sir, the Super's on her way.'

'I wouldn't expect owt else. She's on the ball, as always.'

Stephen Danskin turned full circle, looking out across Fellside Road, along Oakfield Road, and back to the Clavering Centre.

'We could do with some intel on the victims. See if they're known to us.'

'They're not, sir. Ravi Sangar's already run the checks. All clean.'

'Aye, officially, mebbe. That's not to say there's not a wrong 'un amongst them. We need some local insight.'

'Where will we get that from, sir?'

'From DS Jarrod, that's who. This is his territory.'

**

From his position on the sharp gravel of the railway crossing, Ryan mumbled into the ground.

'What do I have to do?'

'Whatever you're told.' Geordie Amos still sat on the bridge rail. He'd swung one leg outside, the other dangled trackside. He scratched at his ear. 'And don't come any closer. I've all you've got if you want your family back.'

'You're not going to jump, are you? You never were. This is all to get me out here.'

'No. No, you have to think better than that or you'll lose the game…'

Ryan shot to his feet. 'Game? This is no fucking game!'

'Okay. But stay where you are, or I'll go over. I promise, I will. I haven't lied to you.'

Ryan tugged at his hair. 'Why me?'

'Like I say, they have their reasons. Just like they had their reasons for sending me up here to get you.'

'What reasons, man? We're going around in circles.'

Geordie Amos remained silent astride the bridge as if he were riding a pony.

'Geordie – tell me what you know.'

'I can't.'

'Who chose us?'

Geordie shook his head.

'They're not here. They won't know what you tell me.'

'Of course they're here! They're fucking everywhere, man. They know everything.'

'How?'

Geordie let out a moan so protracted Ryan's blood curdled. 'Don't even try second-guessing them. All you have to do is play by their rules. Do that, and your dad and brother will be safe.'

'You don't know that.'

Geordie tossed his head. Hair flared out like a solar storm. 'True, but I'll know soon enough. If you do what they say, so will you. If you don't, you set off a shitstorm and you never see your family again.'

He met Ryan's eyes and Jarrod saw a steely determination in them. 'Now, are you ready to hear your instructions?'

Ryan drained the last dregs from his water bottle. 'Tell me.'

Geordie took a moment to gather himself. He stared at the ground. Toyed with the green and white scarf around his throat.

'There's a lorry on a ferry on its way from Amsterdam. It'll dock at the Port of Tyne as soon as the tide's right.'

'And?'

'It's got to get through customs.'

'How the hell am I going to do that? They've picked the wrong bloke. I've got no jurisdiction over customs, man.'

Geordie Amos raised his head from the gravel. He gazed downriver, where the ferry port lay hidden around a sweeping S-bend.

'True,' Amos said. 'You haven't.'
He turned his head until he locked eyes with Ryan.
'But your girlfriend does.'

CHAPTER FOUR

Hannah Graves stood, hands on hips, looking out the glass-fronted watchtower towards the derelict dry docks on the Tyne's south bank.

The brown-field site opposite her, off South Shields' West Holborn, was a desolate wasteland populated by a solitary odd-shaped building which stood alone against a backdrop lifted from a Mad Max set.

Sod's Law instructed the lowering sun to catch the building's octagonal roof and direct spears of light into Hannah's eyes. She slipped on a pair of mirrored shades and continued to study the debris desert. She wasn't looking at anything in particular. Not really. She was taking stock of her first two months in the job, that's all.

When Superintendent Sam Maynard first 'encouraged' her to assume responsibility for establishing spans of control at the Port of Tyne Authority, Hannah knew it wasn't a long-term assignment. Get in there, sort it out, and move on. Or, preferably, move back. That was her plan.

If only it were that simple.

On her arrival, Hannah recognised stewardship of the port was a hotch-botch amalgam of several separate bodies working against, rather than with, each other.

The Borders Agency led on ferry passenger immigration whilst an HMRC presence watched over import and export transits. Site security was hived off to a private security company, and a uniform police presence offered lip-service support to all.

The trouble was, each authority worked in its own chimney. Left hand and right hand were disassociated. The place was a shambles with several roles being duplicated and gaping holes left in others. It was an arrangement easily exploited by any OCG worth its salt.

By the end of her first week, she'd met with the Higher Executive Officer from the Border Agency and the Senior Executive of HMRC. Both were full of puffed-up self-importance, but neither keen to assume responsibility for anything outside of their own job description.

'Jobsworths,' Hannah told them to their face. Shelly Mason from the Borders Agency threw her toys out the pram whilst HMRCs Dave Needham didn't give a toss.

The upshot was, after much huffing and puffing, Hannah Graves successfully won the portfolio to head up cross-agency activity – on the proviso she agreed not to interfere directly.

Hannah wasn't entirely sure how she won the battle, but she assumed the fact that two of the four PCs under her direct control were firearms officers and bore arms with the swagger of Rambo clones may have held sway.

So, despite her Detective Sergeant rank being on a par or slightly below her Civil Servant counterparts, Hannah Graves became the big cheese at the Port of Tyne.

Unfortunately for her, Sam Maynard was so impressed with her efforts she'd asked Hannah to sort out a similar mess at the Port of Blyth. As she looked out over the waters of the Tyne, Hannah knew her secondment to the ports would be longer than planned or desired.

She checked her watch, realised she had time for a break before the next dock, and headed for the coffee shop.

Amelia Curry, port intelligence officer for HMRC, was being harangued by the staff boor. Hannah rolled her eyes and Amelia gave her a wry smile in return as Hannah joined them.

'Len was just telling me about…,' Amelia began.

'Yeah. I fitted her with Street Glo lights, neon pink and lime. They're on her underbelly, so they are.'

Hannah smirked, her dimple winking at Amelia. 'Lennie, I recognise all of those words but none of the sentence.'

'I decked her out like she was in Fast and Furious. My Toyota Camry. She's not one of those hybrid crap things, either.'

'Oh, you're talking about your *CAR*. I see, now. I thought it was some devilish practice you'd been up to with your girlfriend.' Hannah paused. 'If you have a girlfriend, of course.'

Amelia choked on a laugh.

Len didn't notice the implied insult. 'Ask your boyfriend. He'll know all about it.'

'I doubt it. Ryan's not a petrolhead.'

'He's not into cars? What's the attraction, then?'

'He doesn't refer to a lump of metal by gender, for starters.'

'I take it he drives, though.'

'Yeah. He's just upgraded. Took years of persuasion.'

'Now you're talking, girl. See, he is into cars. I knew it. What's he got?'

Hannah paused for dramatic effect. 'A red one.'

Amelia choked again as Len shook his head. 'What kind, you daft tart?'

Hannah fixed him with a steely gaze. 'What did you call me?'

'Sorry. I keep forgetting your position. You're canny, that's why.'

'I might be canny, and I might be young, but I'm in charge. Never forget it. Okay?'

'Okay,' Len said, humbled.

'Anyway, to answer your question; he's got a Peugeot. A 107.'

Len's jaw dropped. 'And you say he *UP*graded? Bloody hell.'

'Now, Leonard – before you say anything else, remember what I just said.'

'In that case, I'd better disappear quick. Can't trust myself to be civil after that. I'll be seeing you, ladies.'

He left the remains of his drink and walked off, muttering contempt for her choice of boy and his toy.

'What a creep,' Amelia said once he was out of earshot.

Hannah held her cup against the side of her face. 'But he fancies you, for sure.'

Amelia flashed an engagement ring, still sparkling new under the strip lighting. 'I'm spoken for, remember.'

'Not sure our Len's got the nous to take any notice.'

'My parents wouldn't approve of him, that's for sure. It's hard enough getting them to talk to my Andrew and he's the sweetest bloke in the world.'

'They'll come round.'

'I doubt it.'

Hannah scolded herself. She remembered something Amelia had told her. 'Is your sister's lad still giving her grief?'

Amelia nodded. 'Aye. I think my folks see every bloke like Bryn.' A sadness settled on the young girl's face. 'He never allows her out the house. The only place Dawn can go is Asda, and then she has to show him the receipts. She won't even take any of our calls.'

'Amelia, that's domestic abuse. I can send someone round…'

'No! No, you mustn't. Dawn would blame me. She can't see what he's doing to her, but she'd see what I'd done if you interfered. I'd never set eyes on her again.'

Hannah took the girl's hand. 'Amelia, look at me. She never sees you as it stands, anyway.'

'I know, but as long as I don't upset her, there's hope. And Bryn got me this job. I suppose I should be grateful for that.'

Hannah checked her watch. 'Speaking of which, I have my job to do. Listen: if you need me, or the police in general, we're all here for you.'

Amelia nodded.

'Remember, won't you?'

She nodded again.

'Right. I'm off. Take care.'

'I will. Thanks, Hannah.'

The phone rang in Hannah's pocket. She pulled it out. Glanced at the caller ID. Twisted her face.

'Everything okay?' Amelia asked.

Hannah thought before answering.

'I'm not sure.'

**

Ryan shouted to make sure his voice carried above the blustery wind. 'What makes you think Hannah can wave the lorry through? She's not customs.'

'The voices know what she is. They know what you are. They know it all. She runs the show down there, are they right or wrong?'

Ryan dug his heels into the groundworks, bracing himself against the wind and his panic. 'It's impossible, man.'

'No, son; it's not. It's easy-peasy. And that's good; good for the voices and for your family.'

'You don't know her, Geordie. And they, whoever *they* are, can't know her, either. Nobody tells Hannah Graves what to do. I can't just ring her out of the blue and tell her to let this-and-that through. She's stubborn as a mule.'

'Then you've got to be cleverer and even more stubborn. Call her. I don't care how you do it, just get the lorry through. No mention of me, them, or your family. They'll know if you do.'

Ryan stood on the bridge, bereft of ideas. To him, it was a bridge between sanity and madness, and he fast approached the wrong end.

'Look, son, all I have to do is persuade you to convince your girlfriend to let the lorry through. Then, I can get out of your life – everybody's life – forever.'

Geordie watched Ryan chew on the corner of his lip. He saw him give a slight nod.

'That's the fella,' Amos said, breathing in heavily. 'Call her. She'll have an inventory for the *Sea Duchess*. On it, she'll find a lorry belonging to a company called *Tulpen Uit Amsterdam*. It's got to get through customs without being stopped.'

'I'm not buying into this. Tulips From Amsterdam, my arse. What's it really carrying?'

'I don't know, and I don't care. It's best you don't, either.

Now, make the call, make it from where you are, and make it authoritative but cagey as hell.'

Ryan's brain spun like the hair around Geordie Amos's head. 'If the lorry's already flagged for a search, it'll be searched. End of.'

'She has to find a way, or it'll be the *'end of'* your dad and brother.'

Ryan sat cross-legged in the middle of the southbound track, phone in hand.

'Let's find out how much she trusts you,' Geordie said.

He had his fingers crossed. They both did.

**

'Everything okay, Ry?' He never called her at work. Ever.

'We've got incoming intelligence linked to the port.'

Hannah left the coffee bar and nudged open a door marked 'PRIVATE' with her elbow and pushed it shut with the sole of her foot. She stood on a steel platform overlooking the port. 'Well, Hi, Hannah, how are you?' she said sarcastically, miffed at his down-to-business approach.

'You've a ferry due to dock.'

'That's what happens in a port.'

'Look, listen, will you? This is important.'

She rolled her eyes. 'Okay, Ryan. What you got?' She heard him sigh. Or was it the whistle of the wind?

'I haven't got all the answers. In fact, I haven't got any, so don't ask questions.'

'What you talkin' 'bout, Willis?'

'There's a waggon on board the *Sea Duchess*. I need you to make sure it gets through without a check. There's nothing unusual about it so I doubt it will be, but I need you to be sure.'

Hannah sucked in air. 'This is my port, Ry. Customs stop what they want, and I support them in that.'

'I know, but I'm not leaving you out the loop or holding back on you here, this is live intelligence. All I know is, it must be important.'

'No. There's more to this. What aren't you telling me?'

'Jesus Christ, Hannah,' he hissed, 'Trust me, you don't have the resources to do anything about this. If you try to stop the lorry, you'll need more than the cavalry coming over the hill.'

Hannah turned her head to the left. The wind caught in her curls like tats in a brush. She looked in the direction of the North Sea. Somewhere, just out of sight, the *Sea Duchess* was preparing to enter the mouth of the Tyne. May already be sailing by the Collingwood Monument, for all she knew. Hannah had a decision to make.

'I need to know what this is about. I can't interfere in Customs business.'

'Yes, you can. You have to. Like you said, this is your port.'

'I have to work with these guys.'

There was a long silence. She was about to ask if he was still there when his voice came once again, calm, measured and all the more menacing for it.

'If you try to stop this truck, there'll be no guys left for you to work with.'

Hannah massaged her brow. 'This sounds all wrong to me.'

'I understand that, Hannah. I'd probably think it sounded fishy if I was in your shoes as well but remember what it's like at this end. Sometimes, we get half a story and have to react. The intel on this operation comes from way above our paygrade. It's top level, believe me.'

She sucked in salty air. 'Fine. If I do this, I've got to move now. Text me the details.' She ended the call.

Hannah leant across the steel rail. A dozen people emerged onto the harbour side below. Some already wore Hi-Vis jackets, those that didn't carried them. They made their way to their pre-ordained stations.

'A dozen people doth not a SWAT team make,' she said to herself.

She dashed inside. Hurried to the office. Amelia was back at her workstation.

'Amelia, is there a stop and search list for the *Sea Duchess*?' Hannah asked.

The girl stopped polishing her engagement ring. 'Isn't there always?'

'Print it off for me.'

'Why?'

'Just print it, will you?' She softened her tone. 'Sorry. I'd like to see if we can save ourselves a bit of work, that's all.'

The paper was already unfurling from the printer by the time Hannah reached it. She removed the sheet from the tray as it appeared and started scanning its contents as the printer's mechanical clicks indicated a second page followed.

Even by post-Brexit standards, the *Sea Duchess* carried a light load. Less than half the maximum-permitted cargo was on board, and the ferry bore hardly any passengers thanks to Covid travel restrictions on the Dutch side. Hannah couldn't decide whether this was a good or bad omen.

The randomly-generated stop list identified eight trucks for full stop-and-search procedure, equating to 10% of the total HGV cargo. Hannah checked each one against the details on Ryan's text.

She breathed her relief. It wasn't spring again. There were no tulips from Amsterdam.

Hannah retrieved the second page from the printer. This contained a list of manual mark-ups; those not produced by a computer algorithm but based on intuition – sometimes intel, sometimes suspicion, sometimes a lucky dip. These vehicles would be spared a full customs search. Instead, there'd be a cursory weigh-check and a run through the X-Ray scanner.

The page contained only two entries: a car transporter - and a wagon owned by *Tulpen Uit Amsterdam*.

'Hell.'

CHAPTER FIVE

Geordie Amos scowled at Ryan. 'You said too much.'

'What? I told her nowt.'

'You told her enough to make her curious. For the sake of your dad and brother, I hope she isn't too curious. She might do the opposite of what you want.'

'There was no other way of doing it. I had to make it sound official.'

Geordie glanced at his wristwatch. 'I reckon in half an hour we'll know just how trustworthy your girlfriend is.'

Half an hour, Ryan noted. He had half an hour to sort out the mess he was in. Which meant Geordie Amos didn't intend throwing himself off the bridge. At least, not yet he didn't.

'What happens after half an hour? The lorry goes on its merry way, and whoever's got Dad and James just lets them go?'

Geordie looked skywards. 'That's about the size of it. You do what they ask, they let 'em go. They don't want any shit hanging around them.'

'Ha!' Ryan's barked laugh made Amos sway atop the bridge barrier. 'You heard what Control said. They shot a load of innocent people at Whickham. That sounds pretty shitty to me.'

The man shook his head. 'You still don't get it, do you? That's so you know they mean business. If you don't do what they ask,' Geordie released a hand from the rail and dragged a finger across his throat, 'It's goodnight Vienna.'

'And you expect me to believe they'll release their only assets as soon as the lorry gets out of the docks? If they're as bright as you make out, they'll know I could call in the troops and stop the lorry - and its load - five miles down the road.'

'Man, you learn nowt, do you? First off, the voices will already know if you're intent on doing that. They know it all, remember. Secondly, if you do, they'll find your dad and your brother again, not to mention your girlfriend and your Uncle Tom Cobbly, and you won't like what they do to them.'

It was Ryan's turn to check his watch. He forcibly dragged his imagination away from dockside activity and familial mutilations. 'This is big, isn't it? This isn't just your run-of-the-mill dodgy cigarettes or booze. It's got to be people trafficking, drugs – something really big. This lorry has to get through.'

There was a sadness in Geordie's voice when he said, 'For your sake, yeah; it does have to get through.'

**

'Amelia, did you manually trigger a check on a load of imported flowers?' Hannah tried to make her question sound casual.

'Aye, that was me.'

'Did it come from specific intel or just your random choice?'

'Neither, really. There's no intel as such but nor did I pick it randomly. You see, there's normally a convoy of two or three lorries from that company. They come through together. It just seemed a bit unusual for one to transit by itself so, if I must justify my keep, I thought I'd tick that one. I chose the car transporter because…'

Hannah cut short the Intel Admin's explanation. 'Not much to go off.'

'True, but…'

'Like I said, it's a Saturday, it's quiet, and I want to save your customs guys a bit of work. I think we can cross it off the list. Just for today.' She saw Amelia frown. 'It's a good spot, though,' Hannah continued. 'Normally, I'd go along with your call but, like I say…'

'Yeah – easy day. That's fine. I don't mind.'

'It's agreed, then. We take it off the list.'

'It's a bit late.' Amelia gestured towards the dockside activity. 'It's already on the manifest.'

Buggeration.

Hannah nipped the bridge of her nose. 'Never mind. I've a headache coming on. I could do with fresh air. I'm just popping outside, and I'll have a word with the lads while I'm out there. Get them to call off the hounds.'

'Your call, boss.' Amelia gave Hannah a wink and a salute as Hannah pushed open the door and the pungent scent of the Tyne invaded the office.

Hannah scuttled down the exterior metal staircase towards the dock. At the first landing, two navy-blue uniformed police officers gazed downwards as the *Sea Duchess* approached harbour-side. PCs Micky Hopper and John Jeffries wore their firearms uniform with pride, although neither had used their weapons in anger.

Hopper turned at the sound of footsteps clanging on the staircase. 'Ma'am,' he greeted her.

'Hi lads. What's up?'

'Suspicious,' Jeffries said.

'Why's that?' *Do they know something I don't,* she wondered?

''Cos that's what we're paid for,' John Jeffries smiled a gap-toothed smile. 'I wouldn't have one of these if I wasn't suspicious of everything.' He tapped his belted gun.

'Good man.' She hoped she hadn't sounded defensive.

'What you up to, Hannah?' Jeffries asked. Hopper was the formal one, all *Ma'am* and *DS Graves*, while Jeffries didn't give a toss what he said.

'I'm just on my way to change the stop list for the *Sea Duchess.'*

41

The ferry was pulling into dock, the waters churned into a maelstrom as her gigantic twin props fired into reverse. Another ten minutes to complete the docking procedure, a further ten to fifteen to exchange paperwork and, within thirty minutes, the ferry's towering doors – the Linkspan – would lower to form a bridge for her cargo to exit.

'Change the stop list? Now I really am suspicious,' Jeffries said. 'I might just ask one of our uniform guys to make a couple of routine traffic stops.'

Is he joking? Or could my sub-ordinates really know more than me?

'Feel free, John. I'm sure your pals will be delighted to haul themselves away from the match commentary.'

'Oh hell, aye. I forgot about that. Any idea what the score is?' Jeffries saw Hannah's look. 'Aye. That was one of me stupid questions, wasn't it?'

'Just a bit. Now, excuse me, lads. I need to get on.' She brushed between them and took the stairs two at a time.

When she was out of earshot, Jeffries said, 'Lorna's on duty today. She won't give two-hoots about the match. I think I might give her a shout.'

'Howay man, John. The boss'll go ape-shit if she finds out.'

Jeffries studied Hannah as she hurried between customs officers, giving them their revised instructions.

'True. But I meant what I said. She's got me suspicious. There's summat off here.'

**

The occupants of the van huddled together in each other's arms. Outside, they heard indecipherable voices and the footsteps of the men who'd taken them.

There has a heavy thud against the door. The door handle rattled. They watched the door open, inch by inch. Light filtered in; the beginnings of twilight but light all the same. They were surprised. They'd expected it to be dark.

The light faded as three figures filled the van's opening. Hooded, dressed in black, and with guns or blades in hand,

42

they clambered inside. Stooping against the confines of the van's roof, they made towards them.

The men pulled rough hessian sacks over their prisoners' heads and dragged them from the van. Muffled protests came from beneath the sacks, and behind the gaffer tape gags across the couple's mouths.

The couple were pushed across rough ground and sensed themselves pulled inside a building and up a staircase.

It was old. Hazardous. The elder of the couple guessed the building was unoccupied. It didn't feel like a house, didn't smell like a house. It felt derelict.

They hauled them around a corner. Something sharp snagged on the clothing of the young male. Rough hands pushed him upwards once more. He stumbled on a stair. Put a hand down to steady himself, only for his captor to haul him upwards.

They heard a door open. A foot kicked the younger of the couple to a concrete floor, while the elder was forcibly pushed deep into the room.

When one of their captors spoke, the couple both jumped at the sound.

'Listen to me and listen well. If you do what I say, you'll be fine. Do you understand?'

A hessian sack lifted and fell as one head nodded, the other mumbled what could have been a 'Yes' behind their gag.

'Good. Now, this is what's going to happen. Two of us are going to leave you now. I shall remain with you. You are going to count very slowly to one thousand. Do you want to try?'

The elder made sounds. 'Mmm, te, thrmm', it sounded like.

'Too quick!' He kicked the speaker, who cowered away. 'Try again.'

This time, the noises came much slower.

'That's better.'

The younger of the couple heard the echo of footsteps disappearing from earshot.

'Now,' the man was saying, 'You may have heard my friends leave. Trust me, you won't hear me leave. I can very, very quiet when I want to be. But, at some point between one and a thousand, I will go. It might be at ten, it might be at nine-hundred-and-ninety-nine. You won't know when.'

The man strode to the elder prisoner. 'I have a gun,' he pushed the barrel firmly against the head under the sack. 'You feel it, don't you?'

The head gave a nod.

'Good. Now, tell your son so he knows, too.'

'Mmm mm,' the voice mumbled.

'Excellent. You're learning. When I say 'now', you start counting, nice and slowly. Count out loud so I can here you. When you reach one thousand, you can take off your masks. You can remove your gag then, too. Somewhere in the room, I'll leave a phone. When you've finished counting, and you've found the phone, you can call for help. Understand?'

Two hoods waggled.

'Remember, if you remove your hoods before you reach a thousand, and I'm still here, I'll blow your fucking heads off. Now, start counting.'

The guttural countdown began.

The gunman counted twenty grunts then, silent as his word, he snuck away.

**

Ryan prowled back and forth, the shale of the King Edward Bridge crunching beneath his feet. 'It's been nearly forty minutes. Something's wrong.'

'Cool your jets, man. These things take time. Half an hour was a guess on my part.'

Ryan found the man's tone edgy, lacking conviction. Geordie repeatedly glanced in the direction of the Port of Tyne, even though there was nothing to see. From his position astride the bridge parapet, Geordie lay his hands against the outside of his trouser pocket. He tossed aside his hair and looked eastward once more.

Ryan bit his lip. 'They'd better be okay.'

'What do you intend doing about it? There's nowt you can do. You've just got to sit it out.'

Ryan felt his anger flare. He was about to direct it at Geordie Amos when he saw the man jerk upright. Geordie hung onto the barrier with one hand and fumbled in his pocket with the other.

Ryan noticed the man's hand tremble as he brought both hand and phone out of his pocket. Geordie stared at the vibrating object in his hand. Finally, he inhaled a lungful of air and said, 'Yeah?'

Ryan watched, at first puzzled, then concerned, then – as realisation dawned – frantic. He sank to one knee as he searched Geordie's face for clues.

Geordie just listened. Didn't say a word. Finally, he gave the briefest of nods, said 'Goodbye', and looked to the heavens.

Tears flowed from his eyes.

Oh, please God, no, Ryan thought.

At the same time as Geordie's tears flowed, his face creased into a broad smile. A grin, even. Yet still the man cried.

'Are they alright? For God's sake, Geordie. Are they alright?'

Geordie looked at Ryan as if he'd only just arrived at the scene.

'Aye, lad. They're fine.'

Ryan dropped onto his other knee. Lowered his head. His shoulders heaved as he sobbed his relief.

'Listen, lad,' Geordie's voice seemed to be coming from afar. Ryan raised his eyes to meet Amos's. 'See my backpack there?' he motioned to the bag on the tracks beneath him. 'There's some things you'll need.'

Ryan's brow wrinkled. 'I've got everything I need already, now dad and James are safe. I don't need nowt more.'

'You do.'

'Not once I've got you down from here, there's not.'

Geordie shook his head. 'I already told you. I'm not coming down from here. For me, it's over. All of it.'

Ryan found it hard to concentrate on the job in hand. All he wanted was to hug his dad and brother. 'Look,' he said, 'I've got two people back. I'm not going to lose the third. Come on, Geordie. Don't be a dick. Think of your daughter. Think of your grandson.'

Geordie's tears ran free once more. 'I'm sorry, son.'

'No! Don't!'

'The rucksack. When I'm gone, use it. You'll get yours back as well if you do as they say.'

'What d'ya mean?'

'I think you know what I mean.'

Ryan did.

'Oh fuck. Oh fuck. It's not Dad and James that's okay, is it? It's your daughter and grandkid they've let go.'

'Aye, it is. They took mine, an' all. Why else would I bring you up here?'

'They made you do it. They told you the same thing. That's how you knew I'd get Dad and James back.'

'You're smart. That's good. Keep it that way and you'll get yours back, too.'

'But I've done what they asked. You promised if I got the lorry through, they'd be fine.'

Geordie shrugged. 'And they will be fine, once they're finished with you. I'm sorry, but I guess they must want something else from you first.'

Amos tipped his head skywards. Felt the last rays of the sun kiss his face. Let the wind caress his hair. With closed eyes and a look of serenity etched on his previously haggard face, Geordie spoke.

'Son, tell Maddi I love her.'

With that, he tumbled backwards like a scuba diver.

Ryan sprang forward. His knee cracked against the rail track; he dislodged a tooth as his chin hit the bridge's stonework and his arms reached over the barrier.

His hand grabbed thin air.

With neither scream, howl, nor splash, Geordie Amos was gone.

CHAPTER SIX

Ryan lay face down. Sharp, fume-blackened shale dug into his ribs. He spat blood from where he'd chipped a tooth. He rolled onto his back, chest heaving.

Slowly, Ryan's eyes opened. He stared up at a sky hued with a myriad of red, pink, purple and indigo shades. It should have been beautiful. Instead, it was hellish.

He propped his back against the barrier and looked at the cracked face of his wristwatch. It had turned five. Amos had promised him they'd be free in thirty minutes. That was almost two hours ago and, since then, Geordie had disappeared into the void – dragging Ryan's spirit down with him.

It wasn't only Ryan's spirit he'd taken. Hope seeped from him like sweat from a pore. Faith? He'd never had one. As for charity, whoever held Norman and James Jarrod weren't the charitable type.

Maybe he'd have felt differently if he hadn't been alone, but alone he was. Never more alone. And overwhelmingly bereft. He put a hand to his forehead and forced his eyes away from the sky.

The first thing they settled on was the rucksack of Geordie Amos. The dead man's words came to Ryan as if he still stood alongside him.

'There's some things you'll need.'

Still on hands and knees, he crawled towards the backpack. The stones shredded already skinned and bruised knees, but he felt no pain other than that in his soul.

The bag was an old Slazenger one, the type that once had a plasticky wet-look to it. Now, the surface was scarred and pock-marked with age. Ryan tugged at the zipper of an outside pocket and fished around.

When he removed his hand, he clutched half a dozen silver strips holding painkillers of all descriptions. Paracetamol, codeine, aspirin. *'To dull the tumour pain,'* Ryan assumed.

His hand reached into Geordie's backpack again. Out came a small white paper bag. *Lloyds Pharmacy*, it said.

Ryan peered inside. It held a plastic tub containing strong corticosteroid tablets, a pack of unidentifiable material, and a prescription.

Ryan's fingers fiddled with the script. The wind caught the paper and tugged it from his hand. Ryan grasped at it. Once, twice. He caught it at the third attempt. In the top left-hand corner, he found what he was looking for.

The man's address:
Mr George A Amos
Lynn Street
Blyth.

The final item Ryan found in the pocket was a single house key attached to a photographic key ring. It held a sun-faded image of a teenager and a baby.

Ryan turned it over. Beneath the transparent plastic case imprinted with the words *'A Gift From Bridlington 2012'*, lay a printed sticker.
'I love you Daddy.
Maddi - and Lance Little-Legs
XX'

Whatever it was that Geordie Amos thought Ryan needed, it wasn't here.

He turned his attention to the main compartment. The zip fastener caught on its casing and refused to move more than an inch.

Ryan wriggled it back and forth and, finally, pulled the zipper off completely. He tore at the backpack's fabric and ripped the bag wide open.

'What the…?'

He tugged at a long white wire. At the end of it hung a radio transmitter and tiny microphone, taped to the '*On*' position.

Ryan unearthed a green first-aid box at the bottom of Geordie's bag. He flicked open the lid. It held a spongy earpiece and, more intriguingly, a cheap Alcatel pay-as-you-go phone.

Beneath these items lay a sheet of card, face-up. It bore two words.

Ryan Jarrod.

His pulse whistled in his ears as he flipped the card over.

Your assistance is required. Keep the phone on at all times. If you switch it off, your family get switched off. Keep the wire safe. You'll need it when you're told you need it. No-one knows your family are missing. It must stay that way. This is between you and me now. No-one else. Just you and me.

His phone rang.

He jumped like a Jack-in-the-box. 'Crap!'

He juggled the phone. His fingers fumbled with the unfamiliar keypad. Then, he realised it wasn't *the* phone. Not the burner.

It was *his* phone.

Ryan withdrew his Smartphone and took a moment to calm himself.

'Jarrod.'

'Charlie Two?'

'*Thank fuck,*' he thought. 'Control, this is Charlie Two.'

'Your radio is off. Immediate update needed on the suicide risk.'

He'd forgotten all about the radio. He'd also forgotten to call in Geordie's fate.

'Just about to report, Control. Mission failed. We need divers to retrieve a body. Male. A George Amos. Went in the water under King Edward Bridge.' He looked at the tidal flow. 'Probably find him west of point of entry.'

'Charlie Two, DCI Danskin requests urgent assistance on the Whickham shooting. When can I give him an ETA?'

'Fuck Danskin! I've just had a jumper, here. I'm due a mandatory R&R period, then I've a report to compile.'

He looked at the equipment in Geordie Amos's backpack. 'Besides, there's a few loose ends I need to tie up here.'

'Roger, Charlie Two. I'll pass the message on.'

Control disconnected.

Ryan's head spun, not from the dizzying height but from the unremitting tension. More than anything, he wanted to help Stephen Danskin on the Whickham case because he knew the secret to his family's disappearance must hide there. He just couldn't trust himself to remain silent.

If Danskin uncovered anything, so be it. If it led to the release of Norman and James Jarrod, abso-bloody-lutely great.

But, if not, Ryan wasn't going to jeopardise the lives of his family. He couldn't risk involvement.

For once in his life, he wanted nothing to do with Whickham.

**

Photographs of the deceased were pinned on a crime board in the third-floor bullpen by the time Stephen Danskin rallied his troops.

DI Lyall Parker stood alongside Danskin, with Nigel Trebilcock and Todd Robson facing the board. Gavin O'Hara explained the routine to the latest team member. Lucy Dexter, a bright young thing recruited from uniform on the recommendation of DS Ryan Jarrod after her assistance on a recent case, studied the pictures of the corpses with wide-eyed intensity.

'The gunmen hit Alfie and Janet Rogers first. They were sat at an outside table with their granddaughter, Michelle Eddison,' Danskin recapped. 'The Rogers are regular churchgoers. Members of the Immaculate Heart of Mary

Church at Lobley Hill. They appear to be a good, charitable couple so there's no obvious motive for their deaths.'

'What about the lassie? More particularly, her parents?'

Stephen Danskin thought for a moment. 'That's a good point, Lyall. O'Hara – check for info on the Eddisons. If there's nothing on file, liaise with the Chepstow crew.'

'On it, sir.'

DCI Danskin tapped the board. 'The next victim was a waitress, Jodie Callender. A local lass. Quiet, by all accounts. Started at the café to fund her studies then decided to waitress full-time when she flunked her exams. Again, there's no obvious motive.'

Todd Robson threw his two-penn'orth into the mix. 'You said she took up waitressing to fund her academic studies. Did she have money troubles? Debts, perhaps?'

Danskin dismissed the contribution. 'Doubt it. This is all a bit heavy-handed, even for a loan-shark. Besides, they'd never get their money back once she was dead, would they?'

Superintendent Maynard left her office and joined the team, observing and noting the team dynamics. Danskin nodded an acknowledgement to her before continuing.

'The remaining victims were customers who came to the doorway to see what the ruckus was about.' He pointed at their photographs, one-by-one. 'They were a Don Taylor, Warren Pearson, and Andy Lee.'

'What do we know about them?' Robson asked.

'All clean. That's why we could do with DS Jarrod's input. He lives locally. He might know the folk they mix with, give us more avenues to explore.'

'Waste of time,' Todd said.

'What makes you say that?'

'It's obvious, man. If the intended target was one of those three, how could the shooter know he'd just happen to appear in the doorway at exactly the right time?'

Danskin's face sagged. 'Bugger me. For once in your life, you've made a valid point, Robson.'

Silence hung over the group. Sam Maynard fanned her face with a thin folder held in her hands. Lyall Parker pulled at his lower lip. Nigel Trebilcock stared at the board as if the pieces of a puzzle would fall into place on their own. Finally, someone spoke.

'Can I say something, sir?' Lucy asked.

Danskin nodded. 'Please do.'

'What if this has nothing to do with any of them?'

'Some random blokes shoot a bunch of random strangers outside a random café, you mean? It's hardly likely - but go on; what are you thinking?'

'What if it was a distraction to cover up something else? I don't know what, but let's suppose summat else was happening at the same time; something less obvious? You said there was no CCTV footage. No-one would have noticed anything else going on, not with a drive-by hit on their doorstep. Everyone's focus would be on that.'

Danskin raised his eyebrows. 'Something to consider, I suppose.' His gaze drifted to the view of the Tyne through the bullpen window, as it often did when deep in thought. 'But this happened in a quiet village. Whickham's not known as being full of gangsta-types.'

'Neither were Dunblane or Hungerford, sir.'

Sam Maynard lowered her head and smirked at Lucy's riposte.

'Hardly identical cases, Dexter,' the DCI blustered, 'But you make a fair point, all the same.'

Maynard moved away as her phone vibrated. She answered the call on route to her office. The Super's piercing blue eyes scanned the cover of the folder she clutched. Maynard frowned, gave a quick look back at the crime board, and nudged shut her office door with a hip.

Lyall Parker asked Danskin if the family support officer had gleaned any further information from the only surviving witness, Michelle Eddison.

'Nah. Dead end so far. The poor girl's still in shock. There's some hope she'll open up once her parents arrive but who knows - it could have the opposite effect. We'll just have to bide our time.'

'Anything on traffic cams?'

'That's the thing, Lyall. Ravi says he's found bugger all. We haven't a clue where the hit team went. Wherever it was, it wasn't through the village centre, that's for sure.'

'And I guess there's nay way we'll ever find oot,' the Scotsman mused.

'If anyone knows a route to avoid the cameras, Ryan Jarrod's the man.' Danskin turned towards the window again, studying the monolithic bridges spanning the great river.

'Where the hell's Jarrod got to, anyway?'

CHAPTER SEVEN

Ryan Jarrod was in a dark place.

As he followed a blue line on the floor of the gloomy corridor, the only sound was the echo of his footsteps. Automatic sensors triggered lights above his head, one-by-one. When one lit, the previous one dimmed. It was almost as if he had a spotlight trained on him.

The first set of doors swung inward with a sucking noise as Ryan approached. The stark white lighting inside contrasted with the corridor's darkness, and the hairs on Ryan's forearms stood erect as a blast of chilled air hit him.

Inside, a second set of doors awaited. These weren't automated and were protected with metal plates a third of the way up, the metal scarred and pitted by the impact of thousands of trolleys banging against them over the years. This time, it was the smell he noticed; a suffocating, alcohol-like, almost pickled, odour. It reminded Ryan of his old school science lab.

He took a sharp intake of breath and parted a curtain of heavy plastic strips.

Row upon row of filing cabinets faced him. Except, these cabinets didn't contain archived paperwork. They contained archived human beings. Human beings such as Geordie Amos.

Apart from being dead, Amos had been lucky. When Ryan informed control of his suicide, a police launch was little more than two miles upriver investigating a suspected arson attempt at Dunston staithes. It meant the body of George Amos was located, retrieved, and transported to the Royal

Victoria Infirmary's morgue for toe-tagging all within an hour.

Ryan looked at a whiteboard affixed to the wall. He scanned through dozens of names until he spotted *G A Amos: C 21*, and today's date. Alongside the whiteboard hung a blueprint of the morgue layout. C21 was located at the furthest point from the morgue entrance.

By the time he reached Amos's resting place, the realisation of what he was about to do dawned on him. Ryan had no authority to be there, but he also knew he had no choice. Not if he wanted to see his father and brother again in any place other than where he now stood.

Ryan listened for a moment. He heard nothing but the white noise of a refrigeration unit. He slid out the metal drawer which held Geordie's remains and waited for the fragile, twin metal legs to unfold to the ground to support the weight.

He stared down at the body bag before slowly unzipping it from top to bottom. He peeled it away to reveal a second bag, thin and tight enough for him to make out the frame of Geordie Amos.

Ryan screwed his eyes tight, at war with his conscience. He already knew which side would win the battle. He reached out and prepared to unmask George Amos.

'I hear congratulations are in order.'

Ryan's feet left the floor. He grabbed at his chest. 'Jesus!'

'Only Jesus? Whatever happened to Mary, Joseph, and the wee donkey?'

'Elliot, man. Jesus Christ. I nearly shit mesel there.'

Dr Aaron Elliot, chief Forensic Medical Examiner to the City and County Police Force, laughed. 'I saw you'd signed in,' he said. 'Just thought I'd pop by to say well done. The promotion, I mean. Proper Sherlock now, aren't we?'

Ryan rested his back against the morgue units, breathing heavily. Colour gradually returned to Jarrod's face.

'Thanks doc, but there's a time and a place for everything. I nearly needed one of these slabs for myself, there.'

'Feeling a bit jumpy today, are we?'

'It's this place, man. Creeps the hell out of me.'

'I forget you're still quite new to it all. The dead can't hurt you. But they can tell you much. Now, what brings you to my second home?'

Ryan spluttered. He shouldn't be there, but he had to make his presence sound routine.

Amos's body bag lay between him and Elliot. 'This chap's just been brought in. We need to look into his death.'

'Of course, of course.' Elliot flicked aside his long hair. 'What happened to him?'

'Suicide.'

'Really? Why get involved in a suicide?'

'Well, err, dot the I's and cross the t's, you know. Make sure there's no loose ends.'

'I haven't had the pleasure of meeting this one yet. How did he do it?'

'He jumped. From the King Edward Railway bridge.'

'Ouch,' Elliot winced. 'Nasty.'

'Aye. He'll have drowned, I guess.'

'No, no, no. I very much doubt it.'

'How come?'

Dr Elliot paused as he always did before explaining things in layman's terms. 'I suppose you should know if you intend taking a peek at your friend. He won't be pretty under there, that's for sure.'

Ryan groaned. 'Howay, then: do your worst.'

'You see, when he hit the water, your friend's body would have gone from around seventy mph to nearly zero in a nanosecond. The fact he hit water is immaterial at that speed. It would be no different to hitting solid concrete.'

Ryan grimaced.

'The rules of physics and inertia mean his internal organs will have kept going when the rest of him ground to a halt. They'll have torn loose on impact. Imagine driving into a brick wall at sixty without a seat belt. That's pretty much the same thing.'

'Bloody hell.'

Elliot snickered. 'An apt description, Sherlock. Without even examining our friend, I'd bet a small fortune I'll find a lacerated aorta, liver, and spleen. He'll have broken ribs which will have penetrated heart or lungs, or both. We'll find broken sternum, clavicles, and pelvis. He may have a broken neck and almost certainly multiple skull fractures.'

While Elliot spoke, Ryan's face morphed from white, to grey, to green. 'He didn't drown, then,' he whispered.

'Almost certainly not. It's always possible, of course, but highly unlikely. He'll have dried frothy mucus beneath his nose if he has. Assuming he still has a nose.' He looked at Amos's outline beneath the shroud. 'It looks as if he still has one. Should I check for you?' He reached towards the inner bag.

'No! No…just NO. Okay?'

'I'll take that as a *'no'*, should I?'

They stood in silence, both staring down at the body bag. Eventually, Aaron Elliot spoke.

'Well, I've a list longer than the Nile to get through today. I doubt I'll get to your buddy until I'm somewhere north of Cairo, so I'll leave you to it. I just wanted to say congratulations. You deserve it, Sherlock; you really do.'

Ryan gave a wan smile. 'Thanks, Aaron. I appreciate it.'

As Elliot turned to leave, Ryan thought of something.

'From what you've said, I take it we wouldn't be able to tell if he was deaf?'

'Visually? No, of course not. You can't tell if someone's deaf just by looking at them.'

'You can if they wear a hearing aid.'

'Well, yes but…'

'If this fella had a hearing aid, would it have remained intact?'

The FME thought for a moment. 'It's very, very unlikely. It'll almost certainly have been ripped out even before he hit the water, never mind on impact. And the chances are, if it hadn't become detached during the fall, it'll have been driven inside his skull when he hit the water.'

Ryan's mouth formed a grim line. 'Okay. Thanks.'

'You're welcome. Now, if you're okay, I'll leave you to it.'

'I'm okay,' Ryan said.

He wasn't okay. He was from it.

**

An orderly pointed the man in roughly the right direction.

At the end of the corridor, he looked left, then right, and finally at a direction indicator hanging from the ceiling.

He took the right fork.

The man quickened his pace and almost collided with a female volunteer as she pushed a tea trolley through a swing door. The two exchanged words. The woman pointed an arm straight down the corridor and then indicated left with her hand before twisting her wrist downwards.

The man mouthed 'Thank you' and hurried on.

At the foot of a staircase, a nurse clutched a wad of files to her bosom. The man asked for directions. The nurse said something, and the man glanced at the red, grey, and blue stripes on the floor.

He followed them until the red line disappeared through a set of double doors and he was left with only grey and blue. He knew he was almost there.

The grey marker continued straight on while the blue led him down another two flights of stairs at the foot of which he found himself in a silent, darkened corridor.

It ended in a set of automatic doors only vaguely discernible in the distance as his movement triggered the low-lux ceiling lights.

**

Ryan swallowed hard. He hooked his fingers over the shroud and unmasked Geordie Amos.

'Hell's teeth.'

Amos's blank eyes stared out from waxy skin dappled with semi-formed bruising. His cranium was misshapen and bore clear signs of severe trauma. Blood matted Geordie's straggly hair.

Ryan noted the absence of foam beneath the man's nose. Elliot was right: Amos had died on impact, not by drowning.

Ryan tried to de-humanise the object on the trolley and focus instead on what he was looking for.

He gently moved aside the corpse's hair and looked inside the man's right ear. It was clear.

His hands drifted to the underside of Geordie's neck. The muscles had already stiffened, and Ryan found turning the head difficult. Instead, he bent over the body, careful not to breathe in the stench of death, and ran his fingers around the inside of the left ear.

Nothing.

He grabbed the man's neck again and put all his effort into turning the head. The sound it made curdled his stomach, but the head moved sufficiently for Ryan to inspect the ear more closely.

Barely visible, a piece of wire little broader than a hair protruded from the orifice. He nipped it between his fingers, working the wire back and forth until, eventually, a tiny rubber earpiece worked loose.

Ryan gave a taut smile of satisfaction. He'd been right.

Geordie Amos's clothing remained largely intact; his shirt pocket buttoned tight. Ryan patted it down. He felt an object. Small. Broken. Hard.

Ryan unbuttoned the pocket and slipped his fingers inside. Not much remained of the item but, when he withdrew his fingers, they held sufficient for him to identify the remnants of a microphone.

Someone, somewhere, had monitored every word of his conversation with George Amos. Whoever it was had probably fed Amos with information, told him what to say, like an Ant and Dec prank only with fatal consequences.

That's what Geordie had meant by 'The Voices.'

Ryan stuffed his trophies into a pocket, zipped up the body bag and put his hands on the morgue drawer's runners when the voice spoke.

**

'What the bloody hell do you think you're doing?'

Ryan recognised the voice immediately. With his back to the speaker, he hoped the man hadn't spotted the involuntary sag of his shoulders.

'It's something I had to do, sir,' Ryan said.

DCI Danskin watched him with the air of a man who'd been given a plain brown envelope by a stranger. 'So, why not just come out and say it instead of this *'I need my R&R break'* shite?'

'This is all part of my R&R. I built a rapport with him up there. I dunno, I felt I had to pay my respects to him.'

'I see,' Danskin said, wiping a hand across his lips. 'And these respects – it includes searching him, does it?'

'I wasn't searching him.'

'It looked like you were to me, Ryan.'

Ryan pinched his nose. 'How long have you been there?'

'Long enough.'

'Look, it's not what it seems.'

'Isn't it? Then, what is it?'

Ryan felt himself deflate. 'Have you ever been in this position, sir? I mean, responsible for someone's life?'

'Every day. That's what we do.'

'No. Not like this, we don't. Not solely responsible. And, if you haven't, you can't possibly understand how I feel. Even I don't understand; not fully.'

Danskin watched him carefully. 'Look, I really need your help. There's been a major incident in Whickham. You know the place and its people better than anyone. I want your input.'

'Not now, sir. It's too soon. I need time.' *Time to get my family back,* went unsaid.

'Don't you even want to know what's happened?'

'I already know…' Ryan realised his mistake. 'Control told me,' he clarified.

'Look, the Super's got it into her head this is linked to an OCG.'

'No, man. He just jumped, that's all.'

'What? Oh, not this poor bugger. I'm talking about the Whickham incident.'

Ryan sucked in air. 'I'm not ready, sir. I maybe need to talk to the counsellor first. Get this,' he waved a hand in the direction of Geordie's body bag, 'Out my system so I can concentrate properly. Then, if she thinks I'm okay for duty, I'll offer you all the backing you need.'

Danskin cocked his head slightly to one side. 'Sod the bloody counsellor,' he said.

'Sir, I have a right to access support.'

'I didn't say, *'Sod support'.* I said, *'Sod the counselling'.* Look, The Trent House isn't a kick in the arse away. How about I buy you a swift half and we have a chat?'

Ryan knew it was an order, not a question. He glanced at his watch.

'Sounds fine,' he said without enthusiasm.

CHAPTER EIGHT

The Trent House was a tiny, coffin-shaped establishment sat on a quiet corner sandwiched between the RVI hospital and St James' Park.

Its general patronage consisted of a handful of students - except on match days when it filled to the rafters with football fans enjoying their pre- or post-match pints.

By the time Ryan and the DCI entered, only half-a-dozen match-goers remained, the others having drifted downhill to drown their sorrows in the bars of the Haymarket.

Ryan and Danskin took a table out of earshot of the remaining customers. Ryan swigged on ale while the DCI took a sip of lemonade.

'So,' Danskin began, 'What gives?'

'In what sense?'

The DCI sighed. 'You know what sense, Ryan. Don't come the clever sod. It won't wash with me.'

Ryan snorted a bitter laugh through his nose. 'That your idea of counselling, is it?'

'Listen, we've got Major Crime chasing our arse over this drive-by hit and you're moping about over a self-obsessed nutcase.'

'He wasn't self-obsessed!'

The vitriol in Jarrod's voice took Danskin aback. 'Okay. I'm sorry.'

Danskin stared at Ryan. Noticed the absence of returned eye contact. He took a sip from his glass before continuing.

'I get that you're upset. I get that you may feel responsible, even though you aren't. I dare say it's plausible that you followed him to the morgue for closure...'

'It's more than plausible. It's the truth.'

Danskin locked fingers across his stomach. 'You were set on fire while still a Special, you've worked undercover on people-trafficking, you've been shot at on top of St Mary's Lighthouse, and you were working the same case as your predecessor when she was killed by the kid she was trying to arrest. You've done all those things and more yet here you are, a DS no less, ambulance-chasing a silly old codger and telling me you're traumatised as fuck.'

'I'm not…'

'What were you looking for?'

Ryan sat back. 'This is ridiculous.' He was thrashing around like a fish out of water and was just as sure Danskin knew it, even though the DCI said nothing.

'I came here to make my peace,' Ryan continued. 'I thought I could help him, but I couldn't. I felt this is the least I could do.'

'Ever thought you might have helped him, after all?'

'Come again?'

He can't know about Geordie's family, surely? If he does, he'll know about mine and we're buggered, Ryan thought.

'This is what he wanted all along, Ryan. It's why he was up there. It's why he jumped. He's where he wanted to be.'

Thank God: he doesn't know about his family. Either family.

'It's not what his family wanted.'

'Aye, that's true,' Danskin conceded.

They sat quietly for a while, ruminating on the meaning of life.

Ryan broke the silence. 'Y'know, perhaps in the long run, it is for the best. He had brain cancer you know. Terminal, he told me. He didn't want his daughter and grandkid to see him turn into a cabbage.'

'There you go, then. See, I'm right again. After all, who'd want to turn into Steve Bruce?'

Ryan laughed heartily, for a moment his family's peril forgotten. When Danskin saw the grim mask settle over

Ryan's features once more, the DCI asked if he was ready to go.

'I'm ready. But not to the station. I really do need time to myself. It's too late now for me to make a meaningful contribution to the drive-by, anyway. I'll be in first thing. I promise.'

First thing after I get my dad and wor kid back, he thought.

Stephen Danskin gave it a moment's consideration. 'You've got yourself a deal. You get yourself some rest, yeah?'

'I'm going straight home, sir.'

The DCI gave his protégé a warm smile. 'Aye, it's all right for some,' he said. 'I've got myself a long night. Super wants me, her, and Lyall on an all-nighter. I'd best be off.'

'Okay, sir. And thanks.'

Danskin stood and smoothed himself down. 'No bother, son.'

As he left, he turned back from the doorway and spoke again.

'Oh - when you feel like telling me what you're really up to, you know where to find me.'

**

Ryan drove slowly. He continued to the end of the street and performed an awkward three-point turn at the junction with Railway Terrace before parking up the red Peugeot in the shadow of Blyth Sports Centre.

He remained in the car, facing down the row of tiny, terraced houses. Lynn Street was a typical colliery row. Identical two-up two-downs with front doors which opened directly onto an arrow-straight street. Compact back yards rather than gardens, and street lighting barely fit for purpose.

Fortunately, he didn't need streetlights to pick out Geordie Amos's house. The flashing blue lights of the two squad cars parked outside were a bit of a giveaway.

He was so tightly wound he hadn't thought through his approach. He was grateful for the thinking time the police presence gave him, and disappointed when the dirty white front door opened, and two figures appeared.

The light from inside the house was sufficient for him to identify Billy Straker, one of DCI Rick Kinnear's team. He didn't recognise Straker's female colleague.

A uniformed officer slipped out of one car into the other and Straker and friend ducked into the back seat. It pulled off towards Renwick Road at the opposite end of the terrace and indicated left.

Ryan waited in his Peugeot for several minutes, watching. The small crowd of spectators who had gathered in their own doorways eventually slipped back inside.

Still Ryan waited. He had no way of knowing whether the crew who had taken Maddi and Lance were watching. He had to be sure. If they saw him, it would be curtains for his dad and brother.

He gave it another ten minutes, saw or heard no-one, and quietly stepped from the car. He pulled a hoodie over his head, thrust his hands deep in his pockets, and sauntered down Lynn Street as casually as he could.

Ryan hesitated at Geordie's door, glanced around, and knocked twice.

A curtain twitched. Ryan whipped down his hood, stood back, and held up his warrant card. When the curtain closed, he covered his head again.

'What do you want?', a female voice from inside said.

Hoarse, suspicious, even aggressive, Ryan noted.

He opened the letterbox so Maddi could hear him without raising his voice.

'I'm Detective Sergeant Ryan Jarrod,' was as far as he got before fingers snapped the letterbox shut, almost trapping his nose.

'I've just spoken to your lot, man. I'm done with you. All of you. I just want to be left alone, aal reet? So, fuck off and leave me in peace. I've told you already, I've nowt to say.'

'I was with your dad when he fell.'

There was no response which, Ryan assumed, was better than abuse.

'I was trying to talk him down. I'm sorry I couldn't do it. Really sorry. I'm here to try to comfort you, not question you.'

Silence.

He left it for a full minute until a group of chavs gathered outside a beauty salon at the junction of Lynn Street and Chancery Lane. He studied them. They looked more like kids than kidnappers, but he couldn't take the chance.

He risked the letterbox once more. 'I'm putting a card through the door. If, in the morning or any other time, you feel you need to talk, call me. Just so you know, the police have left a car outside. There's no-one in it, but it should be enough to stop anyone hassling you.'

Ryan waited one last time for a response. When none came, he knew there was no more he could do. Not until morning, anyway.

He shuffled back to his car and, this time, he did head home.

**

Stephen Danskin was as familiar with Superintendent Maynard's office as he was his own. After all, he'd occupied it for several months between Connor's resignation and Sam Maynard's arrival. Still, he remembered the courtesy knock before entering.

Maynard sat behind her desk. DI Parker occupied a chair opposite her, and Danskin took the vacant seat next to him.

'We've got a big problem, boys,' Maynard began. 'A problem I believe that's about to get bigger.'

'You really believe there's more to this shooting that meets the eye, don't you ma'am?'

'Yes, Lyall; I do.'

'What makes you think it's the work of an OCG?' Danskin asked.

Maynard fixed him with iceberg blue eyes which never seemed to blink. 'I have my reasons.'

'Which are?'

'I'll get to them in a moment. Have you made contact with DS Jarrod yet?'

'Aye, ma'am.'

'And?'

Danskin shifted in his seat. 'He's shaken up by the suicide intervention. Thinks he's to blame. He promises he'll be with us tomorrow.'

'Good. We could do with him on board if you say he's local to the victims.'

'I didn't want to force him in tonight.'

'That's the right call. He's entitled to trauma time.'

'So, the OCG?' Lyall asked. 'What's the score?'

Maynard ran her fingers through her hair and tossed her head. 'Hits like that aren't random. It's not something an individual would do.'

'Och, wi' respect, ma'am…'

Sam Maynard raised a palm. 'Hear me out, Lyall. You see, that's only one part of a bigger picture.'

'Are you going to join the dots for us, then?'

Maynard tapped an index finger against her lips. 'There's a number of things come together. We all know of the incident in Whickham. What you guys don't yet know is that I've had DCI Rick Kinnear look into another incident.'

'Another shooting? Never in the world.'

'No; not a shooting. A couple – a young woman and her son – had been held captive and threatened by an armed gang. The gang released them late afternoon. They don't know where they'd been held, but they were moved and released at a point South Shields-side of the river. Tyne Dock way.'

'Do we know who they are?'

Maynard looked at the details on her tablet. 'A Madeira Corrigan and her son, Lance.'

'So,' Danskin mused, 'We have a shooting and a couple held hostage. How are they linked? I mean, has someone put two-and-two together and made five, or do we have intel to indicate there's a connection?'

'Not exactly.' Sam Maynard pulled open her desk drawer. 'Listen, what I'm about to tell you is confidential until I get the nod from top brass. I've been in regular contact with the Met. Seems an OCG, a drug cartel, has sprung up, and it's spinning its web far and wide. All forces have been asked to be on covert alert.'

'Right.' Danskin ran a hand over the crown of his head. 'What links all this to our shooting and the Corrigan family?'

Maynard smiled. 'Call it feminine intuition.'

'With respect, again, ma'am, I think we need a wee more than that to go off.'

'One: the hit has the fingerprints of a drug gang assassination all over it, Lyall. Two: the couple were released right across the river from the Port of Tyne. Three: a ferry had just spewed its guts up minutes before the couple's release.'

Danskin raised an eyebrow. 'It's not out the question, I suppose. What's the woman and her bairn got to do with it all?'

'That, Stephen, is the million-dollar question. Rick's got a couple of his crew with them now but they've not been very forthcoming. Whether fear or shock, who knows?' Superintendent Maynard shrugged.

'So, anything else we need know?'

'Yes. Like I told you, this gang are rolling out all over the country. We've got the Merseybeat working on Op Kop...'

Danskin smiled ironically and shook his head.

'There's similar ops in Stoke-On-Trent, Bristol, and Glasgow as well as the Met and City of London's patches.'

She stretched a hand into the open drawer. Handed Danskin and Parker a folder each.

'These are for your eyes only, until we know for sure we're looking at the same thing.'

Danskin glanced at the file cover. Printed across it was a codename.

Operation Sage.

CHAPTER NINE

The sun peeked out from behind a mountainous grey cloud, decided it didn't like the look of the Earth today, and dove back under cover.

Ryan unlocked the front door to the house on Newfield Walk and immediately felt sick. It wasn't the fact he was inside the empty shell of Norman Jarrod's home; it was the smell inside it.

Ryan gagged. 'Shit.'

He was right. It was shit. Dogshit, to be precise.

Spud the pug yelped and whimpered and put his forepaws on Ryan's shins. The poor dog was starving, neglected, and let his feelings be known by peeing against Ryan's leg.

Ryan re-opened the door, and the pet he'd bestowed to his father and brother made a beeline for the gatepost where he cocked his leg again. Ryan, meanwhile, hunted the house for little presents Spud had hidden around the place.

He tipped dried dogfood into a bowl. Spud bounded in at the sound, snorting, eating, and still weeing all at the same time.

'For God's sake, Spud man,' Ryan said, searching for kitchen roll. He was angry at himself, not the dog. He should have known Spud had been left alone all day and night. Rather than toss and turn in his own bed in his own house, he should have seen to Spud last night.

Last night, though, he'd had more pressing things on his mind. Like, how to rescue Norman and James Jarrod.

Subconsciously, his hand went to the phone bestowed on him by Geordie Amos. He illuminated the screen. It remained eerily silent and unused. Waiting for a call to arms by an enemy unknown weighed heavily. Until it came, he had nothing to go on. Unless…

Suddenly, he had a plan. Hardly a route out, but an avenue of hope. First, he had to get to the Forth Street station, and he had to do it without the knowledge of his colleagues.

Three poo bags dangled from his fingers as he locked the door to his father's house.

'You smell nice,' Hannah Graves said as he turned.

'Eau du Crap.' He held the bags up towards her. She pulled away, face crumpling.

'Why's that your job? Can't Jam Jar do it?', she asked, referring to Ryan's brother by his nickname.

He looked at her askance.

'What did I say wrong?'

He paused. Played a dead bat. 'Nowt, man. Just one of the downsides to owning a pet.'

'Aye, but you don't own him anymore. It's not your job.'

Ryan sucked in air, nostrils twitching. 'I like to help out.'

'They're out early today, aren't they? I thought your dad couldn't get out his pit of a morning.'

'He messaged me,' Ryan lied. 'Got an appointment or summat. James has an interview, apparently.'

'On a Sunday?'

Ryan shrugged.

'I see,' Hannah said.

'You see what?'

'You answer your dad's messages but not mine.'

'Oh. That.'

'Yes, *That*.'

Ryan had ignored a couple of Hannah's calls last night. Couldn't face having to lie to her. He'd done that once yesterday and didn't want to do so again.

'It was a busy day. I was shagged out. Sorry.'

She fixed him with a stare. 'So you should be. Sorry, that is. Then, when you weren't at home this morning, I just wondered.'

'Wondered?'

'Where you were. Whether you were okay. You know – the sort of things normal boyfriends and girlfriends worry about.'

'We are normal boyfriend and girlfriend. At least, I think we are. We've had more than our ups and downs but...'

'You're being all weird.'

'How do you make that out?'

'Well, not answering your phone when I ring you, for starters. Then there was your call at work yesterday.'

Ryan rolled his eyes as his stomach knotted. 'We've been through that.' He saw Hannah open her mouth, so he continued, changing the subject. 'Anyway, it's not any of that. I attended a suicide yesterday. It wasn't pretty. I just wasn't in the right frame of mind to talk last night. Sorry.'

Hannah's face sagged with concern. 'God, how awful. Are you okay?'

'Not really, no,' Ryan said, keen to use Geordie Amos's demise as the justification for his taut manner.

'Listen, do you fancy breakfast? That's what I was ringing to ask last night. I know it's your day off, so I thought I'd call round instead. I guessed this is where you'd be when you weren't at home. I'm not on duty 'til late so we've all day to...'

'It's not my day off now. I'm needed.'

'When do you have to be in? You must have time for a cuppa if nowt else, surely? We could go to that cycling-themed café – I like it there.'

'Pedalling Squares? Nah, haven't got time.'

'Okay – what about somewhere closer? There's one along the road, isn't there?'

'No!'

73

'There is, man.'

'Sorry. I just mean I'm not going there. No way.'

Hannah doesn't know about the shooting outside the café. How's Maynard kept it quiet? Dad and James must be caught up in something big - really big - if Danskin's stepdaughter doesn't know about it, even though she's not part of his span of control.

'There must be somewhere we can go.'

'There is. There's plenty of places. There's not the time, that's all. I have to get to Forth Street.'

Hannah frowned, her mouth and jaw set. 'Fine.'

'Look, I'm sorry, Hannah. I'll make it up to you, I promise.'

'Don't bother.' Hannah marched towards her Renault parked close to the Glebe sports field.

'I'll call you,' he shouted after her.

'I'm sure you will. Like next time you want a work favour, for example.'

'Don't be like that, man.'

'We'll talk about this. Check your diary and let me know when you can spare me five minutes. After all, I'm only the woman who put her job on the line for you. I don't expect you to bump me up your priority list.'

Ryan watched her slam the car door shut and speed off with a squeal of tyres.

He turned and kicked the wall of his father's house. Hard. 'Fuck it!'

From behind the door, Spud's frenzied barks carried along Newfield Walk and onto the Glebe beyond.

**

Ryan took the stairs to the first floor of the Forth Street station. Not for him the camaraderie and banter of the third story bullpen Danskin's squad inhabited. Instead, he slipped into the research room and disappeared into one of a dozen cubicles.

The research room was an unassigned space utilised by officers of any rank or division whenever they needed absolute solitude. It offered a space to think through leads, weigh up evidence, formulate plans away from constant interruptions, and an area from which officers contacted informants without fear of eavesdroppers. Sometimes, it was used for the odd powernap or two.

A powernap was the last thing on Ryan's mind as he logged into the workstation. He had no choice but to use his own password and smartcard but, if anyone chose to run a check, he'd be long gone by then.

Once in, he booted up the Automatic Number Plate Recognition database, pinned a number of camera locations around the Port of Tyne, and input a timeframe of two hours after the docking of the *Sea Duchess*.

Ryan's fingers fidgeted nervously as he contemplated what other parameters to set. He settled on two final filters: Scania trucks and Dutch-registered vehicles.

He sipped from a coffee mug as he waited for the system to flag up the contenders. The two-minute wait for the results felt infinite.

Slowly, pixel-by-pixel, six grainy thumbnail images appeared. All bore the code number of the camera at the Port of Tyne exit.

As the six images snapped into focus, another five blurred images from a camera near the Royal Quays outlet fell onto the screen.

Again, as they morphed into recognisable pictures, another two from the Tyne Tunnel entrance cameras slid into view.

Finally, a single image from a camera adjacent to the northbound A19 flyover at Silverlink appeared on screen.

Ryan leant towards the screen.

Bingo!

A box-bodied truck bearing the *Tulpen Uit Amsterdam* logo was captured leaving the dock. It was one of the five also picked up at the Royal Quays a few minutes later.

Neither of the lorries heading south through the tunnel were of interest to him, but the one heading north on the A19, the one belonging to *Tulpen Uit Amsterdam*, was.

Ryan looked at the ceiling and pondered what he'd learnt. The suspect vehicle had been heading north. And that was about the sum total of it.

Somewhere, between Silverlink and John o' Groats, a waggon he'd help smuggle into the country was hiding with its contraband cargo.

Wherever it was, Ryan had to find it. When he did, he knew Norman or James Jarrod wouldn't be inside it, but he might just find the key.

When he looked back down from the ceiling, he was surprised to find three more images glowed from the screen: one from the Silverlink southbound camera, the others from the Royal Quays and the Port of Tyne entrance.

He dismissed them. The shots showed a curtain-sided lorry belonging to a company by the name of *Visscher Zuid-Holland*. It was, Ryan guessed, booked for the *Sea Duchess*'s return journey.

He scribbled a note and readied himself for a long day in front of the ANPR system scouring traffic cameras the length of Northumberland and Scotland for any sign of a Dutch flower lorry when he jumped back from the desk as if hit by lightning.

Ryan didn't know how he realised but realise he did. To be certain, he zoomed in on the number plates.

The registration plate of the curtain-sided truck was the same as that borne by the box-bodied *Tulpen Uit Amsterdam* vehicle.

In the space of ninety minutes, it had made its drop off, adopted a disguise, and was already back, probably abandoned, on some Dutch backroad.

Without the truck, Ryan was lost to the whims of the OCG gangmaster. Worse, so, indirectly, were his father and brother.

Ryan put his head in his hands and wept like a teething baby.

CHAPTER TEN

Stephen Danskin spread his length along the sofa, calves on the arm, feet hanging loose. A mug of coffee, silted and cold, sat on the flooring. A mournful, weeping guitar riff barely ruffled his rhythmic breathing.

The jarring tones of his phone did.

He reached down an arm, knocked over his coffee, and was grateful he'd chosen hardwood over shagpile.

'Danskin,' he said, without opening his eyes.

'Can I pop and see you, sir?'

'Who is this?' He took the phone from his ear and glanced at the caller ID. 'Ryan? Are you outside?'

'No, sir. I'm already in.'

Danskin sat up. Rubbed his eyes and swallowed down a yawn.

'How did you get in?'

'What?'

'How did you get into my apartment block?'

Vince Gill vocals wailed a lament over the background guitar.

'Oh. You're at home. Sorry, sir. I thought you'd still be at work. No, I'm at the station.'

'The Super's given me a late start. I've only been home a couple of hours.'

Danskin scratched facial stubble. 'Anyway, if you're at the station, you'd know I wasn't in.'

'I'm not in the bullpen. I'm in research.'

Danskin pinched the bridge of his nose. 'What you want me for, Ryan?'

For the first time, Ryan heard the song playing in the background as if the forlorn lyrics sang to him.

'I know your life
On earth was troubled
And only you could know the pain
You weren't afraid to face the devil
You were no stranger to the rain.'

'You said I should call you when I wanted to talk. You know - about Amos and stuff.'

'Do you want to come over here? You know whereabouts on Great Park I live, don't you?'

Ryan hesitated. 'Aye, but I'd rather we met at the station. It'll be less obvious.'

Danskin sighed. 'Any particular reason? I mean, I feel like I've just been home five minutes from the Whickham shoot investigation and I need some shut-eye before I go back in.'

'I can't risk being seen at yours, sir. They might follow me. I've got to behave as if everything's normal. There's nowt unusual about you and me being at the station at the same time, but they'd know something was up if they saw us together in your apartment.'

Danskin stood, suddenly alert. 'I don't like the sound of this, son.'

While the DCI voiced his concerns, Ryan heard Vince Gill's sad lyrics float over the airwaves.

'Go rest high on that mountain
Son your work on earth is done
Go to heaven a-shoutin'
Love for the Father and the Son.'

'And I'm not keen on the sound of that either, sir.'

**

Danskin saw Ryan sitting towards the rear of the staff cafeteria. He had his back to the DCI and, when Danskin touched him on the shoulder, he jumped.

When Ryan span towards him, the DCI saw a man under stress. Tight jaw, clenched teeth, pale skin and hollow eyes.

Danskin took the seat opposite him. 'What's this all about?'

'Geordie Amos isn't who he seemed.'

'You mean he was a ringer? Somebody else?'

Ryan shook his head. 'No. It was him, alright, but he wasn't just a random jumper. Somebody picked him out for the task.'

'Wait, wait. What task? You're not making sense.'

Ryan rubbed an eyebrow while he ordered his thoughts. 'Someone wanted me up on that bridge. That's why Amos was there, and why he asked for me specifically.'

'Had on. Why would anyone want you? And why did Amos go along with it? I mean, he could have said 'no', he could have gone home, or he could have jumped straight off. Why'd he feel the need to involve you?'

Ryan shuddered like a leaf in an autumn breeze. 'Because it was the only way he'd get his family back.'

'Back from where?'

'From whoever held them.'

'This is more confusing than Twin Peaks. So, this 'somebody' had Amos's family. Where do you fit in?'

'Because whoever had his daughter and grandkid also have my Dad and wor kid.'

Danskin blinked. 'Shit, man. Are they okay?'

Ryan's vision blurred through his tears. 'I dunno.'

'Fucking hell.'

'Amos told me they wanted me to do something for them and, when I did, they, or he, would release Dad and James unharmed.'

'What do you have to do? When do you have to do it?'

'It's done already.'

'They didn't let them go?'

Ryan shook his head.

'Ryan, I don't think they ever will. We're gonna have to find them.'

'I think they will keep their word. They let Amos's folk go as soon as he persuaded me to help them. I have to believe they'll do the same for me. Amos reckons they must want me to do summat else first.'

Danskin stared across the near-deserted cafeteria. 'Let's find Amos's family. We need to talk to them.'

'You already have.'

'What?'

'Well, Kinnear's lot have.'

Danskin screwed his eyes tight. Stopped breathing. Finally, a light came on. 'The Corrigans.'

Ryan's brow furrowed. 'Who?'

'They live in Blyth, right?'

'Aye, but the name's Amos not Corrigan.'

'First names?'

'Maddi and Lance.'

Stephen Danskin inclined his head. 'Yep. That's the Corrigans. They were released last night on the south bank of the river, opposite the Port of Tyne.'

'That figures,' Ryan said grimly. 'Anyway, they rang him as soon as they were free. No sooner had Geordie taken the call, he jumped.'

Danskin scratched his ear. 'Okay. They took Amos's folk to get to you. A ridiculous way to do it, but I accept what you say. How'd they go on to get your family?'

Ryan fixed his superior with a piercing stare. 'You already know.'

'Look, stop talking in riddles. Me head's all over the place as it is, with the Super involved in some major OCG activity. It's not as if I don't have enough on my plate with the Whickham shoo...'

He stopped mid-sentence.

'Fuck me; that's it, isn't it? The drive-by hit was a cover for snatching your dad and brother.'

Ryan nodded. 'That's what I believe, yes.'

'So, why not join the investigation? You must be gagging to get them back.'

'Of course, I am!' Ryan looked around as a couple of heads twisted towards them.

'Of course I am,' he repeated more quietly. 'But I'm under instructions not to talk. That's why I couldn't go to your apartment. That's why we're having this conversation here.'

Danskin thought for a moment. 'What did they have you do? I mean, it must be something big, something majorly important to them, to go to all this trouble.'

'I don't know how big it is, but they went to more trouble than you know.'

'Spit it out.'

'They fitted Amos up with a wire. Must have been to make sure he did what they told him. I think they were probably listening in, too.'

'How do you know?'

'I know because that's what I was doing at the RVI. You were right. I WAS searching him. And I'm pleased I did because that's how I found out he was wired up like Radio One.'

'I'll get your folks back, but I need you to tell me what you did.'

Ryan couldn't look at him. 'You're not going to like it, sir.'

'I already don't.'

'I was desperate, okay? I still am. That's the only reason I did it.'

'What the fuck did you do, Jarrod?'

**

Hannah leant over the back of the Custom Intel officer's chair.

'Is there any interesting tonnage on here for you?'

Amelia Curry pointed a finger at the screen. 'I've flagged this one up for a manual check. It's a Dutch container.'

'What is it about you and the Dutch?' Hannah snickered.

Amelia stiffened. 'Most of the ferries come from the Netherlands. Stands to reason I highlight more from there.'

'That's true,' Hannah conceded. 'But this one's not a ferry, and it's not heading here. It's due at Port of Blyth. Blyth's a cargo-only port, and it takes stuff from all over Europe. What is it about this one that's grabbed your attention?'

'Are you trying to tell me how to do my job? Again?'

Hannah kept an even tone. 'Not at all. Just wondered why you picked another Dutch vessel, that's all.'

'There's only two due to dock at Blyth today. The *Power Pioneer* and the *Borgvloot*. I've checked the records and we did a manual on the Pioneer last time she docked.'

'I see.'

'Look, do you want me to transfer the marker to the Pioneer? She's a Barbados registered barge, leased to a Singapore company, and arriving from Bergen. Inventory says she's carrying nothing but cabling.'

'What's on the Borgvloot?'

Amelia clicked on an icon and an excel spreadsheet appeared on screen. She filtered it down still further.

'Her cargo's a mix of RDF, fertiliser, and other bagged chemicals. Listen, she's due to dock at the South Harbour's Ro-Ro pontoon any sec now. As well as our guys, there's a fleet of Mafi trailers and forklifts standing by to shift her load. Do you want me to call off the hounds?'

Hannah thought for a moment. 'What have you flagged up for the manual check?'

'The chemicals. I just thought it possible there might be a different sort of chemical stashed amongst it, if you get my drift.'

Hannah nodded. 'No, you're right – let's stick with the Borgvloot.' She patted Amelia's shoulder. 'I like your thinking. Good work.'

Amelia's eyelids slid shut as Hannah moved away to chat to one of the uniform PCs.

**

In the cafeteria of the City and County police station, Ryan couldn't meet Danskin's eye.

'Sir, this lot know what they're doing. They took the trouble to find out all about me. They knew I was on duty; they knew I was a trained crisis negotiator, and they knew I'd respond to Geordie's call.'

Ryan picked at his cuticles as he continued.

'They know my family. They know their habits. They knew Dad and James would go to the match, and they knew where they'd be beforehand.'

'Like I said, they've gone to a helluva lot of trouble.'

Ryan lifted his eyes. They made fleeting contact with the DCIs before his gaze raced back to his fingernails. 'I was desperate, sir. I didn't have a choice.'

Danskin regarded his fledgling DS with concern, pity, and something else. Something more painful.

'You don't have to apologise, Ryan. I understand. I really do. Remember that night Hannah went missing working undercover? How the trap we set went tits-up? God, I still have the nightmares from it. But I got my stepdaughter back. YOU got Hannah back. And I'm going to get your family back in return.'

He reached across the table. Clasped Ryan's jaw. Tilted it until Ryan's eyes met his own. 'But you've got to tell me what you did for them.'

Ryan's eyes shimmered with tears. He let out the cry of a wounded animal.

'Ryan?'

'Like I said, I was desperate. Really desperate.'

Danskin didn't know what was coming, but he realised whatever it was would hit him like a bucketload of shit.

'Sir, these people don't only know about my family. They know about me and Hannah, too.'

The shit hit the DCI right between the eyes.

'They knew Hannah has influence at the port. They made me persuade her to let a lorry through. That's what they wanted from me. I thought once it was done, they'd let Dad and James go.'

Danskin shook his head like a Metallica fan. 'Nee way. They'll never let you go now they've got their hooks into you. It'll be one thing after another until you're in so deep you'll become one of them.'

Ryan began to cry again.

'What was the lorry carrying?'

Ryan shrugged. 'Flowers, allegedly. But I reckon it must be people or drugs.'

Danskin nodded sagely. 'Drugs.'

'What do we do, sir? How do I get my folks back? How do we protect Hannah?'

'We tell the Super, that's what we do.'

'No! They'll know if we do. You're the only one who can know about this.'

Danskin slapped the table. 'I'm telling Maynard. This is all part of something much bigger than you can possibly imagine. It's national. International. And Maynard knows more about it than anyone.'

Ryan was visibly shaking. 'No! You promised…'

'That was before I knew you'd involved Hannah in all this. Everything's off the table now.'

'Sir, I'm begging here, man. You'll get them all killed. Dad, James, Hannah. All of them.'

Danskin's face was ashen. Nerves danced beneath his cheeks like burrowing insects.

'I've got to tell Maynard. I trust her.' In a whisper, he added, 'I hope to God my trust isn't misplaced.'

Ryan Jarrod felt he and Danskin had followed Geordie Amos into the void.

****

PART TWO

'I always thought a man became a cop to shield himself from his own criminality.'

Norman Mailer

CHAPTER ELEVEN

Dawn Curry felt a weight lift from her shoulders as she went about her evening chores. A wash of the kitchen floor, a squirt of bleach down the toilet pan, and a quick dance around the lounge with the Dyson was heaven on earth for her.

Heaven, because she could relax while performing the list of tasks Bryn set her. Heaven, because she was in the house, and he wasn't. She didn't know where he'd gone – she rarely did – but she was free until he chose to return.

Dawn began humming a tune to herself as she looked out the kitchen window of the house on Riverslea, towards the greenery which bordered South Shields' Harton Primary School.

She jumped as her phone signalled an incoming WhatsApp video call. Her heart sank when she saw the caller ID.

Bryn held the phone so near him only a close-up of his face appeared visible. 'Where are you?' he snarled.

'At home, lovely. I'm at home.'

'Show me. Let me see.'

She reversed the camera and gave him a visual tour of the kitchen.

'Lounge.'

'Really?'

'Yes. Show me the lounge.'

Dawn ensured she suppressed the sigh which welled inside her. The camera wobbled as she walked to the empty lounge.

'Now, upstairs. Show me the bedroom.'

This time, she couldn't hide her frustration. 'Bryn, I'm all alone.'

'Prove it, woman.'

She strode upstairs. Flung open the bedroom door. The camera panned around the room. She zoomed in on a pristinely made bed.

'See? I'm home alone, love.'

'Where've you been?'

His question was hidden behind traffic noise.

'Where are you?' she asked.

'Working. To keep you, woman. Now, where've you been?'

'I've been here all evening. Just finished my jobs.'

'How do I know you're not lying? You haven't set your locations.'

Dawn's eyelids fluttered. 'Oh God. Sorry. I completely forgot darling. I'll do it now.'

She fiddled with her phone and switched on the settings.

'Good. That's better,' the man snarled. 'You haven't been seeing that sister bitch of yours, have you?'

'No. I wouldn't do that, Bryn. You told me I shouldn't have anything to do with Amelia and I wouldn't go against you, darling.'

'For your sake, I hope not.'

Dawn just about made out a different sound in the background. Something familiar, but something she couldn't recall. 'Where are you?', she tried again.

'Out. I'll be back when I'm back.'

'Any idea when?'

He spat out a laugh. 'As if I'd tell you. No, it'll be a surprise. Just make sure you're there. And, in case you were wondering, keep your phone on 'cos I'll be checking on you again.'

The screen died on her and, with it, Dawn's sense of contentment.

**

Bryn returned the phone to his pocket and slunk back into the dark blue Subaru.

The vehicle sat alone in a linear car park alongside the A193. Darkness enveloped it, and a breeze strengthened with a change of tide until the car rocked like a cradle.

Bryn checked his watch. The man was late. Very late. He fidgeted with the gold rings on his fingers. His heavy wrist chain jangled. He climbed out the car again, leant over the roof, and drummed his fingers on the surface.

He was about to give it up as a bad job when he saw the glimmer of headlights as a spotless and expensive-looking vehicle turned into the car park and pulled up several bays away.

No-one stepped from the car and the occupants remained invisible behind its darkened windows, but Bryn knew someone was scrutinising him. He felt it in his bones.

Suddenly, the passenger door opened. A muscular figure emerged, stepped to the rear door, and held it open. He motioned with his head for Bryn to enter.

As soon as he did, the man ordered Bryn to take the centre seat before squeezing in alongside him. The driver's eyes regarded him suspiciously through the rear-view mirror, but it was the man on Bryn's right who spoke.

'So, you want to work with me, I hear?'

The inside of the vehicle carried the scents of leather, pine, and fear. Bryn cleared his throat. 'Yeah, I think we can be good for each other.'

The man chortled. 'I'm good as it is. I don't need anyone to help me. You, on the other hand…well, I think you need me.'

Bryn swallowed. The thickset Oriental alongside him was smaller than Bryn had imagined, but significantly more menacing. He'd heard all about 'Mr Yu' – everyone who made a serious living out of drugs had heard of Mr Yu – but few had the privilege of meeting him.

'I hear you've built up a bit of a reputation around these parts,' Yu continued. 'Now, you've obviously heard I'm expanding my little empire. I'm already trading around these parts, but I've no intention of queering your pitch. Make no mistake, I could squash you like an ant if I wished, but I don't. Not yet. You see, I'd like you to do my dirty work for me. Why take the flak if someone else is available, I say?'

Bryn quaked inside but something compelled a display of false bravado.

'I don't take the flak for anybody, pal.'

Mr Yu said nothing. He didn't have to. His coal black eyes did the talking for him. Finally, though, he did speak.

'I'm not your pal,' he hissed.

Bryn swallowed. 'Sorry.'

'I hope you never have to say sorry to me again. Because, if you do, it means you've fucked up. And no-one fucks with me without being truly sorry.'

'Sorry,' Bryn said again, suddenly wishing he'd stuck with a career driving forklifts.

'Are you in?' Yu asked. 'Don't misunderstand me, Bryn. You're not a partner. You're not even a minnow. But I will reward you. Handsomely, by your standards.'

Bryn held out his hand to shake with Yu. The Chinese ignored it.

In the darkness of the vehicle, Yu broke into a broad smile captured by the dashboard lights. 'I want to show you something tonight.'

'Yeah. Sure. Anything's fine by me.'

'Is it, Bryn? Is it really?'

'Yeah. We're…'

'Partners? Oh dear, that's not what you were going to say, was it? I hope you haven't forgotten already. I don't like people who forget their place.'

Bryn looked straight ahead. He felt the man to his left look towards him. Saw the driver still watch him via the mirror, and the gooseflesh on his arm told him Yu was glaring at him.

'Driver, let's show this young man what happens to those who forget their place.'

Bryn felt a dewdrop of urine form at the tip of his penis.

**

Yu's vehicle pulled into another car park barely two hundred metres up the road. Another car sat at the back of the plot with its engine idling, a third parked up a little way from it. Other than that, the area was deserted.

All three vehicles doused their headlights.

'Out,' Yu ordered.

As soon as Bryn, Yu, and the muscle were out, their car reversed across the entrance, blocking it.

Bryn recognised the place well. He didn't need the hint of crashing waves to tell him he was in the Marsden Grotto car park even though he could see only the solid blackness of night in front of him.

Yu spoke over the dull roar of the North Sea.

'I'd like to introduce you to a couple of friends. They're newbies, too. Unfortunately, they forgot their place.'

Bryn felt another dewdrop leak from him.

'Come. Let's meet them.' Yu took his elbow and frogmarched him to the nearest car. Two shadowy figures emerged from the vehicle parked furthest away and joined them.

Bryn peered through the passenger window. A male sat bolt upright. He was about Bryn's age, perhaps a year or two older. His skin was ghostly white, and his eyes bulged with fright.

In the driver's seat, a young woman - early twenties, slim face, dark hair and eyes – exhaled with shallow gasps. Her window was open a couple of inches and Bryn at once noticed a strong smell of ammonia.

The vehicle's occupants had released more than a dewdrop.

Mr Yu tapped on the window. 'Put it in gear, my dear.'

'Please. We talk, no?' The voice was heavily accented. Russian, Bryn thought.

'Correct. We don't talk,' Yu said with a smile. 'You have caused me a lot of trouble, and even greater expense. I didn't bring you back from your little Dutch cottage for us to talk.'

Yu stood and addressed Bryn.

'This doesn't happen often but, when I am let down, I make sure lessons are learnt.' He clapped his hands. Bryn jumped. 'Come. Come with me. Let me show you.'

Bryn followed Yu to the rear of the car. 'Tell me what you see,' the drug lord demanded.

'A car park. Tarmac. A wooden fence. Grass beyond.'

'Look again.'

Bryn screwed up his eyes. Peered into a night as black as ink. Shook his head.

'I'll give you a clue. Look at the fence.'

Bryn saw it. The low-level fence consisted of single logs connected by barbed wire. Except in one place, where a log was missing.

The gap was directly in front of the car.

Sweat beaded the forehead of the man in the passenger seat.

'I have a child. Help us. Please. This must not happen,' he whispered to Bryn.

Yu answered for him. 'If it doesn't happen to you, it'll happen to your child. Which do you prefer? I can arrange a swap if you wish.'

The man closed his eyes and mouthed a prayer.

One of the occupants of the other car approached Yu and whispered something to him. Yu nodded.

'It is time.'

'NO! I can't do it,' the driver screamed.

'You can, and you will. I promise it'll be quick. I'll even ensure I give you a hand.'

The other man unlocked the boot. Bryn ducked out the way as the lid sprung open.

'Release the handbrake.'

Sobbing, the girl obliged.

'Remember, the faster you go, the quicker your death shall be.'

Bryn heard the engine roar. He felt physically sick. Even more so when Yu's accomplice tossed a bottle of paraffin stuffed with a burning rag into the open boot.

The car moved, slowly at first, then rapidly gaining speed as the girl ramped through the gears. The car left the tarmac, bounced and rattled over uneven grassland. Bryn saw the occupant's heads tossed left and right.

Still the vehicle increased its speed until it left terra firma and took to the air above the cliff edge, its engine screaming as the tyres lost traction.

The car seemed to hang in the air for several seconds, the drag ripping open the passenger door, before the bonnet tipped downwards - and the vehicle disappeared from sight.

There was a rending shriek of metal as the car somersaulted against the cliff face followed by a sickening crash as it thundered onto the rocks thirty metres below.

The screech of a hundred seabirds rent the air and a flash of orange and red flame fleetingly lit up the night sky. A silence followed; one so unnerving Bryn wondered if he had dreamt it all.

'I think that concludes our meeting,' Yu said. He squeezed Bryn's shoulder as the entourage returned to their vehicles.

'I'm sure you won't forget your place now, young man, will you?'

CHAPTER TWELVE

'*I need to know. M.*'

A text in the middle of the night normally filled Ryan Jarrod with dread. This time, once he'd pulled himself around from a fitful slumber disturbed by malevolent thoughts and partying neighbours, it signalled hope.

He checked the number and discovered it did indeed belong to Maddi Amos. Or Corrigan. Or whatever name she went by.

He dialled the number.

'Maddi. It's Ryan. Thanks for getting in touch.'

'I don't know if I'm doing the right thing. I don't much care for you lot, but I do – did – care for me Da. I need to know he didn't suffer.'

Ryan ruffled his hair. No small talk. Straight down to business, she was.

'Can we meet?' he asked. 'I don't want to talk about it on the phone.'

He heard her suck in air. 'Aye, I dare say. Come here. First thing. Before I change me mind.'

'No. We should meet somewhere neutral. In case anyone's watching, like, and they think you're getting pally with the police.'

'Don't get yer hopes up. I'm telling you nowt. You'll be the one talking.'

'Still, just in case, yeah? Bring Lance as well. I'm sure you'll be safe, but I don't want him left on his own.'

'He's not leaving my sight. Where do we meet?'

'It's your call, Maddi. Anywhere you like. Make it somewhere public but not overcrowded. Like I say, just being cautious.'

She suggested a location. Ryan knew it, vaguely, but wasn't familiar with it.

'Eight-thirty too early for you?' asked Maddi.

'I'll be there. Thank you, Maddi.'

'Like I say, this is for me; not you. And it's a one-off. I can't have folk round here thinking I talk to the cops. They're your words, Mr Jarrod.'

Maddi disconnected the call leaving Ryan to stare at his bedroom's cracked ceiling while listening to the rest of The Drive party like it was 1999.

The glow from the bedside clock told him it was two-thirty a.m.

He swore and wrapped the pillow around his face.

**

Ryan approached the meeting point via the village of Cambois – a typical, tightly knit community sandwiched between compare-and-contrast landscapes of derelict industrial land and unspoilt sandy beaches.

After passing a restaurant with connections to the Charlton footballing family, he nursed the Peugeot along narrow seafront streets with hilltop dunes on his left, and rows of terraced housing to his right.

He braked suddenly and reversed to make sure his eyes hadn't lied. Yes, there it was: a sign proudly proclaiming Cambois to be the first nudist beach in England. A bitter wind arrowed in from the choppy North Sea and Ryan wondered who in their right mind would get their nob out in this bleakest of locations.

Ahead of him he saw three conical towers which represented the remnants of the former sea terminal for the long redundant Alcan smelting works.

Ryan blinked and missed the tiny settlement of North Blyth, all three streets of it. From there, the road switch bladed across a single railway track. He kept the clifftop railway on his left-hand side as he approached the mud-soaked quicksand of Blyth Harbour's north-eastern outpost.

Across the river, Ryan observed an odd-shaped vessel anchored dockside. Through the fret, he just about made out the legend *Power Pioneer* etched on her bow. Half a dozen cranes towered over the barge like a herd of watchful dinosaur.

Straight in front of him, the ghostly form of an offshore wind turbine beckoned him onwards. Both the road and railhead terminated at the abandoned smelter plant, so he swung left at a crossing and found himself in the roughest of car parks.

The Peugeot bounced across the uneven, crater-strewn surface and pulled to a halt against a barrier of strategically placed boulders beneath which the surf pounded against rocks like Keith Moon on speed.

He clambered from the vehicle and peered over the cliff edge. A woman enveloped by waterproofs tossed a ball for a pair of Bedlington terriers. An old collie padded behind his master, the dog's coat wet and bedraggled. And a skinny woman and young boy stared up from the pebbled beach.

Maddi's eyes never left Ryan as he edged his way down a moss-slicked ramp to the beach. He teetered over rocks, dodging numerous pools which formed around them.

'Maddi? I'm Ryan Jarrod.' He extended his hand.

The woman responded by wrapping her long, knitted cardigan around her slender frame. 'Aye. I guessed it was you.'

'Might be a stupid question, but how are you doing?'

'It's a stupid question,' she said in reply.

Lance stood alongside his mother, hands thrust deep into pockets, eyes downcast.

'You must be Lance,' Ryan smiled at him.

The boy drew circles in the sand with his shoes.

'He doesn't say much,' Maddi explained. 'Even less since…' Her sentence remained unfinished.

All three stared out at the shifting mass of grey water. A cargo vessel weighed anchor on the edge of visibility.

'He used to work the ships, you know; Da, like,' Maddi said.

'No. I didn't. Did he enjoy it?'

Maddi snapped a laugh. 'What is it they say? *'Born in Blyth, made in the Navy,'* isn't it? It didn't make Da.'

'So why sign up?'

She sighed. 'When the pit closed, it seemed a canny option for him, I suppose. Trouble is, he couldn't stand being told what to do without having summat to say back. He didn't last long. Besides, it was work. Da hated work. Didn't like it doon the pit, then he went on the bins… 'Nuff said aboot that the better. No; work wasn't for Da, and Da wasn't for work.'

Ryan itched to quiz Maddi about her abductors, where she'd been kept, everything and anything, really, but he'd promised her he wouldn't question her. Not right away, at least.

'Would he have felt anything?' Maddi asked.

The matter-of-fact tone took Ryan aback.

'No. A colleague and friend, a doctor, told me it would have been instant. He woudn't have felt a thing.' He spared her Aaron Elliot's detailed analysis.

She nodded her head. 'Good.'

'He talked about you, you know. At the end. You and Lance. He asked me to tell you he loved you.'

Tears formed in the young woman's eyes. 'I didn't need you or him to tell me that. I know he loved us both.' She gave Ryan a brief smile. 'But thanks for saying it, all the same.'

'That's why I was so keen to speak with you. I didn't want to break my promise to him.' It was a lie, but only partially.

This time, Maddi's smile was warmer. 'Thank you,' she said again. 'It can't have been much fun for you, either.'

Ryan's face set grim. 'It wasn't.' A nerve flexed at his jawline.

'He was dying anyway,' Maddi said.

'I know.'

'He told you?'

Ryan nodded, and silence descended.

Lance picked up a pebble and skimmed it over the sea's surface.

'Granda' taught me to do that,' he said glumly. 'He taught me lots of things, did me Granda'.'

'That's what they do best,' Ryan agreed.

'Do you play FIFA?'

Random, Ryan thought. 'Not my scene. I prefer the real thing.' He closed his eyes as he added, 'My Dad and brother do, though.'

'Who are they?'

The question perplexed Ryan. 'Norman and James.'

Lance looked at him as if he'd descended from a different planet. 'Na, man. Which teams?'

'Oh. Don't know. I bet you're Spartans, though. Am I right or am I right?'

Lance gave him that look again. 'They're not on FIFA, man,' he said, picking up another pebble.

'He seems to be doing okay,' Ryan said.

'I don't think he really understands what's happened. We'll see how he's doing in a couple of days.'

The threesome wandered northwards, the wind whipping their hair, biting at exposed flesh. Ryan shivered at the thought of the nudist beach.

'Did he really talk about us?' Maddi asked.

'Of course. He was proud of you. You were his world.'

'He didn't have a good life, you know. My mother couldn't cope when he was at sea. She got into all sorts. She met someone else. He was a bastard. He plied her with drugs. She ended up a typical junkie, and her life ended the way most junkies' lives' do.'

'I'm so sorry, Madeleine.'

'It's Maddi. Short for Madeira, not Madeleine. It's where Da and Ma went on honeymoon, I gather.'

'Bet you're pleased they didn't go to the Isles of Scilly.'

Maddi laughed. A genuine, hearty laugh. Her face lit up and, with the smile, she lost half a dozen years in age.

She looked at Lance, trawling a rockpool with his fingers, and sadness overcame her again.

'Do you have kids, Ryan?'

'No. Nearly did, once, but it wasn't meant to be.'

'I've never been so scared when those men came to wor door and took us.'

His heart skipped a beat. She'd opened the door for him, too.

'They came for you?'

'Aye.' She gave a brisk nod.

'To your home? They knew where you lived?'

'Must have, yeah. I was terrified they'd hurt Lance.'

'They didn't, though?'

Maddi shook her head. 'No. Played a bit rough, gave us the odd kick up the arse so I'd go where they wanted - but I've had boyfriends do worse.'

She leant into Ryan. 'I was so scared.'

Ryan slipped an arm around her. Lance looked across for a moment then resumed his pool hunt.

'They said if Da did what they wanted, we'd be fine. I didn't know what they wanted. I still divvent.'

Ryan said nothing. His heart raced. He wanted to learn more. *Needed* to know more, but better it came from Maddi than through questioning.

'There were three of 'em. They moved us around all the time. They kept us cooped up inside the van mostly. Two stayed in the back with us. The other one only turned up near the end. He told us me Da was doing good. Doing everything they wanted.'

Ryan risked a question. 'Did you recognise any of them?'

'Apart from ten seconds when I answered the door, they never showed their faces. Or, if they did, it was when we were blindfolded.'

'Where did they keep you?'

She shrugged. 'Nee idea. Like I said, back of a van most the time. At the last minute, they moved us to a warehouse-type thing and then, before we knew it, one of them told us to count to a thousand and we could go. They left us a phone. I found it, rang Da…' she swallowed, hard. 'And that was the last time I spoke to him. The cops came and took us home. The bastards who took me and Lance warned us not to say owt, so we didn't. I'd seen what they were capable of. No way was I going to talk.' She looked at Ryan. 'Until you came along. Now, I've said too much.'

Her jaw locked as her gaze drifted south, towards her hometown.

Ryan read her thoughts. 'I can get you to a safe house if you're worried. I genuinely think they'll leave you alone now, though.'

'I'm not moving. It's my home. It's me Da's home.'

A trio of yapping dogs snapped Ryan's brain into gear.

'Why are you a Corrigan?'

'What?'

'Your father was George Amos. Not Corrigan.'

'Oh. I see what you mean. That's Lance's dad's name. It's on his birth certificate so I thought it was easier all round if I used his name, an' aal. Stop awkward questions at school and stuff.'

'What was Lance's dad like? I mean, he couldn't be involved in any of this, could he?'

'No.'

'How can you be sure, Maddi?'

The woman looked at her son, chasing seagulls across sodden sand. 'Because he pissed off to Ibiza the day Lance was born, and he's never been back since.'

'What was his first name, just so I can run some checks?'

'Wayne Corrigan. He won't be involved. He's a daft twat but he wouldn't have owt to do with this.'

Ryan wasn't so sure.

'Ryan, I've got to get back yem. I've said too much. If anyone is watching, I can't have them knowing I've been talking to cops. You say I'm safe, I hope I'm safe – but I can't chance it, much as I'd like to make sure this doesn't happen to anybody else.'

Ryan shuddered. 'Too late for that.'

'Huh?'

'Nothing. It doesn't matter.'

Maddi cupped her hand around her mouth. 'Lance! Howay, son. Time to go home and get warmed up.'

The boy trotted over the sand towards them.

'I can get you moved if you want, you know,' Ryan repeated.

'Nah. I'm sure. I'm not running from anybody.'

The words resonated with Ryan. Meant something profound. 'You know, neither am I. Thanks, Maddi.'

He stared at nothing far in the distance before continuing.

'Listen, you mightn't be able to contact me for a few days. I might be away somewhere. If you change your mind about moving, or want to speak to someone who'll understand, dial this number.'

He scribbled something on a scrap of paper and passed it to Maddi.

'I'm not talking to no social worker.'

'He's not a social worker. He's a cop.'

'Even more reason not to talk.'

'He's no ordinary cop. You can trust him. His name's Stephen Danskin.'

Ryan turned his back on the woman and boy to hide the tears brimming beneath his lids.

'He's almost a dad to me.'

CHAPTER THIRTEEN

Stephen Danskin spotted Lyall Parker first. The sun's rays formed a halo illusion as it reflected off the window-table's surface onto the Scot's silver hair.

Danskin averted his eyes and caught those of the woman next to Parker. The DCI mimed a 'drink' signal to her, but Sam Maynard placed her hand over the top of her mug and shook her head. She said something to Parker who looked across before also shaking his head.

The DCI checked the menu at the counter of Carliol Square's Flat Caps Coffee Bar. He ordered a Colombian microlot filter, even though he had no idea what one was, and a blueberry cookie even though he despised blueberries.

His mind was on other things. Specifically, Ryan Jarrod and the mess he'd got himself into.

'Morning ma'am. Lyall,' Danskin said as he pulled a schoolroom-like seat up to the table. 'Why the message to meet you two here?' He raised his eyebrows approvingly as he took a sip of coffee. 'Not that I'm complaining, mind.'

Maynard's eyes swallowed Danskin whole. 'I want your opinion on something. It's Op Sage-linked so I thought it better we met here so I could bring you up to speed on developments before I go public with it to the rest of the crew.'

Danskin gave a whistle. 'You reckon it's live then, this drug cartel?'

'I believe it is, yes. I'll be sending what I know to the Met once we're done here. They'll confirm it but, yeah; I'm pretty sure it's reached Newcastle.'

Lyall Parker peered through the fronds of a dwarf palm tree. 'What ha'e ye got for us, ma'am?'

Maynard pursed her lips, gathered her thoughts, and broke the latest news.

'A traffic officer from the Prince Bishop force found a guy wandering down the middle of a country road. He was dazed and confused, had one shoe missing, and was mumbling nonsense.'

'Drugged up?' Parker offered.

'No. He was in shock.'

'Where was he found?'

Maynard shrugged. 'I'm not familiar with the area but it was somewhere called Whitburn. Do you know it?'

'It's down Mackemland way. Near the Academy of Shite,' Danskin explained.

'In English, please, Stephen.'

'It's where the Sunderland Football Team juniors are based, ma'am.'

'Oh. Anyway, he was wandering all over the road outside a boarding kennels. When the traffic officer managed to get some sense out of him, the man asked for police protection. He claimed people had killed his cousin and tried to kill him, too.'

'Did he say when and how?'

'No. The man wasn't British and, in the state he was in, the report says he was unable to offer much more. Nothing the officer could make sense of, anyway.'

Stephen Danskin rubbed his jowls. 'I'm not getting the link with Op Sage, ma'am.'

'I'm coming to that bit.' Maynard gave a terse smile. 'He says someone smuggled him into the country in a lorry.'

Danskin put his cup down with such force it cracked. Coffee flooded the wooden tabletop and lapped onto Maynard's trousers.

'Shit.' He mopped at it with a handful of napkins. Tried to soak up the spillage. Dabbed the sodden material against Maynard's thigh.

'Stephen?'

'Oh. Sorry, ma'am. Inappropriate, I know.'

'I didn't mean that. I meant, 'What's wrong'?'

'Nowt. Nowt, man. Just don't know me own strength. You were saying?'

'The foreign national was arrested. He's in custody at Sunderland North, but we only have a small window if we're to talk to him.'

'And it's no' oor jurisdiction,' Parker realised. 'How do we have a chat wi' him?'

Sam Maynard brushed a hand against her damp leg. 'That's where the Met come in. They can pass authority from the Bishop force to us if we prove the Op Sage connection. And I'm pretty sure I can.'

'Go on,' Parker encouraged.

'He entered the country illegally, not of his own volition, and my guess is he came in via the Port of Tyne. Which just happens to be right opposite the point where the hostage-takers released the Corrigan family. On top of that, we have the coincidence of the Whickham shoot. Once we get DS Jarrod onto that case, we may have a definite link.'

Maynard looked at Danskin. 'Can you confirm Ryan's back on duty, Stephen?'

Danskin stared blankly across the table, his face ghostly white.

'Earth calling Stephen.' Maynard rapped her knuckles on the sticky table surface. 'Hello? Anyone home?'

Danskin looked up. Blinked. 'What? Oh, I don't know, ma'am. Not had time to check yet.' He breathed a sigh of relief when Parker changed the subject.

'Do we know the nationality of the bloke?'

Maynard beamed. 'Yes. That's what convinced me it was Op Sage-linked. He's Macedonian, name of Pavel Maric. What's more, he carries a PNC intel marker.'

Parker leant towards the Super. 'Aye – and?'

'The PNC marker ordered any stops to be reported to the Operation Tower intel team. That's the national operation for combatting the movement of Class A drugs around the country.'

She looked from Parker to Danskin and back again. 'It's also the mothership enquiry for Op Kop and the like. Including Op Sage.'

Lyall pushed back his chair. 'Then what are we waiting for? Let's do it!'

'Stephen? Are you in agreement?'

Danskin closed his eyes. Exhaled loudly. Squirmed on the hard seat. 'Can I have a word, ma'am? In private?'

'No. You can't. Parker and you are the only ones who know about Op Sage. Everything must be in the open between the three of us.'

Danskin's gaze shifted to Lyall. Parker was Danskin's most loyal associate. They'd worked together since Parker transferred south from the Granite City force. He'd trust him with his life. But this wasn't *his* life. It was Norman and James Jarrod's.

And, possibly, Ryan Jarrod's, too. And Hannah's.

He closed his eyes again as he spoke to Parker.

'Lyall, do you mind? Ten minutes, that's all.'

'Aye. It's nae bother to me. It must be important. See you outside.'

Superintendent Maynard and Stephen Danskin watched Parker cross the café floor. Once the door closed behind him, Maynard fixed Stephen with a gaze as icy as her eyes.

'This had better be good.'

**

Sam Maynard didn't think it was good in any way, shape or form.

While Danskin filled her in on his conversation with Ryan, Maynard's eyes widened at the same time as her jaw dropped. By the time he'd finished, she looked like a Tex Avery cartoon character.

'Jesus. Jarrod wouldn't happen to be H as well, would he?'

Danskin didn't smile. 'So, ma'am. It's delicate. That's why I doubt DS Jarrod will be working today.'

'Stephen, I doubt he'll ever work for us again. Do you not realise the seriousness of his actions? He's put lives at risk, not to mention jeopardising the entire Operation Sage.'

'With respect, what would you have done in his position?'

'I'd have called it in, like any sane officer would.'

Danskin lowered his voice as the Flat Caps café became busier. 'That's just it, though. He wasn't thinking sanely. Not with his family at stake, and the pressure of a suicide negotiation on his hands. Let's face it: who would? Besides, he was being blackmailed into the bargain.'

Maynard reached for her phone. 'I'm calling the Met.'

Danskin grabbed her wrist. 'You're not.'

'Let go of me, Stephen.'

'Not until you promise not to say anything. At least, not yet. Think, man. The gang haven't released Jarrod's folks yet. They must have something else lined up for him. They'll be in touch with him again, which means he can work the case from the inside.'

Maynard looked around the café. 'No.' She shook her head. 'I can't trust him. I thought I could but, after this, there's no way.'

'And what about Ryan's life? You'd be as good as ordering his execution.'

Maynard flopped back into her seat so hard it almost tipped her backwards. After a silence which stretched to infinity and beyond, she spoke.

'I've got to get back to the station. I'll send Lyall on his way, then you and I will walk to Forth Street. That's less than a mile. You've got until we get there to persuade me.'

**

Maynard's anger didn't abate until they were halfway down High Bridge. As they passed the Duke of Wellington, she asked, 'I take it no-one's looking for DS Jarrod's family?'

'No, ma'am. The focus is on the shooting and there's no witnesses to the Jarrod's snatch apart from the little girl who's still saying she saw nowt. The only kidnap incident on record is Geordie Amos's kid and grandson, and we know where we are with that one.'

'Anyone likely to miss the Jarrods?'

'There will be, aye, but I doubt it'll be for a couple of days. Ryan's grandmother is in a care home and hasn't capacity, if you know what I mean. I'm not aware of any other close relatives. Besides, I reckon anyone missing them would go to Ryan first.'

'And if they do?'

Danskin knew the answer to that one. 'He'll put them off. Come up with some sort of cover story. He'll do nowt that'll jeopardise his family. As far as he's concerned, the gang were good to their word with Amos's family. He's got to believe they'll be straight with him, as well - providing he plays by the rules. Those rules don't include us lot.'

They made a quick shimmy onto Pudding Chare. They'd covered half the distance to the station.

'If I'm reading this correctly,' Maynard summarised, 'Ryan helped get the lorry through, but the cartel didn't release his folks. You believe they will if Ryan does what they say. So, they must have something else lined up for him. How do they contact him?'

'Presumably, by phone.'

'More to the point, *when* will they contact him?'

'That, I don't know. But I'd bet my bottom dollar it won't be long.'

By the time they reached the Revolution Bar at the junction with Westgate Road, Danskin knew the clock was against him. Time for desperate measures.

'Ma'am, can I trust with you some private information?'

'I would have hoped you didn't need ask me that, Stephen.'

They remained silent as they dodged the traffic east of the Central Station portico.

'Well, like I say, Ryan used DS Graves to get the waggon through customs.'

'I'm aware of that, Stephen. That's another blatant misuse of Jarrod's authority.'

They turned right into Orchard Street, into the tunnel which passed beneath the East Coast mainline.

'Aye, but there's something else you need to know. By doing what he did, I believe he's also put Hannah Graves in danger. The OCG can use her as a tool to get at him even if and when they release his dad and brother.'

'You think I haven't already thought of that? You underestimate me, Stephen. You really do.'

'Don't you see?' Danskin said as they stepped into pale sunlight and switched right onto Forth Street. 'There's the lives of two officers on the line here.'

Maynard stopped in her tracks. Took him by the arm. Looked at him with eyes which had lost their sparkle.

'And one of them is your stepdaughter.'

The Super walked on. Danskin didn't.

'What? How? When?' he spluttered.

'Like I say, Stephen; you underestimate me.'

'Did Parker tell you?'

He saw her head shake as she continued to walk away from him. 'Nope. I just did some digging. *Proper coppering* is what you'd call it, would you not?'

'Bugger me,' was all he could say.

Maynard stopped. Turned to face Stephen. 'I moved Hannah to the port because of her relationship to you, not because of her relationship with DS Jarrod.'

'Bloody hell. I thought no-one other than Lyall and Ryan knew.'

'Far as I know, they don't.' Maynard looked up Forth Street. 'There,' she said. 'You've made it with two hundred metres to spare.'

She smiled at her DCI.

'Now, let's get in the station - you and I need to work out how we're going to talk to Maric.'

CHAPTER FOURTEEN

Superintendent Maynard breezed through the bullpen, Danskin trailing in her wake.

'Lyall. We're not to be disturbed under any circumstances. Understand?'

'Aye, ma'am.'

'Make sure you see to it.'

Maynard was already closing the blinds at her window before Danskin made it inside the room. She booted up her PC, retrieved the Operation Sage folder from her desk drawer, and poured them both a coffee so quickly her movements were a blur.

'Okay,' she spoke even as she took her seat. 'It says here that Pavel Maric first came to our attention six years ago. He's been arrested seven times in those six years. All but one of those arrests were in London, hence the Met flagging him as a person of interest.'

'You taken a speed-reading course or summat?'

She ignored him.

'I'll put in a request for European records. I bet he's known in his homeland.'

'If they bother to keep records ower there.'

'Stephen – it's Macedonia, not North Korea.'

Chastised, Danskin sipped his coffee. 'What's the intel marker tell us about Maric?'

'Initially, robbery and theft. Latterly, drugs possession. I guess that explains the Op Tower and Sage connection.'

Danskin watched as her eyes flitted across the text on the screen.

'Aha. Maric has links to Yu Tube.'

'I don't get it. I watch music videos on it. I don't reckon I'll have an intel marker against me.'

'Yu Tube – without the 'o'. It's an OCG with roots in Hong Kong. Drug related, hence our interest. Shit!'

'What, man?'

'They have propensity for extreme violence. Beheadings. Emasculation. Torture.'

'Jesus. Ryan can't get to hear this.' He stared at the ceiling. 'Any Triad involvement?'

'Stephen, I'm not the font of all knowledge here. Once we approach Scotland Yard with what we know…'

Danskin scowled at her.

'Don't give me that look. I'll keep Jarrod and Graves out of it for as long as I can. As I was saying, we'll get full access to the Operation Tower file. I doubt there's Triad involvement, but the Tower files will confirm.'

She held up a hand to shush him as she read on.

Danskin swept aside beads of sweat on his forehead and scratched his shaven crown. 'What's Maric's link to this Yu Tube caper?'

'Vague at first. Seems he was dossing at a property in Poland when it was raided. The authorities had a tip-off they were dealing crystal meth.'

'Ah fuck. That stuff again.'

Maynard took her eyes from the screen and file for the first time. She knew what the DCI referred to. DS Sue Nairn had been killed by a kid dosed up on meth.

'Yes. I'm afraid so,' she said. After a moment, she resumed her study of the records.

'Seems the raid also discovered traces of pervitin, but not enough for a charge to stick. I'll find out why once I get permission to approach the European Liaison Unit.'

'Pardon my ignorance, but what's this pervert stuff?'

Maynard chuckled. 'Pervitin. It's basically what Hitler plied the Nazis with on the Russian front. Kept them awake,

111

deprived them of any empathy whatsoever. Effectively, it turned them into pain resistant killer robots.'

'Nice.'

Maynard's focus remained on the files. Danskin watched, impressed and in awe of his new Super's ability. She was a good 'un. He felt sure his faith in her was well-founded. Sam Maynard wouldn't let him down.

'Now, would you look at this? There's some personal intelligence on Maric. He's been involved in the supply of crack cocaine.' She looked at Danskin. 'Along with his cousin, a Silvia Maric.'

Danskin wrung his hands. 'Get onto the Met. Surely, we've enough to link him to Op Sage now, which gets us through the Prince Bishops door?'

Maynard was already speed-dialling.

'Agreed. Let's go get him.'

**

Ryan came in from a quick tour of his small garden in The Drive and began a melancholy round of the house.

He went from room to room, looking all around, taking in every last nuance of each aspect. He closed his eyes and sniffed the air, his senses storing the scent in his memory banks.

He sat on the cream sofa Hannah had bought for him and swallowed down tears as he looked fondly around the lounge she had lovingly designed.

Ryan lingered in the final room. The master bedroom remained unchanged from the time his grandmother had owned the house. He screwed his eyes tight, knowing the visit he was about to make may be the last time he'd see his beloved gran.

Ryan took a final look up at the house as he closed the front door behind him. He wondered how long it would be before he stepped foot inside it again.

If ever.

**

Ryan rang the buzzer and stepped back from the doorway.

'Yes?'

'I'm here to visit Doris Jarrod.'

There was a moment's silence before the voice asked, 'Is that you, Ryan?'

'It is.'

'Oh, thank goodness. It's Angela Doyle here,' the manageress of the home said. 'I've been trying to get hold of your dad.'

A clenched fist gripped his intestines. 'He's gone away for a couple of days.' Ryan hoped Angela hadn't noticed the tremor in his voice.

'Then, when I couldn't get hold of you, either…well, I feared something had happened.'

'Is gran okay?' Ryan's heart thumped inside his chest. He didn't think he could face another family trauma.

The door clicked. 'Come in. I'll meet you in the lobby. Remember you still need a face mask inside here.'

Ryan hooked a disposable mask around his ears and stepped into the luxurious surroundings of the care home.

'What's wrong?' he asked the woman who hurried towards him.

'Your gran's okay but we are obliged to inform all our residents' families when we have a Covid case on the premises.'

'Bloody hell. I thought that would be all over with, now.'

'Sadly not. Everyone's been double jabbed, of course, but we're not taking any risks of it spreading. Your gran isn't on the floor affected. It's been quarantined but we aren't taking any chances with the rest of our residents, so we aren't allowing any room visits.'

Ryan rubbed his brow. 'I really wanted to see Gran. It's been too long.'

'Yes, it has,' Doyle said, abruptly. She saw his eyes flare then die. 'I'm sorry. It's none of my business but you used to be such a regular visitor. And with her illness… sorry to be so blunt, but your grandmother needs to see familiar faces regularly.'

'I regret it, too, but it's the bloody job, man.'

'And then when we couldn't get hold of Mr Jarrod…'

'You could have tried me.'

'I did. Your phone's off.'

Shit. He'd forgotten he'd gone off-grid. Instantly, his hand went to his pocket. The other phone was still there, the one he kept fully charged and with him at all times The one he prayed would ring yet dreaded what the voice would say when it did.

'Yeah. Sorry about that.'

Angela Doyle tilted her head. Smiled. 'You'll want to see her, I suppose?'

'Well, yes…if I'm allowed, with the virus and everything.'

'You'll be fine, in the pod. You know where it is. Make yourself at home and I'll get someone to fetch Doris down for you.'

Ryan muttered his thanks and made his way to the visiting pod.

The pod reminded him of an interview suite at Forth Street. Small, claustrophobic, and with a perspex screen dividing the room in half. He sat one side of it while he waited for 'the prisoner' to be escorted into the other half.

Angela Doyle's words reverberated inside his head. *'Your grandmother needs to see familiar faces regularly.'*

Conversation with Doris Jarrod was well-nigh impossible anyway. If she didn't recognise him, couldn't tell him from Adam, the visit would be untenable.

When the door opened and an attendant wheeled Doris Jarrod in, he held his breath. There was no flicker of recognition, no nod of acknowledgement, no hint of a smile.

'Hello, gran. How you doing? It's Ryan.'

'I know it's you. I'm not stupid, you know.'

Ryan let out a breath.

'So, how are you?' he asked again.

The old woman looked past Ryan as if searching for something.

'You not brought your boy with you? I was looking forward to seeing him.'

'Who?'

She waved a hand in his direction. 'You know, with the daft haircut.'

Ryan gulped. 'You mean James, gran. He's not…'

He caught the carer's eyes. The attendant's eyes smiled as he shook his head.

Ryan remembered. *Don't correct her.*

'James isn't home.' The words were harder to say than he imagined.

'Not to worry. You're here now. What about Ernest? He hasn't visited for ages. I'm a bit annoyed.'

Ernest was Doris's husband. He'd been dead almost as long as Ryan had lived.

'I'm sure he'll come soon, gran.'

The woman teared up and Ryan was pleased when the carer provided solace by laying a hand on her shoulder. Doris responded by resting her mottled hand on his latex glove.

'You two haven't been introduced. Ryan, this is Gordon. He's my special man. Gordon, this is Norman.'

The dark eyed man winked behind his face shield as he said, 'Pleased to meet you, Norman,' he said, going along with Doris Jarrod's faux pas.

'Likewise,' Ryan said, sadly.

Conversation became muted once they'd discussed the weather three times and agreed what an awful woman that Mrs Thatcher is. After little more than quarter of an hour, Ryan stood to leave.

'Gran, I have to go. I'm dropping Spud off at the boarding kennels. I might be away for a couple of days. Possibly longer, who knows?'

He looked at the old woman through a veil of tears. 'Take care, gran. I love you.'

The woman placed her palm against the perspex divider. Ryan matched it on the other side of the screen.

'Bye Norman,' she said.

Ryan turned his back on the room and made for the exit with tears streaking his cheeks.

'Don't worry,' the man called Gordon said. 'I won't let her out of my sight.'

Ryan raised an arm in acknowledgement and stepped from the solitude of the care home pod, out into the roar and the smell of traffic on Whickham Bank.

**

A thought struck Danskin as he drove Sam Maynard towards the police station in Southwick, Sunderland, where the Prince Bishop constabulary held Pavel Maric.

'Ma'am, it's not possible Maric is one of ours, is it?'

She looked up from the tablet she was using for research. 'What's your thinking, Stephen?'

'We seem to have a fair amount of intel on this Yu Tube operation now we've access to the Met files. Maric couldn't be the source, could he?'

'I don't think we've anyone inside this, Stephen. It would be convenient if we had because we wouldn't need lean on him.' She set the tablet on the seat alongside her. 'Yet, it certainly explains away the attempt on his life, I suppose. Revenge is as good a motive as double-crossing a drugs deal. We'll find out soon enough.'

Danskin turned right at the Grange Hotel and headed south on Thompson Road for no other reason than it avoided passing the Stadium of Light. Maynard resumed her research.

'The Bishops are treating Maric as nothing more than a witness at this point. They'd have set him on his way by now if we hadn't pulled those strings. I'm not convinced we'll get much out of him today,' she said. 'I think we should use this chat as an opportunity to win his confidence.'

Danskin craned his neck as he sought a gap in traffic at the junction with Sunderland Road.

'How do you plan to win him round?' he asked.

'Offer him witness protection. You and I know that'll take days to organise, but Maric won't.'

'Unless he is one of ours.'

'True, but I'm confident he's not.'

Danskin eyeballed a group of yobs dressed in red and white shirts congregating on Southwick Green. His remarkable resemblance to Alan Shearer grabbed their attention and they universally flicked the Vs. It wasn't quite enough for him to nick them, unfortunately.

'What if he still won't talk?' he said, turning his attention back to Sam Maynard.

'If Maric doesn't want to play nicely, then we'll take him on a little drive.'

'Eh?'

'We'll ask him to take us to the scene.'

'Does he even know where that is?'

'I'm sure a drive around will help acquaint him.'

As they queued in traffic awaiting access to a B&M store's car park, Danskin said, 'I'm not exactly sure that's the way to win his confidence, like.'

They crawled forward, stopped, and moved off again.

'I'm not comfortable allowing the bad guy to control the timetable,' Maynard responded. 'The OCG are in control of that with Jarrod. I'm not letting Maric do the same with me.'

At the curve of Church Bank, Danskin flashed his warrant card at a camera and waited for the police station gates to swing open.

'If we play hardball, I'm sure Maric will clam up. I vote we wait a couple of days and get him into protection.'

Sam Maynard clicked her tongue.

'Thing is, Stephen, we can't be sure Ryan and his family have a couple of days.'

CHAPTER FIFTEEN

Sam Maynard strode into the Sunderland station's holding cell after a tense stand-off with a local constabulary reluctant to hand over their spoils.

The man inside was a wiry, unshaven individual in his mid-thirties. He wore dishevelled clothing which matched his unkempt hair. His eyes were puffy and red against sallow skin.

'Pavel Maric,' she said. 'I'm Superintendent Sam Maynard of City and County Police. This is Detective Chief Inspector Stephen Danskin.'

The man looked at Maynard warily, then at Danskin, before his eyes shifted back to Maynard.

'You know that is my name.'

The accent was distinctly East European, but his response assured Maynard he understood the English language well enough.

She looked him up and down. 'Bad night?'

'No good,' he replied with understatement.

'I was sorry to hear about your cousin. It must have been hard for you.'

A man in a white paper suit scraped material from beneath Maric's fingernails and popped the detritus into an evidence bag for later analysis.

'I not kill Silvia.'

'Did I say you did? I don't think so. No; from what I gather, the local plod are holding you without charge.'

'Then why this?' his mouth curled at the CSI officer and his probe.

'He's just doing his job. You see, we haven't found Silvia's body. There's no murder to investigate until we find some evidence.'

'And you are looking for this evidence on me. You believe I kill my cousin. I did not.'

Maynard allowed her eyes to sparkle. Gave Maric the warmest of smiles.

'Then help us find who did kill her.'

'I know nothing,' Maric said.

Despite the traumatic circumstances, Danskin chuckled. He couldn't help but think of Manuel in Fawlty Towers, until Maynard shot him down with a single look.

'Pavel,' she continued. 'Whatever you say will help YOU, not me. I believe you know you're in a lot of danger…'

'Here, I am safe.'

'You can't stay here.'

'What if I said I killed Silvia. Then could I stay?'

Maynard and Danskin traded looks. Maric was scared shitless. Time for a different approach.

'Listen,' Danskin said, 'I need to talk to you about what happened, but it takes time. If it was official, like. You'd need a solicitor. We'd have to get an interpreter. We'll make a proper start when they get here, but anything you say before that will be off-record.'

'Solicitor first.'

Stephen Danskin let out an exaggerated sigh. 'Okay, but anything you say then will be on the record. You might just drop yourself into all manner of shit with us, as well as with your cousin's murderer.'

Maric remained unconvinced. Danskin opened the flaps of his jacket. 'See, there's no mic on me. Look around – do you see any recording equipment? Any cameras?'

Maric stared at the cell floor.

'Pavel, you can speak freely. It's not as if owt will get posted on YouTube.'

That got the Macedonian's attention.

'What did I say?' Danskin asked, playing the innocent.

'You tell jokes, yes?'

'No. I don't. Ever. So, have you anything to tell us?'

Maric met Danskin's stare. 'I tell fuck all.'

Maynard stood. 'Come on, Stephen. Let's go.' She directed words at the uniformed officer by the cell door. 'When CSI are finished, book him for murder.'

'No!'

Maric's objections were muffled behind the closed cell door.

'What now?' Danskin asked once they were in the corridor.

'He's our only lead. If we must do this by the book, that's what we'll do.'

'Ma'am, you said it yourself: we haven't got the time. Besides, you saw how he reacted when I mentioned Yu Tube. We need to know more about the operation, and then we have to find Ryan Jarrod.'

'The first bit's easy. From the Op Sage intel, we know Yu Tube began its UK operations in London. There's a lot of competition down south. The Yu Tube set-up quickly realised they had an untapped market outside the capital, ripe for picking.'

'I see where you're going. Operation Tower became a nationwide investigation, managed by local forces.'

'Exactly. Which is how I became involved with Op Sage. Stephen, these guys are professionals. They have business models to make Jeff Bezos envious, cashflow projections like any major company you can name, and a growth market to rival BioNTech. They treat their dealers, all their middlemen, in fact, as well-paid employees – they're almost akin to franchise-holders, I guess. With one important difference: the middle-men work under threat of death if they put a toe out of line.'

Danskin whistled. 'Maric and his cousin stepped out of line.'

'Big time, Stephen. Big time.'

'Why call themselves YuTube? A bit corny, isn't it?'

'Not really. The head honcho goes by the name of Benny Yu. He's good – or bad, if you prefer. All we know about him is his name.'

They stood in the corridor, each working through their own thoughts.

The Super broke the silence first. 'I take it you've heard nothing from Jarrod?'

'He's got his bloody phone off. I've tried Hannah but it seems they had a tiff. Like a typical woman, she's too stubborn to make the first move.'

'She has to, Stephen.'

'She can't. If his phone's off, it's off.'

'In that case, get her to turn up naked on his doorstep with as many sex toys as she can carry.'

Only half-jokingly, Danskin said, 'That's my stepdaughter you're talking about.'

'I don't care. If I thought it'd have the right effect on Jarrod, I'd do it myself.'

'Really?'

'Yes, really.' She looked at him and he drowned in her reservoir eyes. 'You've a lot to learn about me, Stephen Danskin.'

He cleared his throat. 'So, what's our next move?'

'I don't reckon we'll get much more out of Maric today by the time his solicitor and interpreter get their arses into gear. We'll let him sit tight for the night then, first thing, I'm taking him for a little drive. See if we can't locate the alleged murder site.'

'I look forward to it.'

She shook her head. 'Not you, Stephen. It's time I brought the rest of the squad in. I'll leave Ravi and Gav at Forth Street chasing up leads. I'll bring the rest of the crew out here for the road trip. It's high time they got involved.'

'What about me?'

'Nominally, you oversee Ravi and Gav.'

'Nominally?'

'Yes, *'Nominally.'* You convinced me it was useful if we had Jarrod on the inside, but he's no use if we don't know where the hell he is or what he's up to. So, nominally, you're in charge of Sangar and O'Hara. In reality, you're using the time to move heaven and earth until you've located Ryan Jarrod.'

Maynard gave him a solemn look.

'He's going to get himself and his family killed. Find him, Stephen.'

**

Ryan dumped his two bags on a flimsy shelf in the bedroom of a rundown B&B on Gateshead's Durham Road.

He'd convinced himself it was the right thing to do even before he'd visited Doris Jarrod but, now he was here, he wasn't so sure. It wasn't the smell of damp, the traffic noise from the busy through-road outside, or the peeling wallpaper which gave him second thoughts. It was the sense of isolation; the knowledge he was on his own with the destiny of those he loved balanced delicately in his hands.

Ryan drew comfort from the fact Stephen Danskin was on his side; less reassuring was the thought the DCI had trusted Sam Maynard – a woman they'd worked with for a matter of months and who neither of them *really* knew – with the safety of his family.

He was sure both Danskin and Maynard would try to contact him. He thought they'd probably already tried. They'd want him to follow their instructions. Well, they could sod off. They could do their thing, he'd do his.

Ryan believed – had to believe – that two separate lines of enquiry doubled the chances of his folks getting out of this alive. His personal mobile remained switched off. He was totally off-grid; free to do his own thing safe in the knowledge not even Ravi Sangar and his tec guys could locate his whereabouts.

The only regret he had was that it meant he was also out of contact with the few people he really needed: his dad and his brother. And Detective Sergeant Hannah Graves.

Thoughts of her reckless curls, the cheeky dimple when she smiled, and the Chinese dragon tattoo on her midriff were lost amidst fears of what the voices might do with her if he didn't follow orders.

He headed for the shower to wash that girl right outta his hair, only to discover there was no shower. Instead, he emptied his overnight bag. It held two changes of clothing, a couple of bits and pieces he'd picked up from the station, a can of deodorant, and a toothbrush.

The other bag was more important to him, Geordie Amos's old Slazenger bag. All the kit remained intact. Most importantly, the cheap - and terrifyingly silent - burner phone still held 80% charge. Ryan plugged it in all the same. He wasn't about to risk losing signal. At some point - today, tomorrow, next week – they'd come for him.

He flopped onto the bed. The mattress squeaked beneath him. Ryan switched on the TV which hung so low on the wall he had to spread his legs and point his toes so he could see.

He hopped channels, found nothing worth watching, so he closed his eyes and settled down with BBC News 24 as a bed partner. Morpheus had almost wrapped his arms around him when he was roused by the urgent tones of the presenter.

'And we have some breaking news to bring you from the north-east. With the details, here's Megan Wolfe. Megan – what can you tell us?'

The mention of the name grabbed Ryan's attention. Wolfe previously worked for The Mercury newspaper, where she targeted much of her investigative work on the City and County Police.

'Martine, I'm here outside Sunderland North police station where I understand a man is being held in connection with a murder investigation. I'm told police have yet to discover a body, but they are treating the claims seriously.'

'What can you tell us about the man being detained?'

Megan Wolfe pouted at the camera and turned her face slightly to project her best side.

'We are unable to name him for legal reasons, Martine, but I understand he is a foreign national in his mid-thirties.' Megan adopted a stern expression. 'I am led to believe the alleged victim is related to the man – who is yet to face charge – and both have historical links to the use of illegal drugs. The detainee was found wandering the streets of South Tyneside by a member of the Prince Bishop constabulary on a routine patrol. The man is reported to have been in a confused and dishevelled state.'

Wolfe paused for effect while the camera scanned the outside of the Southwick station, picking out the Prince Bishop Constabulary logo. As the camera lingered on the building, Wolfe concluded her report off-camera.

'Intriguingly, I gather the case is being transferred to the City and County police for investigation. This is an unusual move, to say the least, and we don't yet know the reasons for it. I'll keep across the story and update you as soon as I learn more. In the meantime, I'll hand back to you, Martine.'

The blonde-haired woman in the studio returned to screen. 'Megan Wolfe reporting from Sunderland. We'll bring you more on that breaking story as it develops.'

Ryan turned off the TV as the presenter switched to a story about the Royal Family.

His head spun. *Was this linked to his family? What did it mean for them? For him? How did Wolfe get her dirty paws all over a top-secret investigation? Who leaked the story?*

He got some of his answers within ten minutes when the burner phone took its first breath.

**

'You imbecile!'

Yu's henchman flinched.

'He's still alive! Why didn't you check?'

'Sir, you returned to your car. I followed you. You told me I had to follow you everywhere.'

'Not immediately, you incompetent piece of shit. I told you to make sure the job was done.'

'It *was* done. You ordered it, we did it. You saw the car fall from the cliff. You saw the fire. Heard the explosion.'

'Of course, I did! But your job was to make sure the mission was successful. That they were both dead.'

'Mr Yu, no-one could have survived that.'

'The point is, they did.' Yu's eyes flashed like black diamonds. 'You saw the report: they have Maric!'

'It could be a trap, sir. To make us think he's alive. To lure us into making a mistake.'

Yu slammed the table in front of him. 'Nonsense. They have him, I tell you. I'm above shit-shovelling, but now that's just what I have to do. All because you fucked up. You'll pay for this, one day.'

Yu picked up the phone.

**

It didn't make sense to Danskin. Apart from the Whickham incident, all gang-related activity had occurred on South Tyneside, yet ANPR tracked the *Tulpen Uit Amsterdam* truck heading north.

'Sangar, I want you to trace a route for the lorry. We know the timescales, so how far could it have got in that time? Bear in mind it had to drop the Macedonians off, then adopt its disguise before it returned to port.'

'I'll do that straight away, sir. I'll get Todd to give me a hand 'til the guv'nor calls for him.'

Danskin was about to agree when his phone rang.

'Ma'am,' Sangar heard him say.

'You're joking, right?'

Pause.

'Fuck me.'

Longer pause.

Sangar mouthed *'What's up?'* Danskin shushed him.

A 'Yup', 'No', and 'Jesus Christ' followed before the DCI ended the call.

'You going to tell me, sir?'

'Aye. You can forget about Todd Robson giving you a hand. Super wants the rest of the crew ower the river, pronto.'

'Why now?'

'Because that wretched Wolfe woman's just been on the telly. Somehow, she's got a hint of what's up. Told the world – and the OCG - that Pavel Maric is still alive and where he's being held. He's a sitting duck. Super wants the drive-out to happen yesterday, and then we'll move Maric, even if only temporarily until witness protection get him a safe house.'

Sangar swore. 'It's just me, thee, and Gav, then.'

'Wrong. It's just you and O'Hara.'

'What's she got you doing?'

'Me? I'm going to find Jarrod.'

'What do you mean, *'Find him?'* I thought you said he'd got Covid? That's why all the lads took lateral flow tests, wasn't it?'

Bollocks. Danskin had forgotten the story Maynard had concocted to explain away Ryan's absence.

'Just a manner of speaking, Sangar. I'll get him doing background checks on the Whickham victims. He's not so ill he can't trawl the internet now and again. We need all the help we can muster on this one.'

He dialled Ryan's number one more time.

**

Amelia Curry slipped into her coat.

'That's me done for the day, Hannah.'

'Okay. Wish I had flexi-time I could use anytime I fancied an early finish.'

'Steady on. We civil servants don't get many perks, you know.'

'Like I do? I don't think so,' Hannah laughed. 'Go on; get yourself off. Anything special lined up?'

'Andrew's hoping to get a half-day. I thought we might have some afternoon delight.'

Hannah rolled her eyes. 'Too much info. It's alright for some.'

'Oh aye? Your fella not living up to expectations in that department?'

'Err, excuse me – I'm still in charge here, remember; you impertinent minx.'

'That's avoiding the question,' Amelia chided, good-naturedly.

'Ry's been pushing his luck a bit lately so I'm playing hard to get. Let's just say I'm waiting on a call.'

A phone chose that moment to ring. Hannah's heart jumped with anticipation, until she realised it wasn't her ringtone.

'Hi,' Amelia said into her Samsung, an excited note in her voice. 'Well, yeah; I could, I suppose.'

Hannah saw the customs intel operative check her watch. 'Give me an hour, okay?' Amelia said. 'What's this all about?'

She moved the phone away from her ear and gave it a curious look as the caller ended the conversation.

'Lover boy changed his mind?' Hannah joked.

'No. It wasn't Andrew. It was Dawn.'

'Your sister? That's great news.' She saw her colleague's face. 'Isn't it?'

Amelia didn't answer.

CHAPTER SIXTEEN

'Dawn?'

It was the car Amelia recognised, not the girl behind the wheel. They'd agreed to meet in the car park of a Lidl supermarket off Boldon Lane. It wasn't a place the Dawn she knew would ever shop. That, above everything, aroused her suspicion.

Amelia found a bay a few rows behind and approached her sibling's car with a sense of foreboding. When she saw her sister sat upright, eyes staring forward, she knew her intuition was as fine-tuned as ever.

This wasn't the Dawn she remembered. Gone were the long, expensively coloured blonde locks. In their place, short mousey hair which looked as if she'd trimmed it herself.

Instead of her usual low-cut top and exposed cleavage, Dawn wore a Matalan crewneck T-shirt. Her legs, normally tanned and extending to eternity from the briefest of skirts, were covered by cheap tracksuit trousers.

And rather than lie under a portrait of cosmetics, her face was lined; a complex mix of puffy redness around the eyes and waxy tautness at the mouth.

'Dawn!' Amelia said again. She rapped on the passenger side window and saw her sister levitate from her seat with fright.

'Oh God, Dawn – what's he done?' She pulled at the door. Found it locked from the inside.

Dawn woke from her catatonic state and unlocked the car. Amelia climbed in. Dawn locked the door again as soon it closed behind her sister.

'It's something to do with Bryn, isn't it?'

She didn't reply at first. Then, she gave a series of jerky nods with her head.

'What's he done?'

Dawn looked around. Saw no-one near the car. She gripped the hem of her T-shirt and slowly raised it until her plain cream bra was exposed.

'Ohmygod, ohmygod, ohmygod!' Amelia stuttered.

Dawn's entire torso was the colour of a thundercloud. Fresh bruising discoloured her body, cuts wept at the side of her ribcage. Worse, in Amelia's mind, was the fact Dawn's face was untouched.

To the outside world, nothing seemed out of place.

'We're going to the police.'

'No. We can't. Promise me, you won't.'

Amelia sucked in air. 'This was Bryn, wasn't it? What the fuck did he do this for?'

'He isn't normally like this, Amelia. Honest, this was a one-off.'

Amelia tried to open the door.

'Don't! Don't call the police.'

'I'm just going for my bag, for God's sake. I've left it in my car.'

'No. I can't trust you.'

'You can't trust *ME*? Look at the state he's got you in, but it's *me* you can't trust? Jesus, Dawn – he's really got into your head.'

Dawn began weeping. It was a silent cry, but the redness around her eyes shone with tears.

'Right. You mightn't let me go to the police, but I'm not letting you go home. Not while he's there.'

Dawn grimaced and avoided her sister's eye.

'Has he hurt you anywhere else?'

'No.'

'Dawn! Has he hurt you anywhere else? Like, down below, you know?'

She shook her head.

Amelia bit down on her own emotions and waited for her sister to do the talking. Eventually, she did.

'Bryn's always been controlling. I think that's what I liked in him, the fact he was so in control. But it soon took over everything. Became overwhelming. He's never been aggressive before, not physically. Just emotionally. He says things in a way that makes me do what he wants. This time, though, he was different.'

Amelia ordered her thoughts. 'Different in what way?'

'He'd been working. He video-called me and he seemed his usual self.'

Amelia pulled a face but refrained from comment.

'I waited for him to get home. I waited and waited. I couldn't sleep so I got up to make myself a cup of tea. That's when he came in.'

'And hit you?'

Dawn shook her head. 'He was like a ghost. Pale. And sweaty. Agitated, like. Pacing up and down. He looked ghastly. Terrified, I'd describe it as. I knew straight away something had happened. I was worried about him. I asked if he was okay, and he just stood up and walked away from me as if I wasn't even there.'

'Drunk?'

'No. He uses now and again, but not drink. And it's never made him like that before. I followed him through to the kitchen. I couldn't see very well in the dark, but I thought I smelt something. Paraffin, or thinners, maybe.'

Dawn stopped talking. Folk buzzed around the car, but no-one took any notice of them.

'I put on the kitchen light. Bryn had taken off his shirt and was balling it up to go in the washer. It looked like he'd burnt his shirt, so I told him it was ruined. Said there was no point washing it.'

She paused. 'I asked him what had happened.' Dawn took in air as if it were her last breath.

131

'He hit me. Hard. In the stomach. When I doubled over, he kidney-punched me. I remember lying curled up on the kitchen floor, Bryn standing over me. Then, he kicked me. Again, and again. He kept kicking me. I thought he was going to kill me, Amelia. I thought I was going to die.'

She lay her head in her younger sister's lap and cried like a baby.

'Fuck, Dawn; he can't get away with this.'

'I know. I'm not going back. Can I stay with you? I promise I won't get in the way of you and Andrew.'

Amelia stroked Dawn's hair. 'Ssshh. That's the last thing you need worry about. Andrew will be fine. Absolutely fine.'

Dawn raised her head. 'Thanks,' she said simply.

'And I'm staying with you. I'm off the rest of the day and, tomorrow, I'll tell work I've been pinged by track and trace.'

'You don't need do that.'

'Yes. I do have to do that. You're my sister.'

'He won't come looking for me. Even if he does, he'll come with a bunch of flowers and apologies. He always does, and it's always cos I've pissed him off by saying stupid things.'

'Don't go there, Dawn. This is not your fault.'

They fell into silence. Amelia knew what she had to say but didn't know how to phrase it. Instead, she just came out with it.

'Hannah, at work. She's a copper assigned to the Port of Tyne. This isn't her thing anymore but her fella, Ryan, I think he's called is a Detective. He sounds canny. I could ask her to have a word with him, off the record…'

'NO! Absolutely not. You promised you wouldn't.'

'I don't think I did, actually.'

'Well, promise me now. Don't go to the police.'

Amelia sighed. 'Okay. I won't go to the police. Now, let's get out of here. Follow me home, if you trust me enough.'

'Amelia, it isn't only you. I don't trust ANYONE, not anymore. Not after this. I know you're all I've got. I'll follow your car. Go, quick, before I've time to change my mind.'

'Okay, but it'd help if you unlocked the door.'

Dawn almost smiled as she pressed the release mechanism.

'Follow me,' Amelia said. 'I'll keep you in sight. If I do happen to lose you, I'll wait for you until you catch up. It's only a few miles. Nothing will go wrong, I promise. I won't let it.'

Dawn flinched. 'I don't think that's something you can promise.' She hugged her stomach. 'You see, my baby's in here. At least, she was. I don't know if she's still with me. I really don't know.'

Amelia had no words for her sister, only tears.

**

Stephen Danskin gave up his attempt to contact Ryan after the fifth time the automated voice told him it hadn't been possible to connect the call.

Instead, he rang Hannah Graves. Asked if she'd heard from him. She said she hadn't, that it was up to Ryan to contact her, and why did Danskin think it necessary to call at her work about it?

He very nearly told her, so he ended the call before temptation won.

'Sangar,' he called as he left his office, 'Is it possible to trace a mobile phone if it's switched off? Yes, or no?'

'Depends.'

'That's not one of the options.'

Ravi Sangar spun to face the DCI. 'That's as maybe, but it's the only one I can give you, sir.'

Danskin's mouth formed a straight line and he snorted from his nostrils. 'Go on, then. Explain.'

'Tracking a switched off phone is difficult. It'll stop communicating with mobile towers so it's only possible to trace the location it was at when last switched on.'

'So, the answer is *'No'* not *'It depends'.*'

'It depends.'

'For fuck's sake, Sangar, don't play games.'

The DCI's tone took Ravi aback. 'If the phone's Bluetooth was set to on at the time the device was switched off, it's technically possible to trace it. Difficult, but possible.'

Danskin nodded and scratched his stubble.

'But,' Sangar continued, 'If the device was set to air-plane mode, all bets are off. It's absolutely not possible to locate its whereabouts.'

Decision time. Danskin either gave Ravi Ryan's number – which would prompt a tumult of questions Danskin couldn't answer – or he came up with something else.

While he considered the matter, he paced to a whiteboard. On it hung a map of the region dissected by a semi-circle drawn in blue marker ink. Danskin knew it represented Ravi Sangar's estimate of the *Tulpen Uit Amsterdam* truck's journey limit.

As he pondered his next move, his eyes followed the arc of the line. It extended west to Hexham and Bellingham, both quiet, rural towns, and north as far as Otterburn and Rothbury. Neither of these locations seemed a likely destination for drugs or for Pavel and Silvia Maric.

Ravi's line extended eastwards to the Northumbrian coast as far north as Warkworth and Amble.

South of these lay the urbane market town of Morpeth, and the former mining community of Ashington.

None of these rang alarm bells with Danskin. The sight of the town situated five miles south of Ashington, though, prompted a surge of electricity inside Danskin's brain.

It was the town of Blyth. Home to the late George Amos.

Danskin spoke as he headed for the bullpen exit.

'Sangar, I need a favour...'

CHAPTER SEVENTEEN

Stephen Danskin signed out the keys of an unmarked Ford Focus and tore up the A189 Spine Road towards Blyth.

It was a town he wished he knew more about. He'd had ample opportunity to find out from Hannah, but they'd made a pact not to talk shop to each other ever since Sam Maynard moved her to the Ports Authority.

It was a lost opportunity. All he had to go off were limited childhood memories of a lonely fish and chip shop standing back from the dunes, the remains of wartime defence pillboxes on the beach and, for some surreal reason, he remembered Blyth once had an Approved School with an odd statue of a young boy in a Jack Tar uniform at its gatepost.

At one time, he'd worked with a DS from Blyth, and he remembered he lived on somewhere called South Beach Estate. From memory, he recalled it was a pleasant location. He'd also heard good things about a newish estate up by Asda, though he'd never been. Where he brought the Focus to a halt was neither South Beach nor newish.

This was Lynn Street, and he was parked at the exact spot Ryan Jarrod had when he'd called on Maddi Amos. Or Corrigan. Christ, Danskin didn't even know what he should call her. At least, he didn't until Ravi Sangar rang him with the information he'd requested back at the station.

As soon as the call ended, Danskin stepped from the Focus into the shadows of Lynn Street. The door opened barely six inches. In a parody of Hammer horror movie from the sixties, a woman's face appeared at the crack.

'Yes?' she said.

'Maddi Corrigan?'

'You lot again. I've got nowt to say, man. Give it a rest, will you?'

Danskin smiled to himself. He hadn't shown her his warrant card, yet she'd instantly known.

'It's okay. I'm not here to ask you anything. Just making a routine check to make sure you're okay.'

'I've just lost me frigging Da. I'd hardly say I was okay, like.'

He tried to look reassuring. 'Of course. You can tell me to go away if you like, Maddi. I don't need to talk to you. I just came to see how you were getting on and nobody was giving you grief.'

The door shut in his face. *'Bugger,'* he thought, while saying, 'If you need owt, just ring Forth Street and ask to speak to me. Stephen Danskin's the name.'

He put his hands in his pockets and contemplated his next move. He didn't have long to wait. The door opened again.

'So: you're Stephen Danskin, then.'

The comment surprised him though he tried not to show it.

'I am,' he smiled while showing her his ID.

'What do you want?'

'Like I say, I'm just here to make sure you and Lance are coping.'

'That makes a change for you lot. You're persistent fuckers, I'll give you that.'

'*Persistent fuckers*' is a lot more polite than some call us.'

Maddi chuckled and began to cough. 'I was making a cup of tea. Fancy one?' She opened the door wide.

'Aye, ta. I wouldn't mind.'

Danskin followed Maddi into a living room covered in dust and a trip-hazard carpet. All four corners of the room were piled high with junk.

A young boy sat inches from a TV screen, a games console clutched in his hand. He gave an anxious start but quickly turned back to the screen and continued zapping a zombie horde.

Danskin gave Maddi a quizzical look. She tipped her hand a couple of times. He interpreted its meaning as '*So-so*' and followed the stick-thin young woman into a tiny kitchen.

'Sorry it's a mess. I'm usually not bad at the housework. I just haven't been arsed these last few days.'

'I can only imagine. Don't worry about it.'

'I didn't sleep much, neither.'

'It'll take a while to get over something like this. Don't overthink things, and don't apologise for anything.' He lowered his voice. 'Remember you've got Lance, though. Don't go doing something stupid.'

'Like throwing mesel off a bridge, you mean?' she bristled.

Danskin tipped his head towards a bottle of Malibu next to the kettle. 'No. Like drinking. It won't help. Trust me, I know better than anyone.'

'You had your share, an' aal?'

'Messy divorce. Nearly lost me daughter to a maniac. Yeah, I've had my share.'

She smiled. 'Not to mention losing your prospective grandkid, eh?'

'Sorry?'

'Ryan told me all about it.'

Danskin's jaw dropped open. 'You've spoken to DS Jarrod?'

'Aye. It's the only reason you're in here. He said you were canny. Like a dad to him, I think his words were.'

Maddi poured boiling water into two cups. She left the teabag in hers and carried it into the living room. Danskin left his on the bench and trailed behind her like an inquisitive mongrel.

'When was this? What did he say? What did you tell him?'

'Whoa, hang on. You said you weren't here to ask questions. That's three, straight off.'

'It's important.'

'Sorry to disappoint you, but I didn't tell him much and he told me even less, apart from the fact he might be away a couple of days and, while he was, I could trust you.'

Danskin prepared to call Sam Maynard as he asked, 'Where was he going?'

He let go of the phone when she replied, 'I divvent knaa. He didn't say.'

Stephen Danskin felt a headache coming on. He slumped forward, rubbing his brow.

'Listen, Maddi: I know I said I wasn't going to quiz you, but we haven't got much to go on. I'm sure you want the bastards who took you and Lance, and did what they did to your dad, put away. Is there anything at all you want to tell me?'

She shook her head. 'I told Ryan I wasn't running away, but I'm not stupid, either. Folk around here gossip.'

'Same as anywhere, Maddi.'

'Nah. Not like here. Don't get me wrong, they're the salt of the earth, but they're bloody nosey fuckers, the lot of 'em. They see cops coming round, it'll be all over Facebook before you can say shit the bed.'

'I can get you somewhere safe.'

'No. I'm not running.'

'It's not running. Call it lying low. I'm not talking witness protection or owt. Christ, tectonic plates move quicker than that lot, but I could get you into a hotel somewhere.'

She gave him a glacial stare.

Danskin held up his hands. 'Okay, okay.'

She sipped her tea while he listened to a silence broken only by the sound of exploding zombies and Lance's cheers.

'Your dad knew he was going, didn't he?'

'What do you mean? Anyway, that's another question, innit?'

He ignored her. 'Look, we know those people contacted your dad. Set it all up. It didn't all just happen on Saturday. This has been planned for a while.'

She stared at the ripped carpet.

'Maddi, I know how much you got out of this. One of the lads at the station checked it out. Ten grand landed in your account yesterday.'

'Get out of my house!'

'Ten grand. You can do a lot with that. Set Lance up for a start in life, it would.'

'Fuck off!'

She launched herself at him. He grabbed her wrists. Pulled them against her sides. She was sobbing hard while she screamed at him. Eventually, she lay her face against his chest and sobbed so much she couldn't speak let alone swear.

Danskin wrapped his arms around her.

'It's okay, Maddi. It's okay. I know you didn't want this. Tell me what happened, then I'll leave you.'

The commotion even roused Lance from the zombie apocalypse. Maddi despatched him to his bedroom. The boy went without protest.

Maddi sought the Malibu after all. Her lips curled around her teeth as the neat liquor hit the spot. When she spoke, even Maddi Corrigan had adopted the voice of the living dead, lifeless and flat.

'He didn't want any money. Me, neither.'

'Tell me about it, then. Tell me how it came to this?'

Maddi made a noise like a deflating balloon.

'Da was approached about a month after he'd been diagnosed. Like I say, nowt stays secret round here.' She took a second slug of the alcohol. 'Look, the money and stuff - it's not how it seems.'

Danskin said, 'You mightn't have wanted the money, but you took it.'

Maddi let out a deep sigh. 'Da changed with the diagnosis. He wasn't worried about himself, but he couldn't bear the thought of Lance seeing him end up a vegetable. He wanted to live life as best he could.'

'I don't see how that fits with him being on that railway bridge.'

'He knew he couldn't beat it, but he wanted quality time with Lance.'

She took another swig.

'He was doon the club when this lad approached him. Said he'd heard aboot the cancer, and he had some pills that would take away the pain. Da would never do drugs, not like cannabis or cocaine. But this stuff seemed to numb the dreadful headaches. The lad kept giving him the stuff, for free, like. I should've known nee bugger would hand over drugs for nowt.'

'Do you have a name?'

She shook her head vigorously. 'No names. Na. This is all off the record, but if you dig deep enough, you'll find him. He's got a record.'

'Which means you know who he is.'

'Course I frigging do.'

'His name, Maddi. I need his name.'

'Nee chance.'

Danskin sighed. 'Madeira Corrigan, you're under arrest for perverting the course of justice. You are not...'

'You're fucking joking me, right?'

'A name, Maddi, or you come with me to Forth Street and Lance goes into foster care.'

'You wouldn't!'

'Try me.'

'You bastard. Ryan said I could trust you. He promised me.'

'This isn't just about you. Other families are involved.'

She looked at him blankly.

'Yes, Maddi. That's right: they've taken someone else's family.'

'No way. Who's? I suppose it doesn't matter.'

'Aye, it matters. It matters to me, and it should matter to you. The other family belongs to Ryan Jarrod, that's who's family they've got.'

'Oh fuck.'

'Yes, *'fuck'*. Now: a name.'

'Stuart. Stuey.'

'Stuart who?'

'He stopped giving Da the pills. Said he had to do something in return if he wanted more of them. Da told him to piss off, but the lad came back the next day and offered him money. Ten grand. Now, Stuey hasn't two coppers to rub together, so I know it isn't his money. Anyway, Da wasn't having owt to do with it.'

She held the Malibu bottle up to the light before continuing.

'I suppose that's where Lance and me came into things. Insurance, like. Or assurance. I divvent knaa which is which.'

'So, they told him to stand on a bridge and ask for Ryan Jarrod, and they'd give him ten grand. Why?'

'Don't ask me. You're the copper roond here. All I know is, Stuey must have told 'em where we live cos a bunch of them knocked on the door and took us just like that. Just like you came knocking on my door. And Ryan before you, and all your other mates.'

'Why did your dad jump?'

'How the fuck do I know? I'm not bloody psychic. He's dead: I can hardly go asking him, can I? Maybe he really couldn't stand the pain. Maybe he was thinking of Lance.'

'Or ten grand.'

'No. Not that. Maybe they told him he had to jump for them to let me and Lance go.'

'I need that name, Maddi.'

'I just told you the name.'

'Second name.'

She shook her head.

'Do you want someone else killed? I need his surname.'

Maddi rocked back and forward on her heels.

Maddi, the name.'

'Hetton, for fuck's sake, man! Stuey Hetton.'

Danskin let himself out.

CHAPTER EIGHTEEN

Two uniformed officers led a handcuffed Pavel Maric to the rear passenger side of the unmarked vehicle. Once the Macedonian was settled in the seat next to Lyall Parker, one of the uniforms fed the seatbelt to Parker who buckled Maric in.

Sam Maynard half-turned and offered Maric a reassuring smile. 'Sorry about the handcuffs,' she said, 'But until you tell us more, I'm not taking any chances. Imagine my paperwork if we lost you.'

'I do not wish you to lose me.' Maric peered out the window, eyes darting back and forth as if he expected an Orc to appear at any moment.

One of the uniformed officers returned to the station, while the other slipped into the driver's seat of a marked car which already held Todd Robson and Lucy Dexter. Maynard had allowed the Prince Bishop constabulary to have a token presence and the driver – PC Joey Brooks – was it.

Brooks pulled the patrol car in front of the unmarked Vectra. Its radio crackled into life.

'You lead us out of the town. Once clear, let us pass and we'll take our lead from Mr Maric. You follow,' Superintendent Maynard instructed.

'Excuse me, ma'am – Sunderland's a city, not a town,' the constable shot back.

Todd Robson stifled a laugh.

'Just follow instructions, PC Brooks.'

'Yes ma'am. Understood.'

Brooks steered the car out of the compound, the Vectra close behind. From the Southwick station, the mini convoy passed the Stadium of Light and took the A1018 northbound.

From there, Maynard instructed PC Brooks to take the B1299 until they reached the point where Maric had been found wandering.

'Okay, PC Brooks. We'll take over from here,' Maynard announced over the radio.

Brooks allowed the Vectra through and drew the patrol car up behind it. Both cars waited with their engines idling.

'It's over to you now, Pavel,' Maynard said.

Maric said nothing. Maynard tried to catch his eye in the mirror, but Maric stared resolutely ahead.

'Okay. Have it your way. Let's just drive, DC Trebilcock. Let's see where we end up.'

Trebilcock slid the car into gear, with no clue where to go. The Cornishman began with a loop of Boldon Golf Course. Maric gave no glimmer of recognition. They took the main road through East Boldon via the Grey Horse. Still the Macedonian remained silent.

'Och, we could be here all day and night, man,' Lyall Parker said. 'Ye must recognise somewhere.'

'I do not want to say anything. I must not help you. They will find me and kill me.'

'Not if we find them first. Help us oot here. They killed your cousin. Do you want to spend the rest o' your life hiding from them?'

Maric stayed silent. Parker harrumphed and folded his arms as Trebilcock meandered the streets. All the while, Maynard studied the prisoner; his face pinched and drawn, expressionless and resigned.

Trebilcock reached a decision. A murder was unlikely to happen on an open road. He steered the vehicle onto a country lane heading south-east. Trebilcock slowed until he was sure the patrol car followed. He crawled down the lane. The silence inside the car suffocated them.

They passed a brown direction indicator half-hidden by overhanging branches. *Cutthroat Dene*, it signalled.

Maynard saw Maric swallow hard.

'It not here,' the Macedonian said, glumly. 'It happen near ocean.' His face contained a *'What have I just done?'* expression.

'It's near the coast,' Maynard said into the radio as Trebilcock increased the Vectra's speed.

'Copy,' Robson's voice came back. 'Put your foot down, you Mackem bastard,' she heard him say before he shut down the radio.

Maynard shook her head.

Trebilcock wasn't familiar with the area. Maynard, neither. Lyall Parker directed them to Seaburn and suggested they head north.

'Tell us when you recognise anything, Pavel.'

He gave no sign whether he would or wouldn't. Until he gave a whimper when he saw the red and white hoops adorning the Souter lighthouse.

Maynard spun in her seat. 'Here?'

He shook his head. 'Near,' he added.

The radio crackled into life.

Joey Brooks.

'I think I know where we're going, ma'am.'

The patrol car zipped ahead of the Vectra.

**

Darkness fell at a breakneck pace. Streetlights flickered alive and sent long, spectral shadows across the tarmac surface of the clifftop car park. The sound of a calm sea lapping ashore far below them seemed to whisper a hushed warning.

Todd Robson's voice came over the radio, startling the Vectra's occupants.

'Is this the spot, ma'am?'

Maynard knew Brooks had been on the money. Maric visibly quaked in the back seat, shivering as if he were an Antarctic explorer.

'Seems that way.'

'What does that mean?'

'Our friend hasn't said as much, but if it's not the right place, then he's just seen a ghost.'

'Interesting spot for it.'

'How come?' Superintendent Maynard asked.

'You wouldn't know, being a Cockney and all.'

'Essex isn't Cockney, Todd. Anyway, go on.'

'Marsden cliffs is more a location for suicide than murder. Renowned for it, it is. Mind you, they reckon there's a fair bit of dogging goes on in this car park, as well.'

The radio clicked off, then instantly came alive again.

'At least, that's what I'm told, of course.' Robson added.

Maynard heard Lucy Dexter giggle in the background. 'This is serious, guys. You've had your fun, now concentrate on the job in hand, yeah?'

'Ma'am,' a suitably chastised Robson replied.

'PC Brooks, drive through, please. Check for vehicles. Give it a mile or so.'

The marked car rolled through and shrank out of sight.

Brooks reported back within a couple of minutes. 'Nothing doing ahead, ma'am. It's all clear.'

The marked car reappeared.

'Good,' Maynard replied. 'We've got a clear line of sight up front should anything approach.' She looked over her shoulder. From the car park, the Coast Road curved gently away. 'We've got a blind spot behind, though. You guys hold round there and make sure nothing comes by.'

'Copy that.' The patrol car disappeared from view less than a hundred yards down the road.

'We're in position, ma'am.'

'Thanks, guys.' Maynard switched off the radio. 'Time you told us exactly what happened, Pavel.'

**

Todd Robson swivelled in his seat, one arm over the headrest.

'What do you make of the job so far, Lucy?'

The new recruit smiled. 'Let's just say I wouldn't get a job like this if I was still in uniform.'

'And what about the lads? They treating you well?'

'They are. I thought they might be a load of sexist sods but they're not. Apart from you, of course.' Lucy smiled again.

'*Canny set of gnashers on you, pet,*' Todd thought. 'I'm not sexist,' he said.

Lucy Dexter laughed.

'I miss Ryan, though.'

'Oh aye? He's spoken for, you know.'

'I didn't mean in that way. I like him, that's all.'

'What? 'Cos he got you the gig, you mean?'

'No. I just like the way he does things. Still, hopefully he'll be back soon if it's just a minor dose he's got.'

Todd opened his mouth to speak.

'Don't even think it, Todd.' They both laughed, but the comment went over Brooks' head.

'What do you make of Foreskin?'

Todd aimed the question at Lucy, but it was Brooks who asked, 'Who?'

'The DCI,' Todd explained.

'Why do you call him that?'

'Why'd you think? Because his name's Danskin and he's a dick.'

'Actually, you know,' Lucy said, 'I think he's okay.'

Todd nodded. 'Aye, he is, as it happens – but why let the truth get in the way of a good nickname?'

Lucy thought for a moment. 'I think he fancies Superintendent Maynard.'

'You don't say? It's bloody obvious the way he follows her round with puppy-dog eyes, man. He's got no chance, mind.'

'You reckon?'

'Nah. He's got a face like an elephant's knee.'

Lucy burst out laughing.

Todd half-turned to say something over his shoulder. He sensed, rather than saw, movement before the rear windscreen became obscured by a black shadow as a Toyota Landcruiser, lights off, rammed into the rear of the patrol car, fast and hard.

The impact shunted the patrol car several yards up the road.

Lucy screamed as her head bounced back and forth. Todd felt a sharp pain in his neck before it froze solid, his head facing Brooks.

Despite his seat belt, Joey Brooks shot forward. His forehead hit the steering wheel with such force the airbag exploded into his face, sending him backwards in his seat. The back of his skull hit the headrest and he slumped in his seat, oblivious to all.

Todd's own pain disappeared momentarily as his twisted neck forced him to stare directly into what had once been Joey Brooks' face. It would be a long time before it became recognisable as a face again.

Todd Robson was vaguely aware another vehicle, bottle green in colour, had drawn up alongside – so close that opening the driver's side doors was impossible.

Lucy screamed again as their car began to shake, the roof banging.

Todd could move only his eyes, which was just as well because the windscreen imploded as something heavy came through it and bounced off the dash – and Robson's fingers.

He yelped in pain.

Boots appeared on the bonnet.

A figure dressed entirely in black dropped to his knees. 'Don't fucking move!' a male voice said from behind dark material pulled tight over his face.

Lucy screamed again.

Todd swore again.

'Move out of this car in a second less than twenty minutes and..' he drew a gloved finger across his throat. 'Understand? Twenty minutes.'

The man jumped from the bonnet and made a shooshing gesture with the same finger. He tiptoed backwards from the car, a gun trained on its occupants, until he disappeared around the bend in the road.

No sooner had he gone, Todd moved into action.

'Twenty minutes, my arse.' He reached for the radio as best his bent frame allowed.

A tap on the passenger window stopped him in his tracks.

Robson turned his entire body in the direction of the sound and froze at the sight of another masked figure. And a gun aimed at his head.

'Oh, fuck it,' he groaned.

**

'This is the place, for sure.'

Pavel Maric's voice, hushed at first, became more animated when he asked, 'Can we go? Now, please.'

'Not until you tell me what happened.'

Maric knew Maynard was in no mood for messing. He sucked in air.

'We park here. Silvia was driving. The men, the bad ones and the one who looked scared, they tell Silvia to drive.'

'Where to?'

Maric's eyelids fluttered shut. He motioned with his head.

'What? Over the cliff?'

He nodded; eyes still closed. A tear squeezed between his lashes.

'Good Jesus,' Parker whispered. 'They made her drive over the cliff?'

Maric nodded again.

'And what's the best way to hide a murder?' Maynard spoke almost to herself. 'Make it look like suicide. Remember what Brooks said? That's what this place is known for.'

'How could the wee bastards be sure you'd die?'

'They put something in the, how you say, boot, yes? They set it on fire.'

Lyall traded in his *'Jesus'* for a 'Shitting hell.'

Sam Maynard broke the silence. 'If I'm to believe you, how come you got out?'

He shrugged. 'I get lucky. When car go over cliff, door open. I fall out. Land on grass ten metres down. The car landed next to me. I saw Silvia's face. I have not seen that look anywhere. I do not want to see it ever again. It was not human. The car creaked and rolled over. It went over the edge. It went over the edge…' he broke down, his words lost in sobs.

'I'm sorry, Pavel. Where did it go over? We need to find the car, and we need to retrieve Silvia for you.'

He raised his cuffed hands and pointed them towards the fence.

Trebilcock flicked the car's lights onto full beam. Through the circling haze of mist and fret, they saw the missing fencepost.

Maynard opened the door and took a step across the car park, heading for the cliff edge.

'Get back in the fucking car! Don't move!'

A fist forced Maynard to move, backwards and into the car, her lip split and already swollen.

A figure stood over her.

'Stay where you are, bitch.'

The man pointed a snub-nosed revolver at her. Through her pain and confusion, she was aware of movement behind her. Recognised Parker's voice, but not his words as another hooded figure rammed the butt of a gun into his temple.

'Stay here for fifteen minutes. Don't move. Don't do a thing. We'll be watching. We've better weapons than these and, if any of you move, it will be the last move you make.'

The man took a pace back from Maynard. 'Fifteen minutes.'

With that, the man was gone.

Sam Maynard felt the car rock as if someone had just got in. In fact, someone had just got out.

She watched as Pavel Maric was frogmarched between two henchmen, out of the car park, and into a vehicle hidden from sight.

The Super risked moving an arm. Flicked on the radio. 'Robson! Dexter! How the fuck did you let them through?'

Silence.

'Are you receiving?'

Nothing.

'Shit. The radio's not working.'

Warily, she reached for her mobile. Brought it from her pocket, careful not to move any part of her body but her hand. She glanced at the screen. It was blank. No service.

'Nothing's fucking working!' She let her phone drop to the floor.

'What do we do now, ma'am?' Trebilcock asked.

'We wait. Twelve minutes, by my reckoning. Then, we go find out what the hell's happened to the patrol car.'

CHAPTER NINETEEN

Maynard, Parker, and Trebilcock didn't need wait that long. After ten minutes, the patrol car came to them. At least, its occupants did. Two of them, anyway.

Lucy Dexter led the way, Robson's hunched and twisted frame limping behind her like an am-dram performance of Quasimodo. There was no sign of Joey Brooks.

When their arrival wasn't accompanied by a burst of gunfire, warning shots or fallen bodies, Superintendent Maynard jogged to meet them, a tissue pressed against her bloody lip.

'You okay?' were her first words.

Robson gave a half laugh. 'We'll live, if that's what you mean.'

'Brooks?'

'He's unconscious back in the car. He's a mess but not critical.'

'What the hell's just gone on here?'

Robson tried to raise his head to meet Maynard's eyes, but it was stuck fast. 'We got rammed up the arse by a 4x4. Another penned us in. They told us to wait twenty minutes. Left someone behind to make sure we behaved. When a car pulled up and sped off with our guard, I guessed it was safe to ride to your rescue.'

'I presume you called it in?'

'Aye, but just a couple of minutes ago. Radio got fucked by the ram and there wasn't a phone signal 'til I got round the corner.'

Maynard shook her head. 'They took Maric.'

'Aw bollocks.'

'That's not the half of it, Todd. We've got some explaining to do to the Met. They won't be happy Op Sage has fucked up so royally.'

Todd ran a hand around the back of his locked neck. 'Their trucks are still round the corner. We might get some forensics from them.'

'Doesn't matter, though, does it? They'll be long gone by now, and they've got our only lead, Pavel Maric, with them.'

Lucy Dexter was in her own state of shock, mumbling to herself and anyone else who would listen. 'How did they know? No-one could have known we were coming here. Not today. How did they find out?'

'They're questions for later, Lucy. We're okay, that's the main thing. Assistance is on the way. We'll get Brooks seen to, then we'll put together how we let this happen.'

**

Stephen Danskin was on his way back to Forth Street from Blyth when he heard the commotion over the radio. When a second update announced there'd been casualties, he flicked on the lights concealed in the front grill of the Focus.

The traffic cone elves had been out in force again, reducing the Spine Road to a single lane in both directions for no obvious reason. Even with his car lit up like a Christmas tree, Danskin found no way through the queuing traffic.

'Come on, come on!' he yelled, slapping the steering wheel in frustration. He bypassed Control and patched his radio straight through to Sam Maynard.

'Ma'am, you okay?'

'I'm surviving, but no; I'm not okay. Far from it. They got Maric.'

'I heard. How?'

'Smash n grab. Blocked in our back-up. Threatened Todd and Lucy – Robson will need a neck brace I think but Lucy's just shook up – then they hit on us. Armed to the teeth, they

153

were. Whacked Lyall on the head – he's with the medics now but he'll be fine – and took Maric with them.'

'What about you?'

'I took a smack in the face but, apart from looking like I've OD'd on collagen fillers, I'm as good as can be expected.'

Danskin heard the whump-whump of a helicopter rotor and the snarl of police dogs over the radio, grateful that the background noise hid his sigh of relief.

The traffic edged forward. Danskin drummed his fingers impatiently. Light drizzle splattered the windscreen, enough for him to flick on the wipers, but insufficient for it to moisten the blades. The annoying screech on the glass riled him further.

'They knew what they were doing, Stephen.'

'Aye, for sure.'

'You don't know the half of it. It was a well-timed, simultaneous hit on both vehicles. They blocked the patrol car in and used a third as a getaway car. They threw jammers under our cars, so the radios were kaput. Even blocked our mobile signals.'

Danskin steered the Focus through the cones into the empty lane, flicked his headlights to full-beam to ensure there wasn't a workforce in the road, and floored it.

'I'm on my way. I'll be at the tunnel in ten minutes,' he said as he cut across traffic to take the A19.

'No. I don't need you here. I want you back at the station, directing Gavin and Ravi.'

'Are you sure?'

'Yeah. Lucy came up with a good question: how did they know what we were doing? Our recon mission was deliberately low key.'

Their chat was interrupted by Control feeding information from a Prince Bishop patrol. The vehicles involved in the hit, a black Toyota Landcruiser and green Land Rover Discovery, had been stolen from *Sixteen*, a 4x4 specialist dealership located on Newcastle Road, Tyne Dock.

The officers reported that the trucks were stolen from where they'd been parked: on display on a grass slope at the front of the dealership, out of range of the forecourt's CCTV.

Danskin whispered 'Shitballs and piss,' and cursed the inadequacies of private CCTV surveillance.

Sam Maynard overrode the announcement. 'Stephen, we're on private here. Get back to the station and learn what you can about the theft. There's a third car, too. A getaway vehicle.'

'Can O'Hara and Sangar not handle that themselves?'

'Yes. That's not why I want you at Forth Street.'

'It's not?'

'No. Listen, whoever did this knew what we are up to. If they know how to jam a radio, they're also able to listen in to our conversations. That's how they knew where we were. They're more than professionals.'

Danskin was ahead of her. 'You're thinking it's an inside job?'

'Yes; I am. Someone leaked the whereabouts of Maric to that damn reporter. Someone knew what we've been doing every damn step of the way. I reckon it's one of the Bishops.'

'Seriously?'

'Seriously. They didn't want us involved in the first place. They put every obstacle in our way. They're jealous of us taking *'their'* case at best, or someone is in cahoots with Yu and his gang at worst. I want you to run checks on a Joey Brooks first, then anyone else who's been at that fucking station in the last forty-eight hours.'

Danskin pulled the Focus off the A19 at the Killingworth junction.

'On my way, ma'am.'

He was on his way, but not where Maynard expected him.

If this was an inside job, Stephen Danskin was pretty sure it wasn't anyone inside the Prince Bishop force.

He steered the Focus back onto the A19, this time heading in the direction he'd just travelled.

Whoever set this up had a much stronger motive.

Someone like Ryan Jarrod.

**

'You've had quite a time of it, haven't you?'

The voice in the earpiece sounded middle-aged, but it was hard to tell through the static.

'What do you want from me now?'

'Straight to business. I like your directness, Mr Jarrod.'

'Just tell me what you want me to do so I can have me Dad back. I'm not interested in owt else.'

'You have an intriguing accent, Mr Jarrod. Common, but intriguing.'

'Get to the point, man.'

'Good. You're doing very well so far. Next, I want you to go to the Travelodge at the MetroCentre. I know you'll know where it is. After all, it's near where you live.'

Ryan shuddered. He'd done the right thing by not returning to Whickham. They knew where he lived. Of course, they did – this lot knew what they were doing.

'I know you're used to hotels,' the voice continued. 'You've been staying in one on Durham Road, haven't you? I must say it looks even worse than a Travelodge. I hope you appreciate the upgrade.'

Ryan squeezed his eyes tight. Could he ever outsmart this gang? He doubted it, which is why he jumped at their every word.

'You have a reservation. It's made in the name of Mr Ryan. Yes, I know it's neither original nor subtle, but it serves a purpose.'

'I'll need to show ID…'

'You won't. I've checked. You just need to give them your name and ask for Room 101. I think that's a very appropriate room for you, is it not?' The voice cackled. It sounded like dry tinder.

'Listen…'

'No. YOU listen, my friend. There'll be a package waiting for you. You'll need its contents for your next task. You'll learn what to do with it when we speak again.'

'Wait, let me speak to…'

The voice was gone, the earpiece silent.

Ryan trudged back to the car and got into the driver's seat.

'You kill me now?'

Ryan locked eyes with Pavel Maric in the rear-view mirror. Maric sat at an odd angle, one hand cuffed to the door handle, the other around the front seat headrest.

'I don't kill you, full-stop.'

'I don't believe. You talk to them. If you don't kill me, they do.'

Ryan swivelled in his seat.

'You're alive, aren't you? Just think of your cousin and be bloody grateful you're still breathing.'

He saw a muscle twitch in Maric's cheek and Ryan felt an instant pang of regret over his words.

It was a feeling he'd become accustomed to, but one that never became any easier. Ryan Jarrod fought back tears for the umpteenth time.

He had not the faintest idea how he was going to get himself out of the mess he was in.

**

The row of pebble-dashed council houses made Lynn Street look like Knightsbridge.

Danskin had obtained Stuey Hetton's address from Ravi Sangar. Maddi Corrigan had been right – Hetton had more form than the Racing Post.

In the darkness emphasised by broken streetlights, the DCI trod warily over an obstacle course of upturned wheelie-bins, discarded bikes, and curdling vomit pools.

Someone slipped out the door of a nearby Labour Club for a fag, allowing drunken laughter and raised voices to momentarily echo around the narrow streets before the door swung shut.

The lights in the address were on, but when Danskin's knock was answered by a woman of undeterminable age, her blank eyes told him no-one was home.

'What you want?' the woman slurred.

'Is Stuey home?'

Danskin studied the woman while he waited for his words to register. She was podgy, ill-suited to the tight jeans and vest top she wore, but at least it provided a distraction from her bad skin.

'Who?'

Danskin sighed. He'd heard that evasive response a thousand and more times. 'Stuart Hetton. I know this is his address.'

'Is he getting nicked?'

What is it about folk round here? Can they smell coppers from miles away like sharks detect a drop of blood?

'He's not, no. I wouldn't turn up by myself if I was here to nick him, would I? You should know that by now. Stuey's been arrested enough times for you to know the score.'

'He doesn't like you lot. Nowt personal, like.'

'I'm sure it is.'

'He's not in.'

Danskin took a step back and raised his eyes skywards. The woman began to close the door. Danskin stepped forward and put a foot over the threshold.

'If he's not in,' he said, 'Who you got hidden away upstairs? Net curtains are the worst thing you can hide behind, do you know that? Nobody can resist pulling them aside to have a peek out.'

'You're not coming in without a warrant.'

'Why would I need a warrant? Like I say, I'm not here to arrest Stuey. But I do need to talk to him. Let's say it could be mutually beneficial.'

'What the fuck does that mean?'

Danskin rolled his eyes. 'There could be something in it for both of us, yeah? Understand now?'

A toilet flushed upstairs, followed by a gruff male voice. 'Let the bugger in. Might as well hear what he's got to say. We've nowt in the hoose to interest him.'

'Not now you've flushed it down the bog,' Danskin thought. 'Good lad. You know it makes sense.'

Danskin brushed past the woman and looked up the staircase to see a rough, scruffy-looking bloke in his underkegs, his hands down the front of them.

'Stuey Hetton?'

'Aye, that's me.'

'I'm Stephen. I wonder if I can have a word with you?'

Stuey Hetton pulled a pair of trackie bottoms over scrawny legs. 'What for?

Danskin was about to explain when Hetton answered his own question.

'It'll be aboot the daft fucker who chucked himsel' off the bridge in the Toon, I bet.'

'Now, what makes you think that, I wonder,' Danskin thought.

'And a few other things, besides,' he shouted up the stairs. 'Can I come up?'

'Aye, why not? I could do with a laugh.'

Danskin stopped on the third stair. Looked long and hard at Stuart Hetton.

'Something tells me you won't be laughing for long, sunshine.'

CHAPTER TWENTY

'There's a family in danger,' Stephen Danskin began. 'I think you can help me find them before they get hurt.'

'I don't know nowt about any family,' Hetton sniffed noisily from the bed.

'No, but you know about the new set up, don't you? Goes by the name of YuTube.'

'If you say so.'

'I do say so. I think that's who you're working for.'

'I've always been self-employed, me.'

Danskin rested his backside against a cigarette-burnt dresser. 'You said I'd come to see you about Geordie Amos. Tell me about him.'

'He's dead. Suicide. Is that enough for you?'

'No. Because his death isn't being investigated as a suicide, that's why. He was forced into it. Someone egged him on. Threatened, even.'

Hetton put a finger against each nostril in turn and sniffed. 'So?'

'So, I know you couldn't give a toss about anyone's family, but I think you'd do a lot to protect your own arse.'

'Waddya mean, like?'

'I mean, there's serious offences involved there, Stuey. Add blackmail to the list, accessory to murder, manslaughter. Need I go on? Funnily enough, yours is the only name I have.'

Hetton jumped off the bed. 'You said you weren't here to nick me. Fuck off out of here, okay?'

Danskin held his hands aloft. 'I'm not nicking you, Stuey. Let's take a chill-pill. All I'm here for is to find out who put up the money.'

'What money?'

'The ten grand you offered to Amos.' DCI Danskin looked around the dingy room. 'Now, this place doesn't make me believe the money came from you. Whoever put the cash up isn't plucking deals out of his arse for a tenner a shot. All I want to know is where I can find the man.'

Hetton sneered.

'A name, Stuey. That's all I want. An address would do.'

'Why the fuck would I tell you?'

Danskin locked eyes with him. 'Because my next stop after this will be the new crack house in town. I'll get a team despatched to insert fingers up backsides, and while they're doing it, I'll let slip that we got the info off a Mr Stuart Hetton.'

He'd taken a punt. He had no idea whether a new set-up existed locally. Hetton's reaction told him there was.

'You twat!'

'Aye, I can be. I reckon there'll be some horrible fuckers in there who you wouldn't last two minutes with. I'm a desperate man, Stuey, and when I get desperate, I do desperate things.'

Hetton dropped to the bed.

'Aal reet. Just don't go dropping me in the shite with them, okay?'

**

The Travelodge carpark was at the rear of the building, next to the Skiff On The Tyne bar. Fewer than a dozen cars and a workman's van occupied the bays. Ryan glanced at the dashboard clock and, judging by the time, reckoned that would be the hotel's capacity for the night.

'What you do now?' Maric asked.

'We check in.'

'Oh no. You may, I will not. I going nowhere with you.'

Ryan unlocked the cuff attached to the door handle and wrapped it around his non-dominant wrist. The other, he clamped around Maric's right hand. He slid off his jacket and folded it across their arms, hiding the cuffs.

'I not come. I shout for help.'

Ryan struggled to get his ID out his left pocket with his right hand. He flipped the wallet open.

'You go ahead and shout. I'm a police officer and if anyone challenges me, I'll show them my warrant card and say you're under arrest and we're taking a toilet break on our way to the custody suite.'

Maric's eyes yawned. 'You are a cop? No, I do not believe.'

'Believe what you like, pal, but I am. I work for Witness Protection.'

'Protection? You kidnap me. That is not protection.'

'Yeah. Sorry about that but we have info that the gang you worked for, the people who are after you, have infiltrated the police. We couldn't run the risk, and we had to make it look good.'

Maric breathed in relief. 'You succeeded, for sure. You release me, yes?'

Ryan stood alongside Maric in the gloomy car park, the murky river behind them revealed only by the reflection of the lights from the former Vickers factory on the opposite bank.

'Not yet. You see, I don't know you well enough to trust you. For now, we stay hooked together. Let's see how it goes from there.'

'What about the other men who took me? They police, too?'

'Aye. Undercover. Took a shitload of planning, I tell you.'

Ryan set off towards the hotel entrance, the shackled Maric trailing awkwardly a pace behind him.

Inside, the Travelodge was the same as every other hotel in the chain, anywhere in the country. The reception desk was a tiny, box shaped affair leading directly into a back office.

'Can I help, sir?' the receptionist asked. She was young, attractive in a subtle way which reminded Ryan of Hannah.

She wore a name tag which told him her name was Diana, and a uniform like a Tui travel rep. Diana's wrist bore a tiny rainbow tattoo which matched the clip holding back her hair.

'I have a room booked. 101.'

She clicked a mouse. 'Your name?'

'Mr Ryan.'

'Ah yes. I'd almost given up on you,' she smiled.

'Better late than never.'

'Indeed. Now, it's for three nights, yes?'

'Err, aye. That's right.' *Three nights? Why on earth book three nights?* he puzzled.

The woman swiped a credit card-like object through a reader. 'Your key card, sir.' Her eyes flitted to Maric standing up against Ryan. 'Would you like a second card?'

'No. Just the one, thanks,' Ryan said.

'Enjoy your stay.'

'Oh, I believe there's a parcel for me?'

'Ah yes.' The receptionist disappeared into the office. She re-emerged with an envopak holding a package which could have been a large toiletry bag.

Ryan took it from her with one hand. Its weight surprised him.

'Thank you.'

'You're most welcome, sir. Your room's on the first floor. The lift is just through the door to your left, or the stairs are right there.' She pointed across the lobby.

'We'll take the lift, ta.'

He headed for the door the girl had shown. As he and Maric waddled ungainly towards it, the girl spoke again.

'Excuse me saying, but you needn't be so coy, you know.'

'Sorry?'

'I think it's cute.'

'I'm not following.'

'Holding hands. You don't need hide it.' She waggled her tattooed wrist towards them. 'Loud 'n' proud, I say.'

Ryan blushed furiously as he and Maric disappeared through the door, Ryan's jacket still folded over their arms.

**

The hotel room was a bog-standard Travelodge affair. Large enough, freezing cold, and a small bathroom with a noisy fan which wouldn't switch off.

There were two single beds, a slim desk on which sat a Samsung flatscreen TV and an ancient remote control.

Ryan dragged Maric to the door, double-turned the deadlock, and struggled to insert the security chain. Only then did he release the cuffs.

'You stay far side of the bed furthest from the door, Pavel. For now, at least.'

Maric obliged, rubbing his chafed wrist.

Ryan dropped his bag and the parcel on the other bed. 'I'm parched. Fancy a coffee?'

Maric nodded enthusiastically. Ryan picked up the kettle. Shook it. It was empty, which meant one of them would have to leave the main room to fill it in the bathroom.

He glanced down at the condiments. 'Aw man,' he said. 'No coffee?'

'No coffee, no tea, no nowt. Look what the maid's left.' He pulled out the contents of the condiment jar. Held them up one by one.

Salt, pepper, two sachets of mayonnaise, another of HP brown sauce, and three of ketchup.

'We ask at reception for more, no?'

'No is right. We don't. We're not leaving this room.'

He looked at the objects in his hand. 'Could rustle up a quasi-tomato soup with the ketchup if you're desperate.'

Maric snickered. 'You funny guy.'

Ryan adopted a serious look. 'You mean, let me understand this cause, ya know maybe it's me, I'm a little fucked up maybe, but I'm funny how, I mean funny like I'm a clown, I amuse you? I make you laugh, I'm here to fuckin' amuse you? What do you mean funny, funny how? How am I funny?'

Pavel looked shocked. 'I sorry. I meant nothing.'

Ryan laughed out loud. 'No, man. Joe Pesci. Goodfellas.'

Pavel's brow wrinkled.

'You know, man. Goodfellas. It's a quote from a movie. Oh. Never mind.'

Ryan pinched the bridge of his nose, the tension and the stakes suddenly overwhelming.

'Listen, Pavel, there's something bigger behind this than just keeping you alive.'

'You need me to talk?'

'Yes. Urgently. The more you tell me, the easier it'll be for me to understand the OCG.'

'OCG?'

'Sorry. Organised crime group.'

'Ah. I understand.'

'Do you, though? We need a lot more intel – that's intelligence, information – before I can keep you safe. What are we up against?'

'Animals!' Maric spat out the word. 'These people kill many. They kill my cousin. I saw her face just before she died. They try to kill me. I told your other people I talk only when I am safe. This,' he pointed around the room, 'Is not safe.'

'It's the best I can do for now, Pavel. Who wants you dead? It's very important to me that I know.' Ryan swallowed hard. 'You could say, it's life or death.'

'These people give very bad death.'

'Who are they? Give me their names.'

'Bad men.'

'That's not a name.'

Maric said nothing. Ryan banged his fist on the paper-thin wall in frustration, leaving a dent behind.

It had the desired effect. 'No names but he works in drugs. He is big in cocaine. In London. Europe. Everywhere. If you buy cocaine in south of England, it will come from him.'

Ryan whistled. 'Where does he get his supply from?'

'Direct from Colombia, some. The rest from Poland. Or Amsterdam. They deliver it among other things. Beer, meat…'

'People. Flowers.'

'Yes. In that lorry, I was surrounded by maybe five million Euros-worth of drugs.'

'Five million Euros-worth of cocaine? Jesus.'

Maric shook his head. 'Not cocaine. Outside of London, money is a problem. Cocaine, it is expensive. He supplies heroin, too.'

Another whistle.

'There isn't enough money in heroin for him. It too cheap. He mixes heroin with another, cheaper drug. It, how you say, maximises rewards.'

'You came in a lorry full of heroin.'

'Not heroin. The cutting agents, Pervitin and fentanyl. One is meth, the other opium.'

Ryan's brain clicked into gear. 'Pain medication, right?' *At last – a link. Geordie Amos, the brain tumour, pain relief, and the unidentified substance amongst his medication.*

'It is much more than pain relief. Fentanyl is one hundred times more powerful than morphine. This is a hit like no other. And it is cheap to buy on the black market. It makes a little heroin go a long way. This is how he makes his money. But it is dangerous. Very dangerous. Mix fentanyl with pervitin AND heroin, *boosh!* – it blows your mind.'

'All drugs are dangerous, Pavel.'

'Not like this. People die making it. Pervitin and fentanyl, they are a powder. Pervitin it is not too bad. But fentanyl? It gets on hands. It soaks through skin. People who handle it, they wipe their mouth – in seconds it is in their system. A horrible death for who get it wrong, but rich rewards for those who trade.'

The walls of the hotel room seemed to pulse in and out, as if the room was a creature breathing its last.

'That's why he wanted the lorry to get through customs.'

'Yes. He has been stopped many times. This only happen recently. Something has changed. He knows he has a problem, and he wants it to end.'

'Bloody hell, Pavel. No wonder he wants you dead.'

'It was not me. It was not Silvia either. It is someone else, but this man stop at nothing. Anyone who it could have been, he wants out the way.'

'Hang on. He doesn't know it's you, he just thinks it might be, so he goes to the bother of dragging you over from Amsterdam so he can kill you just in case?'

'For sure. That is how he runs his business.'

'Fucking hell.'

'It is a fucking hell.'

'You still haven't given me a name. I need it.'

Pavel paused as if considering his options. Realised he had none.

'He goes by name of Benny Yu.'

The name meant nothing to Ryan.

'Now, I feel dirty. I need bath.'

Ryan rushed to the bedroom window. Slid it open four or five inches. If Maric needed a bath, he needed to vomit.

He did so. Explosively.

CHAPTER TWENTY-ONE

Ryan entered the unlocked bathroom with two motives in mind. One, for a tumbler of water to rinse away the peppery taste of stale vomit; two, to check Maric was doing what he said he was doing.

Pavel Maric was indeed in the process of taking a bath, whilst covering his genitals and muttering 'Get the fuck out, yes?'

Satisfied the Macedonian would be a good twenty minutes, Ryan got the fuck out and delved into Geordie Amos's old Slazenger bag. He removed the wire, switched it to '*On*', and tucked the power pack into his rear pocket. He struggled with the plastic tag which held the coiled mic wire before unravelling it and clipping it to the inside of his shirt.

Next, he pulled out a couple if items he'd purloined from the station and placed them under a pillow. Finally, he unlocked the cheap burner phone which had never left his side and typed a five-letter text message.

'*Ready.*'

While he waited for the voice to pierce the static in his earpiece, he stuck his fingers through the envopak and ripped it apart. Inside was an Amazon box sealed with brown parcel tape.

Ryan peeled off the tape, opened the box – and sat back on the bed, hard.

The box held a handgun.

Blowing air through his teeth, he lifted it from the box, weighed it in his hands, and flung it down onto the bed. Beneath the gun he found a zip-sealed bag containing two pairs of disposable gloves inside a shrink-wrapped packet, a cloth, and a roll of Gaffer tape.

'Hello, Ryan.' Jarrod jumped at the voice. 'I trust you have our friend.'

'Aye,' he replied simply, swallowing down the contempt he held for the man who'd taken his family.

'I didn't anticipate needing your help with Mr Maric, but I appreciate it all the same.'

'When do I get my Dad back?'

'Oh, you're a little premature, Mr Jarrod. The task is not yet complete. Not by any means.'

'You bastard. One task you said. That's two already – the port, and Maric.'

'One more task, then you have your family back. I give you my word.'

Ryan looked up. Listened intently. He heard the sound of water lapping around Maric as he washed himself.

'What frigging task?'

'Finish the Maric issue.'

'I have done. He's here. He's in the bath. All I need do is step outside, lock the door, and he's all yours.'

'Very good, Ryan; but there's a flaw in your logic. You see, I don't want him. Not while he's still alive.'

Ryan's eyes were attracted to the gun like iron filings to a magnet. He knew what it is was for. In truth, he had done from the moment he opened the box.

The voice whispered into his ear, so quiet it deafened him. 'Handle the weapon with care. It's loaded. You need to kill Maric, then leave.'

'Don't be stupid, man. I can't shoot him.'

'You can, and you will.'

Ryan listened to the Macedonian splashing bathwater behind the door next to him.

'I can't kill a man!'

'Remember the stakes, Ryan. Just one squeeze of the trigger, and you'll have your father and brother back. If you don't, I'll be the one squeezing the trigger and one of them will be gone.'

'You bastard!'

'Is that a yes, Ryan?'

'No!'

'Do it now. I advise you very strongly not to say 'no' to me again.'

'I can't!'

'You must.'

'How many times, for Christ's sake? I'm a Detective. I can't take a life.'

He picked the gun off the bed. Threw it back down as if it were a dead rat, disgusted.

'Do you have your phone close by, Mr Jarrod?'

'It's never left me.'

'Good.'

An unearthly howl - a high-pitched, inhuman scream - screeched through his earpiece, followed by a whimper, then a silence which made his skin crawl.

'Jesus, no. Leave them alone. Leave them alone!'

Static filled his earpiece once more. Ryan threw himself on the bed, sobbing. The cold steel of the handgun pressed into his ribcage.

His phone chirruped. Ryan levitated from the bed. His heart pumped against his chest wall as he retrieved the phone.

He'd been sent a picture message.

'Please God, no.' He couldn't bring himself to open it. Didn't dare look at whatever Benny Yu had done to his father, or James – or both.

His brain forgot to tell his fingers. They accepted the message.

Against his better judgement, Ryan's eyes slid downwards.

The image wasn't Norman Jarrod. It wasn't James Jarrod. Ryan should have felt relief.

He didn't.

He recoiled from the image in front of him, fresh from the knowledge that the voice truly could get anyone – anything – any time he wanted.

It was the image of an eviscerated animal.

A dog.

A pug.

Yu had sliced open and disembowelled Ryan's beloved Spud.

**

Ryan lay on the bed, his diaphragm rising and falling like a piston; his whole being preoccupied with the image of Spud, spatchcocked as if ready for the barbeque.

The sound of an initial rush of water, followed by a gurgle as Maric's bathwater spiralled down the plughole, roused him. Ryan's fingertips brushed the handle of the gun, felt beneath the duvet, probed beneath his pillow.

He sat up, startled, as the voice returned.

'Are you dealing with Maric? Yes, or no?'

Ryan's lips moved. No sound left his mouth.

'Remember the photograph, Mr Jarrod. Remember who's in control here.'

Ryan made a guttural noise.

'I need to know: is it yes, or is it no? You must tell me now.' Yu hissed in his ear.

'Let me talk to my Dad first. Please.'

Every sound, every movement, became amplified in Ryan's mind. He heard the water glug as its last drops entered the decrepit plumbing system. Pavel Maric's towel made a rasping noise as he dried his torso.

And he heard Benny Yu speak again.

'No deal, Mr Jarrod.'

'Please.'

Ryan heard a rustle as Maric pulled dirty, four-day old clothes over his clean body.

'Yes, or no?' Yu kept up the relentless pressure.

Ryan clamped his eyes shut. He leant on the headboard for support. Pressed his face into the rough fabric.

The bathroom door opened.

'Ah, that is better.' Maric said. He saw Ryan curled up in a foetal position. 'You not feel good?'

Ryan hurriedly flipped the duvet over the objects on the bed.

'Been a long day,' he said, his voice quavering.

Maric agreed.

Ryan heard the voice take an intake of breath; a hissing sound like a snake about to strike.

'Deal with Maric. Do it now. I will not ask again.'

Silence.

'Is that a yes?'

Silence.

'Think of your dog, Ryan. Think of your father. Think of your brother. Think of them with me. Now, is it a yes?'

'Yes,' Ryan whispered.

Maric turned towards him. 'You say something?'

'Yes,' Ryan said again, stronger this time.

He tugged at the bedding. His hands fumbled beneath it. Found what they needed to find.

Maric was a blur to him, nothing more than a shapeless mass, as Ryan held up the weapon.

He pointed it towards the Macedonian.

And pulled the trigger.

**

Benny Yu heard two muffled explosions, little more than loud pops.

He'd heard the sound many times; the sound of a gun being discharged into a pillow to silence it. *Mr Jarrod knows how to make a kill. I'm impressed. I could do with someone like that on my side.*

'Sounds as if you made the right choice. Good man.'

All Yu heard were rapid, shallow breaths from the man wearing the mic.

'You excite me, Mr Jarrod. Only next time, I implore you not to hesitate so long. The consequences could be dire.'

'Next time? There is no fucking next time.'

'Really? We shall see.'

'You promised…'

Yu interrupted. 'I need proof. Use the phone to take a picture of Maric. Send it me. Do it now, Ryan.'

Yu stared at the phone intently for several minutes.

'I don't see anything. That is not a good sign, young man. I urge…'

The phone pinged.

Yu looked at the screen.

Maric lay with his feet on the bed, the rest of his body hung over the side. The man's arms were splayed out on the hotel room floor. Red gore seeped through his shirt and coagulated on his stomach. Another patch of redness, a cleaner wound, shone from the centre of his chest.

Yu smiled.

'Good work, Mr Jarrod. Very good work.'

'When do you release my Dad?'

'All in good time.'

'No! Now! Please – let them go now.'

'You need to get out of there, Ryan.'

'Not until I speak to them.'

'Not yet.'

'Bastard!'

Yu chuckled. 'Yes, I am, aren't I? You need to go NOW. You don't want to be arrested for murder, I'm sure. I don't need tell you what that would mean for your father and brother.''

'They'll find the body. They'll know he checked in with me. They'll know it's me. I'll be arrested anyway.' Ryan's voice broke with emotion.

'No, you won't. There's someone on their way to clean up your room right now.'

Of course, they both knew there wasn't.

'Where do I go?'

'Anywhere, my friend – providing you take your phone with you. I shall call you at three p.m. Don't miss my call, will you?'

Yu ended the communication.

Ryan was left alone in the world with nothing but static in his ear, the stricken Pavel Maric in his eyeline, and desolation in his soul.

****

PART THREE

'Police officers see everything, and they experience everything - which means they don't always act correctly.'

Cheo Hodari Coker

CHAPTER TWENTY-TWO

A hand-written sign informed Stephen Danskin that the Forth Street lift was out of operation for routine maintenance.

He took the stairs to the third floor two at a time, waited several moments while he regained his breath, before pushing the bullpen doors wide open.

He didn't see what he expected to see.

The litter of crime boards holding photographs, maps, and notes scrawled in marker pen, were scattered around the perimeter of the room as normal. It was the absence of people which threw him.

An incident of this magnitude should have seen the bullpen seethe with activity, even at the pre-dawn hour. Instead, there were only two.

'Where is everybody?'

'You're looking at them, sir,' Gavin O'Hara mumbled through a yawn and a stretch.

'You and Sangar – that's it?'

'Aye. Just us.'

Danskin looked at O'Hara. 'You look like shit, O'Hara.'

'I feel it, sir, but I'm still looking into where the leak came from in Southwick.'

Flustered, Danskin told him to forget it. There were more important things to consider.

'I'm not sure the Super would agree, sir.'

'Remind me who you report to, O'Hara?'

'Well, technically, DS Jarrod…'

'…and he's isolating, Parker's not around, so who's next up the chain?'

'You, sir.'

'And I'm telling you to stand down.'

Danskin's eyes roamed to Ravi Sangar. Despite being a renowned and inveterate insomniac, Sangar looked worse for wear, too.

'Does that apply to me, an' aal? Super's given folk time off to recover.'

'No chance. We can't afford to step back altogether at this stage.'

'To be fair, sir, Super didn't have much choice. Lyall's on a concussion break for a couple of days, Todd's getting all sorts of scans done on his neck, and Lucy's in a state of shock. She'll be in tomorrow, I think.'

'Treblecock?' Danskin asked, referring to Nigel Trebilcock by his station nickname.

'Maynard told him the same thing: *'Get some rest, and come back tomorrow as per.'*

Danskin puffed out his cheeks. 'And then there were two', he muttered.

'It's not all bad news, though. Maynard's called in Rick Kinnear's crew for the day. They're overseeing things for her.'

'We're the MIT squad, Sangar. Nee disrespect, but DCI Kinnear's mob aren't equipped for something like this.'

'Sir, there's nowt I can do about that. You need to take it up with the Super.'

'She's here?'

Ravi's head motioned towards Maynard's door. Danskin made a beeline for her office. He entered without knocking.

'What's this I hear about…bloody hell, that looks nasty.'

Sam Maynard looked up from her paper-strewn desk, her lower lip bruised and swollen. Blood seeped from the corner of her mouth. Her eyes bore deep shadows, and her hair was tangled and windswept.

'It's okay,' she said.

'Here, let's have a look.'

177

He walked behind her desk. She lifted her head towards him. Danskin placed his hand under her chin and tilted her face upwards. He stared down into tear-filled eyes which glistened like clear blue tarns in the morning sunlight.

Danskin swallowed hard. He felt something he hadn't experienced for years. The sudden, urgent need to kiss a woman.

'Aye, you'll live,' he said, stepping away from her; confused, concerned and not a little embarrassed.

'I take it you want something, Stephen.'

'*Oh, that I do*', he thought. 'Yes, ma'am. A couple of things, actually. Why've you put DCI Kinnear in charge of the case? He isn't MIT.'

'I am aware of that, Stephen. I also know your guys need a rest. They've been at it non-stop for more than forty-eight hours. They need a break. I need a break. YOU need a break. Kinnear's only heading the operation for today.'

'With respect, ma'am, he doesn't know what's at stake. Only you and I know about the implications for Jarrod and his family.'

Maynard looked away. 'I know. It's only for a day, though, Stephen. Besides…' She hesitated.

'Go on: say it.'

'Perhaps it's too close to home for you.'

Danskin gave a harsh laugh. 'You're not questioning my professionalism, I hope.'

Calmly, rationally, Maynard continued. 'Of course not. But, when we're tired, we all tend to think with our emotions, not our brains.' She tapped her forehead. Smiled at him. 'And I need your brain on this, Stephen.'

She pushed back her chair.

'That's an order, not a request. Get some sleep. That's where I'm heading.'

'Okay, okay – but I said there were two things.'

She let out a sigh and sat back down with a thud. 'And?'

'I've been to see someone. Let's call him an informant at this stage. I got more information about the cartel. That's where I was when Maric was snatched.'

She ran her fingers through her hair. Toyed with a strand. 'Is it crucial? Is it a breakthrough?'

'Not exactly, but…'

'Then it can wait. We're passed the Golden Hour and I need sleep, Stephen. Four hours, that's all I ask. I'll see you back here in four hours.'

Danskin's lips curled inwards. 'I guess I don't have a choice. But can we make it somewhere else, in case we're overheard? After we've spoken, you can decide whether we go public with it.'

'You have yourself a deal, Detective Chief Inspector. Now, go – before I give you a lip like mine.'

**

Ryan checked his watch. Every second lasted an hour, and there were still four of those to go before Benny Yu would call again.

Four hours to lie low.

He knew how difficult staying undiscovered would be with a major investigation into his actions in full swing. He really had no-one to turn to now: not Danskin nor Hannah; most of all, he didn't have his father or his brother.

The passenger seat of the stolen car lay strewn with the wrappings of a McDonald's breakfast he'd picked up from the MetroCentre drive through. He slurped on the last dregs of a full-fat Coke and fished the ice-cube remnants from his cup. He pressed them against his forehead.

Where could he hide out, unseen, for four hours?

It came to him in a flash. But, first, he had to get rid of something. He flipped open the glove compartment. The gun was still there.

Ryan adhered to the fifty-mph limit along the A1, drove by Team Valley and up the Bowes Incline where he took the exit, along with several other vehicles keen to avoid a tailback at Washington Services.

For a moment, one of the cars triggered a memory, something vague in the recesses of his mind, then it was gone as he concentrated on the complex junction by the A1231.

A number of lanes merged, traffic lights and roundabouts added to the confusion, and cars cut each other up like enthusiastic butchers.

Ryan turned sharp left and bounced the stolen vehicle along a rough-track surface. When he reached the small, crescent-shaped carpark, he found two bays already occupied by vehicles.

He hesitated for a moment before stepping from the stolen car. He knelt on its bonnet, then rose to a standing position from where he had a clear view of his surroundings.

To the north, a group of three men sat beneath green canvas shelters, rods dangling in Lookout Lake, part of The Angel of the North fishing farm. Further on, another man sat on a fold-out stool, threading a line.

The second lake, Bowes Lake, lay to his right-hand side. It appeared deserted. Tentatively, Ryan wiped the gun with the cloth Yu had provided before wrapping it around the weapon to conceal it.

As casually as he could, he set off around the lake.

Ryan realised how conspicuous he looked - he had no fishing tackle, no dog trotting alongside him. Rather than appear furtive, he began to whistle brazenly, as if to say, 'Look, I've nothing to hide. I'm not suspicious at all; I'm letting you know I'm here.'

As it turned out, there was no-one to hide from. The shore of the southern lake was indeed deserted.

He unfolded the cloth and, still holding the handgun by it, threw the pistol as far as he could; overarm, like a boundary fieldsman. He watched it spiral through the overcast air until it slipped silently into the dark water.

For a second, he felt the weight of the world lift from his shoulders, until he remembered Benny Yu still had his family.

He raised his eyes skywards. Caught a glimpse of the rusting shape of the famous Angel of the North statue. Memories came flooding back.

For Ryan, this was where his career had taken off. How ironic it was also likely to be the place it ended.

He set off on foot towards it, knowing refuge lay in its surrounding woodland.

**

Stephen Danskin arrived first, ordered an iced water much to the barman's disgust, and took a window table offering panoramic views of Grey's Monument and the apex of the twin archaeological splendours of Grey Street and Grainger Street.

Danskin sipped his water, pretended it was his Corsodyl alcohol-substitute, and stared up through the glass domed roof of The Botanist at an array of clouds scudding across a grey sky.

He tapped the frame of his phone on the tabletop. His call to Jarrod had gone unanswered, as he knew it would – but he had to try.

Sam Maynard turned from the bar and looked around. Danskin swept aside a triffid and beckoned her and her rhubarb gin over to him.

'On duty? Really?' he questioned.

'Today, I'm doing what I want. Just the one to pull myself together.'

He studied the dark shadows beneath her eyes. 'I have to say you don't look much better for the sleep.'

'Thanks,' she chortled. 'Neither do you, by the way.'

'Probably because I didn't get any.'

'Stephen…'

He held up a hand. 'Enough already. Straight to business. We've wasted too many hours.'

'We haven't wasted anything. Rick's been looking after the shop.' When she saw him arch his eyebrows, she changed tack. 'Okay. What did you discover?'

Danskin ran through his conversation with Stuey Hetton in chronological order while Maynard watched the throng of people bustling in and out of Eldon Square, buzzing around the Monument Metro like bees to a hive.

'You think you can trust him?' she said when he paused for breath.

'Not likely. Having said that, he's between a rock and a hard place. Tell us too much, and Yu and co will have him somewhere in the foundations of the new gigaplant factory up his way. Tell us too little, and he thinks I'll tip the gang off and he'll end up under concrete anyway.'

'Where does that leave us?'

'I dunno. Sorting the wheat from the chaff, I suppose. I'm pretty sure the addresses he gave will all be a waste of time. He wouldn't be that stupid. I'm also confident he's the go-between when it comes to supplying the cutting agent. He all but admitted it – but who he goes between is anyone's guess.'

Maynard sipped gin through a straw and more greenery than the contents of the nearest plant pot. 'More to the point, it does nothing to help us recover Ryan's family,' she said.

'I'm not so sure.'

'Tell me more.'

'Well, Hetton admitted he met up with the *Tulpen Uit Amsterdam* lorry.'

'We kinda' already suspected that.'

'Aye, but he said summat else. He said the only cargo it held was the cutting agents. He said nothing about Pavel and Silvia Maric, yet we know they were in the truck.'

'If Maric is to be believed…'

'True but listen: he also said there were two vans with the lorry. What if Yu's people had already transferred them from the lorry into one of the vans? And, what if the other van held Maddi and Lance Corrigan? She told me they'd been moved around a lot. If I'm right, it could mean Jarrod's folks are also in the back of a van.'

'For a man who says, *'Don't see what you expect to see'* all the time, that's a helluva lot of what-ifs.'

'But we've nothing else to go on.'

'That's very true.'

They sat in silence while The Botanist filled around them.

'What did the Met say? About the Maric heist?'

Maynard sucked in air. 'Fortunately, that's above my pay-grade. I'm pretty sure they'll be redrafting Operation Tower as we speak. Probably to exclude us.'

Danskin shook his head, smiling. '*Operation Tower*', he repeated in a voice laden with sarcasm. 'Well, if I get kicked out the force over this, I'd love a new job in the acronym department, or whoever makes up these bollocks name.'

'They aren't bollocks, as you put it. They're quite astute.'

'They're bollocks,' he said again.

'Trust me. They all make sense. The overall project is called Operation Tower because of its familiarity with the London locale, but also as a tongue-in-cheek reference to the fact everybody else thinks the Met sit in their ivory tower doing nothing.'

'So, they make a joke of it? I don't think Class A drugs, or murdering and kidnapping folk, are anything to joke about.'

'True. But it also explains their role in all this: they overlook all the other Ops feeding into the overall picture. They take a helicopter view or, if you prefer, a view from a tower.'

Danskin puffed out his cheeks. 'I suppose I'll give you that one. But Op Kop? Howay, man.'

'It stands for *Knowledge of Possession*. Their role is to keep tabs on where the Merseyside drugs end up. That's what they do. They garner knowledge of possession – and attempt to trace the chain from bottom up.'

'Bugger me.' He stared out the window. 'Okay – why do we get named after a building that looks like a silver slug? Apart from the fact it's local, like. SAGE has nowt to do with Chris Whitty and that JVT fella, I hope.'

Maynard stared at Danskin, a faint smile on her lips. He thought he'd drown in her eyes.

'What do you make of Ravi Sangar?' she said, out the blue.

'That's random, but Sangar's bloody good. The best I've ever come across in his line. Mind, I'm no cyber criminologist.'

'Nor me, but I know a good 'un when I see one. And so do the Op Tower guys.'

He crunched on an ice-cube. 'So?'

'So that's why I've kept him working while everyone else has time out. Top brass needs him. You see, Operation Sage is named after the original Sage computer system, which stands for *Semi-Automatic Ground Environment.* It was a system set up in the States in the sixties.'

Danskin stifled a yawn as Superintendent Maynard continued her explanation.

'Basically, it was a massive tracking system. Planes, telephone systems, troop movements; the works. You see, Ravi's role is to track traffic into ports. Not just here, but throughout the country. Whatever freight comes in, Ravi knows. He doesn't know whether it contains contraband of course, but he knows what vessels are going to which port, and where from. It all helps Operation Tower build up the overall picture.'

Danskin had stopped listening. He was reaching for his phone. Dialling.

'Sangar – stop playing Battleships and Cruisers for a few minutes, and don't you even think about taking a break. I've got some proper work for you. Firstly, I need you to get O'Hara…'

'…O'Hara's gone, sir.'

'In that case, I want YOU to find out what vehicle Yu's mob used as a getaway car during the Maric snatch. I don't care how you do it; but I want it done. Next, I want an ANPR marker on it. I want to know everywhere it's been.'

He thought for a moment. 'Make that a silent marker. Only you, me, and the Super must know.'

'That's highly irregular, sir.'

'Just fucking do it! Next, I want you to run over the footage of the flower lorry. I want you to keep running it until you find two vans following the truck. They might be right behind it, they might ten minutes behind it – I don't know. You put that on ANPR, too. That one's not silent, okay? I want you tracking them everywhere, and I want every uniformed bugger out on call looking for those vans. Understand?'

Danskin heard Ravi draw breath through his teeth. 'Is that all, sir? I mean, you don't want me to rescue any remaining collaborators still in Afghanistan? Eradicate Covid? Name you an honest politician?'

Despite the circumstances, Danskin laughed. Softened his tone. 'Okay, Sangar. I know it's a big ask, but it's important. What's more, you're the only guy for the job.'

He ended the call. Saw Sam Maynard's eyes question, doubt, and admire him all in one look.

'I like this Operation Sage lark,' Danskin said. 'I knew it was a good name all along.'

CHAPTER TWENTY-THREE

A strengthening wind blew across open land. It became tangled in the branches of trees and ripped away their leaves, still green and alive.

It was the first gale of autumn, and the first significant leaf fall fluttered down on the huddled form of Ryan Jarrod, adding to his concealment.

Ryan sat with his back against a Sycamore, his chin resting on his knees. His head slipped lower as he succumbed to sleep. Ten minutes later, the burner phone jolted him awake.

'I've done what you wanted, when you wanted. Now, you do what I want. You keep your end of the bargain. You release my family,' he said, all drowsiness blown away with the wind.

'Tut, tut, tut. Remember who holds the aces, Ryan. I still have a task for you. THE task: the one I want you for. Mr Maric was, shall we say, a little bonus. Do this one thing, just one little thing, then you get them back – just like Geordie Amos did.'

Ryan bounced his head off the trunk of the Sycamore. 'These are innocent people. They've done nothing to deserve this. Geordie Amos, the Corrigans, Dad and James – you can't do this sort of thing and get away with it.'

Yu laughed. 'You seem to forget. I have got away with it.'

Ryan knew when he was beaten. He let out a long sigh. Closed his eyes, and said, 'What do you want?'

'That's more like it. It's quite straightforward. All I want is a swap.'

Ryan's fingers brushed off a handful of leaves as he ran his fingers through his unwashed hair. 'I don't know what you mean.'

'It's really very simple. Someone who works with your girlfriend is the cause of many problems. I need to know who it is, and I want them forwarded to me.'

'*Forwarde*d? This is a person we're talking about, not an e-mail.'

'Semantics, Ryan. Bring them to me. Delivered. Handed over. Whatever term you wish to use, that's what I want from you.'

'I can't go picking people off the street and *forward* them to a lunatic.'

Yu paused before saying, '*Can't* is uncomfortably close to saying no to me. Remember what happened last time.'

Ryan moaned like the wind through the trees. 'Who is it you want?'

'You're the detective, I believe.'

'What? You don't even know who it is?'

'Let me tell you a story, Mr Jarrod. As you know, you helped me get a lorry through port. That's the first I've got through for a while. Now, there's always a risk of a stop and search, but it's happened too frequently to be random. It's cost me a lot, and someone needs removing from their position. I have a leak in my set up.'

'Cut the crap. Who is it?'

'Your girlfriend is the obvious choice.'

Ryan's stomach knotted.

'…but we gathered a lot of information around her. We watched her. You really don't know how close you came to losing her. My normal method would be to eradicate her anyway, to be on the safe side. However, if it turned out not to be her, I realised we'd be no better off. So, we deliberately arranged for a consignment to be sent when we knew she'd be off duty. We still got stopped. She wasn't the source, but she can provide leverage – which is what brought us to you, Mr Jarrod.'

'You used me to get your filth through port.'

'Yes, I did. More importantly, it showed me I can trust you. Which is why I need you to use your connections to the port to find out who is the cause of my problems.'

'I've got no authority down there. I can't tell you who's stopping your bloody lorries.'

'Hannah Graves does. You've proved you can get her to do what you want. All you have to do is convince her again.'

'How do you propose I do that?'

'Not my problem, Detective Sergeant; not my problem at all.'

'Assuming Hannah does as I ask, that I find out who the mole is, what happens then?'

'You bring them to me. And you get your brother and father back. Buy one, get two free, if you like.'

'What do you do to that person?'

'I haven't decided yet – but I'll take pleasure in it, whatever it may be.'

Ryan breathed noisily.

'Goodbye, Mr Jarrod. Call me the moment you have what I need.'

**

Ravi Sangar was good. Bloody good. By the time Danskin and Maynard had climbed the subway steps of the Central Metro station after their one-stop trip, Sangar had something for them.

The moment DCI Danskin's phone regained signal, it rang.

'You got something already, Sangar?'

'Don't get too carried away. It's only a possible, sir.'

'Tell me.'

'I drew a two-mile circle around the scene of the hit, and I checked all reports of stolen vehicles within the boundary line. Turns out there were three vehicles reported taken: an Astra, a Honda Civic, and a Mini Cooper.'

'Sangar, you're a bloody genius.'

'Hold on, sir. Do you want me to look further afield?'

'Negative. Check ANPR for the Astra and the Civic first. If they come up with nowt, we'll extend the search. I'm not convinced we've got enough time to do much more.'

'What about the Mini?'

'Too small. Besides, it's only getaway material in the Italian Job.'

'Sir, would they all fit into one car? Seems like there were a minimum of four guys involved in the hit, plus Maric - and a getaway driver.'

'Shit. You're right again. Okay – get a marker on all three. And, silent, yes? Only the three of us to be informed.'

'Sir.'

Danskin updated Maynard as they made their way beneath the railway bridge.

'You're quite sure about the silent marker, Stephen?'

'Aye.'

'I guess all we can do now is hope Ravi comes up with something on the vans. If Hetton was spreading bullshit, all our eggs are in the getaway vehicle unless Gav unearths our Sunderland leak. Or, of course, Ryan turns up somewhere.'

The echo of their voices in the tunnel became drowned by an Azuma train as it thundered overhead, its steel wheels pounding out the rhythm of a mechanical heartbeat.

Danskin swallowed hard. Took in air as if it were his last breath. 'Look, there's something I need to tell you.'

She snickered. 'What? That you've fallen madly in love with me and want to spend the rest of your days with me?'

Maynard saw his mouth open and close like a goldfish.

'Don't look so worried. I'm only joking. Now, what is it you want to tell me?'

'O'Hara's not looking for the mole. I stood him down.'

Maynard stood stock still. 'What? Why?'

'Because I know who leaked the plans. I know who's behind the heist.'

She looked at him, expectantly.

He couldn't meet her eye.

'DS Jarrod,' he mumbled.

**

'It makes sense, ma'am.'

Sam Maynard had stormed ahead and hadn't spoken a word until they were safely ensconced in the Super's office, blinds closed.

'What? That my Detective Sergeant smacked me in the face? That he kidnapped the only witness we have who can bring Yu and his gang to justice? I think you need to look up the definition of sense, Detective Chief Inspector.'

He held up his hands. 'I know, I know – but listen, okay? Just listen. Whoever took Maric knew how to jam our radios. They had the foresight and the knowledge to scramble a mobile signal. They also were able to listen in to our operation. They knew the route we were taking.'

'We were already aware of all that, hence the probe on the Prince Bishops. Now you tell me Ryan Jarrod's behind it all. He's one of ours, Stephen, and I'm not having it. That's criminal behaviour from someone who should defend and uphold the law.'

Danskin scratched the back of his hand. 'True. But Jarrod isn't thinking rationally. Put yourself in his shoes. Someone's got your family – what do you do? You'd do anything to get them back.'

'No, Stephen. I wouldn't break every rule in the goddamn book. I wouldn't interfere with an inquiry. I wouldn't hand a witness over to the OCG we're investigating.'

He searched her face. 'Wouldn't you? Wouldn't you, really? Can you honestly say you wouldn't do whatever it took to get them back?'

Sam Maynard vibrated her lips. 'He hit me, Stephen. Assaulted me.'

'Nah. I don't think so. They wouldn't risk you or the others recognising him. My guess is, he drove the getaway vehicle, and no more.'

The Super considered her words. Said almost to herself, 'Hence your order for a silent marker on the car.' She poured herself a glass of water. Her hand shook as she brought it to her lips.

'Another thing, ma'am. I'm pretty sure Yu has been in touch with Ryan again. I think that's what they wanted from him. They wanted him to get Maric.'

They were interrupted by an urgent knock on the door.

Rick Kinnear poked his head into the room.

'Sorry, ma'am. You need to know – we've found Maric.'

'Alive?'

Kinnear looked from Danskin to Maynard and back again.

'It's not good news.'

**

'A maid found him. He was half on / half off the bed. He'd had a huge wad of bog roll stuffed in his gob, and his hands were cuffed.'

Maynard sat with lips pursed tight. She glanced at Stephen Danskin, but he didn't respond. He had his eyes screwed shut.

'The maid alerted the manager after she'd wet herself, and the manager called out local uniform.'

'How did he die?' the Super asked.

'Die? He's not dead.'

Danskin's eyes shot open. 'What? I thought you said it was bad news.'

'It is, but Maric is alive and well. Reasonably so, anyway.'

'What's bad about that?'

Kinnear looked sheepish.

'He said it was one of our lot.'

'Our lot, what, man?'

'Well, Maric said someone kidnapped him. Locked him in a hotel room. After he'd taken a bath, he said someone calling themselves Ryan Jarrod tasered him. That's the last thing he remembers.'

191

Danskin half-smirked. Sam Maynard sighed with relief.

'With respect,' Kinnear continued, 'I don't think it's funny. He says when he came round, his shirt had been covered in tomato ketchup.'

This time, Danskin and Maynard laughed hysterically, more a release of tension than anything.

'Is there something I don't know?' Kinnear asked, confused at their response to a fellow-officer's involvement in something so heinous. 'There's also the small matter of a missing handgun. Two rounds were discharged from it into a pillow, and through the wall. Feathers and plasterboard everywhere.'

Danskin and Maynard chuckled again.

'We've got our answer, ma'am,' Danskin said. 'The OCG obviously have contacted Jarrod again. He's faked a kill. I suspect they wanted photographic evidence he'd killed Maric, just as they'd demanded, which goes to explain the cover up.'

The Super smiled, the sparkle back in her sapphire eyes. 'Ketchup equals blood.'

'Exactly, ma'am.'

'That takes a bit of doing, some nerve, with everything he had at stake. He's bloody good, isn't he?'

Stephen Danskin basked in Ryan's reflected glory. 'He is, indeed. Let's hope he's been so convincing even someone like Benny Yu keeps his side of the bargain.'

CHAPTER TWENTY-FOUR

The moment DCI Rick Kinnear left Sam Maynard's office, she leant over the desk, palm aloft.

Danskin accepted the high-five on offer and sat back, temporarily relieved. 'At least we know Jarrod's still with us, and it looks like he has his own plan.'

'I agree, Stephen, but he needs back-up. If he tries to tackle the entire Yu Tube set up by himself, he'll end up getting killed.'

Danskin's relief left him like the soul from a corpse. 'Aye – and if Yu realises Maric isn't dead, same result. Bugger.'

'I'll make sure Maric doesn't go anywhere. This time, he's staying with us, where we can see him and keep him from everyone else's view.'

Danskin placed his hands flat on the arms of the chair and pushed himself from it. 'I'll talk to him. Find out what he knows.'

'Sit down, Stephen. I don't think he'll tell us anything. He didn't talk last time we had him, and since then we've let him be kidnapped by another officer who went on to taser him and fake his murder. I think Maric is a dead-end for us.'

'I've got to try…'

'No. Rick will try; not you. He's leading today, remember. I'll make sure he keeps Ryan's involvement in all this quiet. The fewer who know, the safer Jarrod is.'

'But ma'am…'

'That's my final word on the subject.' Maynard waited until she was sure she had his attention. 'Besides, you and I need confront the elephant in the room.'

Danskin's brow creased. 'What elephant?'

'The elephant called Hannah Graves. Your stepdaughter, that's who.'

'I'm not following.'

'I think you are. When you first told me what Ryan had done, I was furious. I told you he'd put two lives in danger – his own, and DS Graves. Stephen, Yu is targeting those closest to Jarrod. That puts Hannah pretty near the top of the list.'

Danskin supported his forehead with his fingers. 'I've thought of nowt else, man. And, you know what, because of all that thinking, even at my most pessimistic, I reckon Hannah's okay – for now, at least.'

'How long for? Yu isn't one to mess around.'

'As long as we keep the Maric thing quiet, we've got some time. Yu got Ryan and Hannah to ensure his drugs got through. He knows he can use that path again. I reckon as long as Yu has Jarrod's folks, Hannah's going to be okay.'

'That's one hell of a risk you're taking.'

'Don't you think I don't know? I've been over it, time and time again, putting myself in Benny Yu's shoes. If I were him, I'd keep Hannah alive because I could use her as leverage again.'

'Jesus, Stephen. I didn't know you were a gambler.'

He met her eyes. 'I'm not. That's why I'm confident I'm right.'

Maynard rose from her seat. Walked to the full-length window overlooking the Tyne. She stood with her hands on hips, the exact stance Superintendent Connor would have adopted.

'She needs to know, Stephen. At the very least, she needs to know. It's the only way she can be sure to keep herself safe.'

Danskin tipped his head over the back of his chair and exhaled loudly.

'I don't disagree, ma'am, but we have to be careful how we handle it. If she knows Ryan's taken her for a ride, she won't act naturally if he needs her again. That'll see them both in the shit, along with Norman and James Jarrod.'

Sam Maynard turned back from the window and lay against it. 'Couldn't you just call her? Tell her to be on her guard?'

'You don't know Hannah at all, really, do you? It wouldn't wash.'

'She needs to know, Stephen.'

'Let me think, for a minute.'

His thinking was interrupted by an urgent knock on the office door.

Sangar marched in.

'Sorry to interrupt, ma'am, but it's important.'

'It'd better be, Ravi.'

'It is.' He addressed Danskin. 'Sir, the silent marker on the getaway vehicles has come up trumps already. We've had a ping on the Civic.'

Both senior officers stood.

'Where?'

'Port of Tyne entrance.'

Stephen Danskin barged past Ravi and raced towards the bullpen exit.

**

Ryan parked as far from the CCTV security cameras, which radiated all around the port perimeter and its buildings, as he could. He was pretty sure they'd have picked him up on his approach; he just hoped the City and County lads hadn't identified the vehicle yet.

He checked his appearance in the rear-view. It wasn't a pretty sight. Bloodshot eyes set in a haunted, line-drawn face etched with tension.

Ryan vigorously rubbed the palms of his hands against his face to bring temporary colour to his pallid cheeks. He dried beads of sweat from above his upper lip, and combed fingers through his tangled hair.

Just as his eyes were about to leave the mirror, he saw it. It was only a fleeting glimpse, but it was enough.

A car drove by the port gates almost at a crawl. He'd seen it before. Three times, now. And, unlike on his approach to the fishing lake, this time he was certain. Someone, most likely Yu or his cronies, was keeping tabs on him.

There hadn't been time for him to register the make or model of the car, but he knew it was definitely the same one he'd seen before. For now, the only other thing we was certain of was its colour: a gleaming white.

If he did have a shadow, he'd see the car again. Next time, he'd learn more. And, perhaps, he could work that to his advantage.

Firstly, though, he had to work Hannah Graves.

**

'You said you would call me; not that you'd turn up at work unannounced.' Hannah looked him up and down. 'Especially looking like a tramp.'

Ryan sensed the room still as everyone stopped work and settled their eyes on him. 'Is there somewhere we can talk?'

Hannah flounced ahead of him. He followed her into a side room and heard the office murmur begin even as he closed the door.

'I'm busy. What do you want, Ryan?'

He didn't really know what he wanted, or how we would get it. He heard himself stutter nonsense words. Felt as if his legs were about to give way. The room began to spin. Ryan lay his fingertips on the surface of the desk between him and Hannah. Hannah's voice seemed distant, and her face swam in and out of focus.

He collapsed into a chair; head bowed.

'Ry? Ryan? Are you okay?'

No response.

'Can you hear me? What's wrong, Ryan?'

He brought his head up, slowly and with huge effort.

'Huh? Oh, yeah. I'll be okay.'

She gurgled chilled water from a dispenser into a plastic-cup and brought it to him. His hand shook so much, half the contents spilled into his lap.

'Jesus. What's up, man?'

'I'll be okay. I'm just knackered, that's all. Work, man. You know what it's like.'

She hunkered down in front of him and appraised him, her hand lying gently on his knee.

'Come on,' she said, 'It's me you're talking to here. Never kid a kidder.'

Despite everything, Ryan took comfort in her presence. He even managed a smile - and hated himself for the lie which followed.

'I think it's just the shock of seeing that bloke go over the edge. I reckon I mustn't have got to the bit in the course where it tells you how to deal with it.'

Hannah brushed a hand against his cheek. 'I can't imagine what it must have been like for you,' she said softly.

'Nowt can prepare you for it, I tell you.'

'Have you booked your counselling session? That's got to help.'

He shook his head. 'Too much on.'

Hannah sighed, overcome with remorse for insisting he was the one who made contact first. She'd been selfish, pig-headed, and uncaring.

'I'll come over tonight, yeah?'

'No!' He saw the shocked look on her face. 'I mean, I'm okay. There's no need. I just need some '*me*' time.'

'If you're sure.'

'I am.'

Hannah thought he looked neither sure nor okay.

'Talk to Stephen, then.'

'Nah. I'll look soft.'

'Come on, Ry. This is Stephen Danskin we're talking about. He'd do owt for you.'

197

Ryan plucked an eyebrow. Time was pressing, and he'd made no headway with her.

'Your dad, then; or even James.'

He began to sob. 'I can't tell them.' His shoulders heaved.

'Oh Ry.' She put a hand around his neck to pull him close, then instantly retracted it. 'Your hair! It's soaked with sweat. Get home. Now, go on – no job's worth making you ill.'

It was now or never for him.

'I promise I will, after I've done what I came here for.'

'I thought you were here to see me.'

'That's an added bonus.' He offered Hannah the feeblest of smiles. 'I'm here for work.'

Hannah glanced up at the wall clock. 'I haven't much time, Ryan. I've a ferry landing in half an hour.'

He swallowed down the rest of the water. 'I'll make it quick.'

She waited for him to continue. 'Well?'

'I know I was arsey last time we spoke. You know, letting the lorry through and all that.'

Hannah fought down the urge to agree. 'I can't do it again, if that's what you're here for.'

'No, no. Nowt like that – but it is connected.' He shifted in his seat. Gathered his thoughts.

Hannah broke the silence. 'Your guys stopped it, I guess,'

'No. That's just it. Like I said at the time, it wasn't City and County business, but it is now because it was us who fouled up. I'd like to set up an official meeting. Me and whoever supplies the intel down here. You can sit in, if you like.'

She gave him a quizzical look. 'Yes. I do like. This is still my jurisdiction, even if I don't call all the shots or any of the stops.'

'But your intel officer does, yeah?'

Hannah nodded. 'Those that aren't system generated, she does.'

'What about *that* lorry? Had she marked it up for a stop?'

'As a matter of fact, she had. She's had some good stops lately. It went against the grain interfering like I did. She wasn't happy.'

'What sort of success? Drugs?'

'Whoa, down boy. I thought you said it wasn't City and County business.'

Ryan frowned. 'Okay. I'll save it for the meeting. Set it up, Hannah.'

'I'll check my calendar…'

'No. It has to be in the next fifteen minutes.'

Hannah shook her head so strongly her curls fell into her eyes. 'Not possible.'

'Please, Hannah. This is really important. Once I've talked to her, I'll go get some rest.'

A face appeared at the window. An arm followed, and a finger pointed at a wristwatch.

'That's HMRC. The ferry's on its way in. I need to go.'

He grabbed her wrist as she began to stand. 'And I need to speak to your intel officer. Go do what you have to do but leave her with me.'

'No, Ry. You don't understand. You can't meet her because she's had Track and Trace on her back. She's self-isolating. Or, so she says.'

'You don't believe her?'

'Let's just say I'll be having words. She told me her sister was with a wrong 'un. Don't ask me why, but I think that's the real reason she's not here.'

Ryan's heart raced. The woman Yu wanted was home, alone. This was an open goal. He couldn't miss.

'Can you give me her 'phone number? Even better, her address?'

'You've no call on her, Ryan Jarrod. She's my responsibility.'

The door opened.

'DS Graves, we really need you to oversee the offload. Ferry's docking as we speak.'

'On my way.'

The door closed.

'Hannah: your intel officer – what's her address?'

DS Graves flounced to the shared workstation in the room, hit the '*Personnel*' hyperlink from the home screen, input her password, fingers ablur.

She hit print. 'There. Now, I've got to go. The details are on the printer. Get them and go, then get yersel' home. I'll be checking on you later.'

Hannah Graves logged out and dashed off to attend to her duties.

Ryan flopped back, exhausted. He gathered himself, walked to the printer, and asked Google maps for a route which avoided major highways.

Fifty-four minutes. *What the fuck?* Far too long.

He knew he'd have to get there quicker, even though it meant exposing himself to traffic cameras.

He tapped on '*Fastest Route.*'

That was better. Much better.

Amelia Curry lived sixteen minutes away.

CHAPTER TWENTY-FIVE

'Are you sure Andrew's not upset at me staying?'

Dawn Curry stood at the head of the resin-coated driveway to her sister's house. The expansive bungalow, its white frontage gleaming in the spotlights trained on its entrance even during daylight hours, sat amidst lawns better manicured than Rylan Clark-Neal's beard.

'He's not, Dawn; honest. He stayed at his mam's last night just to give you some time to settle in. He'll be back today.' She glanced at her wristwatch. 'Shouldn't be long, actually. He said he'd get away early if he could.'

The bungalow Amelia shared with Andrew was tucked away behind the Methodist church in Cleadon Village. The desirable location came with premium prices. Dawn wondered how they could afford it.

'Andrew must be doing well for himself. You've struck lucky there, girl.' She succeeded in keeping the envy out of her voice, but not the hurt.

'Accountancy has its benefits, I guess. Boring as Keir Starmer, but it pays well.'

'I could stay at Mum's, you know.'

'What? And have her tell you she told you so? I don't think so. If anyone's going to say that to you, it'll be me.'

Dawn heaved a sigh. 'Am I the only one who didn't see through him?'

'Listen, madam: let's have none of that, do you hear? We'll clear the rest of our junk out of your room and then we'll get this chicken in the oven.' She held aloft the farm shop carrier bag.

Amelia made towards to the front door. She was conscious her sister wasn't following her.

'What?' Amelia asked.

'Thanks, Amelia. For all this. I don't deserve it. I've treated you like a leper for so long.'

'You have, yes. But it was him, not you.' She walked to Dawn. The girls leant into each other and hugged as best they could without squashing their dinner or Dawn's bruises.

'I just wish I knew.'

For a moment, the comment threw Amelia. Then she remembered. 'I'll book you in with our doc tomorrow. She'll set your mind at rest about the baby.'

'That's not what I meant, sis. I wish I knew what happened to Bryn that night.'

'Never mind about Bryn, what he did to you was always going to happen, sooner or later. I doubt whatever happened that night – if anything – had much to do with it.'

Amelia led the way to the front door. Placed her key in the lock. And the door eased open without her turning the key.

She froze.

'What's the matter?' Dawn said. She was behind her younger sister and watched as Amelia used one finger to swing the door fully open.

'Andrew?' Amelia called out. 'Drew? You home already?'

She stepped through the front door; Dawn up close behind her. There were two doors off to the right, three to the left, and one directly in front at the end of a corridor running the full length of the house.

All doors were closed.

'He might be asleep,' Dawn suggested.

'Back garden's my guess. Still, he usually locks the door.'

Amelia pushed open the first door on the left. She leant into the lounge, and back out again. She tried a room to her right. Empty. She left the door ajar.

The next door Amelia came to was the room Dawn slept in the previous night. She hoped he wasn't going through her things.

He wasn't, because the room was unoccupied.

'Andrew? Honey, I'm home!' Amelia called.

Again, no response.

Amelia pushed open another door. The main bedroom. The king-size was fully made-up, everything as it had been when they'd left. There was no sign of anyone having used the en-suite: the shower floor dry, toilet seat down.

She was aware the downy hairs on her forearm were erect, the flesh on her shoulders puckered.

'This is the part where the mad axe-man jumps out at us,' Amelia said.

Neither of them laughed.

Amelia edged towards the remaining door, the one at the end of the corridor. Dawn crept behind her on tiptoe, feeling foolish yet sensing it was the right thing to do.

Amelia nudged at the door. 'Andrew – are you in here?'

She widened the gap. Saw the French windows which led to the conservatory. Andrew wasn't there, either.

The conservatory blinds were raised. She could see into the garden. No Andrew.

Amelia stepped into the kitchen – and stopped dead.

Dawn could tell something wasn't right.

'What's up?' She followed her younger sister into the kitchen. Pushed beyond her.

The floor tiles were a delicate coffee shade, wall tiles similar but darker. A breakfast bar separated the dining area from the rest of the kitchen which had gloss-finished units and appliances, buttermilk in colour, with avant-garde red whorls to provide striking contrast.

Red wine had stained the floor, the only blemish in an otherwise pristine world.

Except, it was anything but pristine.

It was the metallic scent which alerted Dawn. That, and the fact the kitchen units had been plain when she'd been shown around Amelia's home last night. No red swirls. Or spilt wine, for that matter.

She took a sharp intake of breath. Felt Amelia's hands lay gently against her back.

'Drew?' Amelia's voice was a whisper. 'Where are you?'

Dawn knew where he was.

She edged forward until she could see what was beyond the breakfast bar.

She'd found Andrew, propped against the island, head lolling forward. Blood still seeped from his body, rivulets adding to the spillage she'd observed from the kitchen entrance. Thick, heavy drops dribbled from his mouth.

'Amelia, can you call an ambulance, please?' She couldn't believe how calm she sounded. 'The police, too.'

She heard Amelia approach. Dawn turned and held her hands out. 'Don't look, love.'

Of course, like someone warned by a 'Wet Paint' sign, Amelia had to look. Dawn lightly grabbed her sister's elbow. Realised it was futile.

Amelia's face was a blank canvas before reality hit her. Her hands rose to her face, her scream echoed around the kitchen, then it morphed into uncontrollable sobs.

She sank to her knees. 'Andrew? Wake up, love. Andrew. ANDREW!' She grabbed his shoulders. Shook him.

His head fell to one side, a red river spilling from his mouth.

'No! No, no, no. NO!'

Dawn backed away, the view of her distraught sister and her dead fiancé shimmering through her own tears.

She continued to back away until the blow landed in her lower back, forcing the air from her lungs. Dawn stumbled from the punch. Felt another, this one to her side.

Her legs gave way. She was on the floor. A dark presence loomed over her.

Another blow came. Dawn raised her arms. Caught the next one on her hands and felt the following hit on her neck.

She moved her hands to the site of the blow. Her neck stung; a sharp, piercing pain she'd never experienced before. Something wet and sticky flowed between her fingers.

The pain in Dawn's back was now excruciating. She heard Amelia calling her name, repeatedly. But the voice was becoming distant. Amelia seemed to be moving further and further away, just as her own pain was relenting.

Another blow landed, this time to the centre of her chest, but she didn't feel it. It must have been aimed at someone else, not her – yet the same familiar warmth ran from her chest, over her stomach, and pooled between her legs. Another strike. Same spot.

She closed her eyes. It was time to sleep, now.

'Goodnight, little one,' she whispered to the dead baby inside her.

**

It took Stephen Danskin ten minutes before he spotted a gap in the HGV traffic trundling off the ferry. Once through, he parked up on the yellow hashed markings of a loading bay to avoid wasting further time.

'Hey,' a voice called over the noise of the port activities, 'You can't park there, mate.'

Danskin looked up. 'I'll be ten minutes, tops,' he yelled back.

'No, you won't. This is a restricted area,' PC John Jeffries warned, hand close to his firearm. 'Public parking's ower that way.' He pointed his non-dominant hand in the direction of the public car park.

'I'm not public,' Danskin said, reaching inside his jacket for his warrant card.

'Freeze!' Jeffries yelled, struggling to raise his gun from its belt.

'We're not NYPD, man. We don't say, *'freeze'* in this country. Besides, if I did have a gun, you'd be deed by the time you got that thing into a firing position.'

Jeffries opened his mouth to reply when Danskin's words registered. *'We?* You said *'we'.'*

'Very observant. I'm DCI Stephen Danskin, City and County CID. Now, if I may, I'd like to show you my warrant card. Do you want me to give you time to get that gun of yours out first?'

John Jeffries shook his head. 'Just do it slowly, yeah?'

He did. Held it up for Jeffries to see.

'Sorry. Can't be too careful, y'knaa.'

'It's sorry, *'Sir'*, to you but I accept your apology. Now, I need to see DS Graves urgently.'

'Follow me,' a contrite Jeffries said, still forgetting the *Sir* bit.

**

The pitter-patter of fingers on keyboards was music to Danskin's ears compared to the racket outside.

Hannah stood with her back to him, and only turned when Jeffries said, 'You've a visitor.'

'It's 'You've a visitor, *ma'am,*' Danskin whispered to him.

Jeffries shrugged and left them to it while he continued his rounds.

'Sir?' she said, eyebrows raised in puzzlement.

'Can we have a chat, DS Graves?' he said, conscious of the formality. 'Somewhere quieter?'

She led him into the room she'd occupied with Ryan not fifteen minutes earlier.

'What's going on? I'm guessing it's summat to do with what Ryan's just been to see me about.'

'Sit down, Hannah.'

She took a seat. 'Shit. I don't like the sound of this. Is Ry in trouble?'

Danskin sat next to her. Played with his fingers. Finally, he looked Hannah in the eye.

'Yeah, he is.'

'Shit, man. Ryan? He'd never do anything wrong...'

'Hannah. Please. Listen, okay?'

'Oh-kay.'

'Ryan's been targeted by an OCG. I can't say too much, in fact I don't really want to say anything, but I've no choice. You see, he's involved you.'

'What? Me? How?'

'This OCG want Ryan to do things for them. Help them out, as it were.'

'No! He never would.'

'Hannah, he already has.'

She sat back, an incredulous gawp on her face.

'I understand he asked you to let a lorry through port.'

'He did. Said you had intelligence on it...'

'No. We didn't have any intelligence. That was a lie, and it's how he helped the gang.'

'Jesus Christ.' She hung her head low, hair dropping forward.

'I'm sorry, Hannah, I can't tell you anymore, but believe me – he had his reasons for doing it and, more importantly, he's still on our side.'

'Ha! Are you sure about that?'

'Yes. I am.'

Hannah puffed out her cheeks. 'He was acting weird when he was here. He said it was to do with that suicide. I wish I'd asked him more.'

'Don't beat yourself up. He wouldn't have told you.' He reached out to touch Hannah's arm. 'I've only told you because I want you to be careful. They obviously know about you. They know your connection to Ryan. They might come after you or try to use you in some way.'

'Howay, it's me you're talking about here. I'm not letting them use me.'

'Five minutes ago, you wouldn't have believed that of Ryan either, would you?'

She made a hissing noise as she breathed between clenched teeth. 'Right. We need to find him.'

'*I* need to find him. *You* need to act as if none of this conversation took place. Now, what did he say when he was here? Did he tell you what he wanted?'

Hannah sat up straight, suddenly alert. 'He wanted a meeting with the Customs Intel Officer, Amelia Curry.'

'Does he know her?'

Hannah shook her head.

'What's her role?'

'Well, among other things, she flags cargo with manual markers for stop and search.'

'Like *Tulpen Uit Amsterdam* on the *Sea Duchess*?'

'Yes. Exactly like that.'

'I need to see her.'

She shook her head again. 'She's not here. I told Ry she was supposed to be self-isolating, but I didn't believe her. Her sister's boyfriend's pissing her about. I think Amelia's trying to sort things out for her. He's a wrong 'un, by all accounts.'

'Is he known to us?'

'Stephen, man: why would I check up on that? I wouldn't check even if it had been Amelia's boyfriend, never mind her sister's. It's nowt to do with me.' She looked away from Stephen Danskin. 'All I know is his first name. Bryn.'

'Okay. So, you don't know where Ryan went after he came here?'

She snapped her fingers. 'I've got a pretty good idea. I gave him Amelia's address so he could go talk to her.'

'I need that address, and I need it now.'

Hannah logged into the Personnel system again. This time, she didn't wait for the printer to go through its motions. She scribbled the address on a post-it note and slapped it onto the back of Danskin's hand.

'Go find him for me.'

'I intend to.'

He turned to leave. Hesitated.

'One more thing,' he said. 'Not a word to anyone about this and, more importantly, be careful, yeah? Don't be the one to meet visitors. Don't go outside alone. Don't interview anyone alone.'

She pursed her lips. Folded her arms across herself in a '*I know what I'm doing*' pose.

Danskin held her shoulders.

'I mean it, Hannah. Do not mess with these people. They mean business. Trust me; they're nasty sods.'

CHAPTER TWENTY-SIX

All petrol stations have security cameras, so stopping for fuel was the last thing Ryan wanted. The Civic, though, was running on fumes and, although the Honda's built-in sat nav told him he was tantalisingly close to his destination, he couldn't take the risk.

As it transpired, it was the best thing he could have done.

While he refuelled at the Jet garage, he saw the flash of a familiar white car zip past, too quick to identify it formally - but enough for him to know it was the same car he'd seen on numerous occasions.

He rattled the pay-at-the-pump nozzle back into its holder and pulled away, buckling his seat belt as he went.

Opposite the petrol station, a Toby Carvery sat at the point where the A1018 temporarily divided. The Carvery was on the opposite side of the road, but he saw it clearly enough: a white BMW, facing outward.

He gave a surreptitious glance towards it.

'Shit.'

The registration plate was hidden by a *Welcome Back* sign.

Nevertheless, he had a make and model, which is more than he had two minutes ago.

**

'Ma'am, I need you to run a name through our systems,' DCI Danskin said into the radio even as he drove away from the Port of Tyne. 'It's an Amelia Curry, a Customs officer.'

'Are you onto something, Stephen?'

'Might be…'

Another voice in the background interrupted his flow.

'Stephen, Ravi's here. He's got news for you.'

'Fire away, Sangar.'

'Sir, things are moving at pace here. You need to know I've got an ID on one of the vans you asked me about. Sure enough, there were two on the way out, but I could only trace one on the way back south. The other one may have been disguised like the flower lorry was, but at least I've traced one. It's definitely the same vehicle.'

'You're sure? Did you get the reg plate?'

'Aye, sir. They were garage plates. False ones, at that. I reckon they'll have ditched the plates already, but I've fed 'em into ANPR anyway.'

'Good man.'

Danskin slalomed his way through stationary port traffic and bore left at a busy roundabout leading to the A19.

'There's more, sir. We've found the stolen Astra. Burnt out, it seems. Forensics are all over it, but I doubt it's any involvement with Op Sage.'

'The Mini?'

'Nothing, sir. But here's the thing: the Civic's pinged again about twenty minutes ago, entering the Tyne Tunnel. I'll try to pick it up on the other side.'

'Don't bother, Sangar. Focus on the vans.'

'You sure, sir?'

'I am. I already know where the Civic's headed. Put the Super back on.'

'Maynard here, Stephen.'

'I know what's going on. I reckon Ryan's got another task, and it involves this Intel Officer.'

Maynard whistled. 'It doesn't sound good for her.'

'No, it doesn't. I think this Amelia Curry is how Jarrod gets his dad and brother back.'

**

It would have been easier for Ryan to turn in at Front Street, but that was too near the Toby.

Instead, he continued a little further and turned in right onto a narrow lane next to the Methodist Church. The lane led him into an estate full of Lake District names.

He meandered back and forth a while until the was sure he wasn't being followed by the BMW, then he picked up the sat nav instructions again. They directed him to an expensive-looking driveway leading to an even more expensive dwelling.

The whitewashed, double-fronted bungalow was something poor Geordie Amos could only dream about. Ryan thought of him, and his own family, as he parked a little further up the road. He had to remind himself why he was doing this. It was the only way for him to remain sane.

Ryan walked down the centre of the drive, glanced inside a car which looked as if it had just been abandoned. He saw the front door of the house stood slightly ajar, but he rang the doorbell anyway and stepped back to observe from a social distance.

No-one came.

'Hello? Amelia? Anyone home?'

He pushed the door fully open.

'Everything okay in here?'

He stepped into the hallway. As he did so, he heard a shuffling noise at the end of a long corridor. A woman appeared, looking back into the room she'd just left.

'Can I help you?' She didn't come any closer. Still stared fixedly into the room behind her.

'Are you Amelia?'

'It's a bad time,' Amelia said.

Ryan saw the woman gnaw down on her top lip as she turned towards him for the for the first time. There was something about her eyes…

'Okay. Sorry. Hannah suggested I come see you, that's all. I'm Ryan, by the way.'

'Oh. Okay. Not right now, though. It's really not a good time.' Amelia glanced behind her again, rictus-faced.

'Are you sure everything's good?' He took a step towards her.

'Don't come in! You can't!'

Ryan retreated. 'That's fine. Don't worry. I can stand here and talk if you like.'

Amelia's eyes, puffy behind messed-up mascara, flicked left and right.

'Please. Not now. Go, please. Close the door behind you.'

'No bother. I will do. Let Hannah know I've been, yeah? You can get my number from her when you're up for a chat.'

Ryan walked down the drive as casually as he could, hands thrust deep in his pockets.

Someone was in the house with her. He'd known it from the moment he'd set eyes on her. Who, he wasn't sure. Not one of Yu's cronies, for certain. Yu would have no call on his services if his people already had her.

A rival gang, perhaps? If it was, that spelt trouble with a capital F.

Could it have been the sister's boyfriend? He was an abuser, so anything was possible. Or, perhaps, Amelia Curry simply had something to hide and wanted Ryan out the way, pdq.

No, he dismissed the last theory. She'd been scared witless by something – somebody - before he'd even revealed who he was.

As soon as Ryan turned left at the end of the drive and was hidden from view of the house, he broke into a jog - and then a sprint.

He reckoned the house backed onto, or adjacent with, the grounds of the church. A quick loop-the-loop around the estate brought him to the front of the village's Methodist church.

Brick-built with a typical apex frontage, the main entrance was to the right of the property. Leaf fall from four mature trees littered the grounds like confetti and gathered around brick gate posts.

The low metal fence, painted black, bordered the church. The gates were open. He didn't expect to see any CCTV cameras, and he wasn't wrong.

Ryan wandered into the churchyard, squeezed between the main entrance and a high wooden fence to its right, and crouched as he approached the rear of the building.

From the shadows, he appraised the properties beyond the church. He was disappointed to discover the rear of the church afforded little cover. A patchwork quilt of lawns interspersed by young fir trees and a second, higher metal fence was the best it offered.

Ryan tried to gauge which of the neighbouring properties was that of Amelia Curry. The sound of a car pulling into the churchyard spurred him into action.

He climbed the fence and dropped into the first garden.

A kiddie's slide and a jumble of tricycles and pedal cars was sufficient to inform him this wasn't Amelia's.

A dry-stone wall separated this home from its neighbour. Too high to see over, he listened intently.

Silence.

He took a run towards the wall, launched himself at it with the pose of Superman in flight, lay his hands on the wall's rough surface, and sprung off it as if it were a vaulting horse at his childhood gymnastics centre.

Ryan perfected his landing, sticking on his feet. Which was just as well as it enabled him to sprint away from the bull mastiff bounding towards him.

Ryan hurdled the adjacent fence and landed noisily in a cluster of rose bushes. Thorns pierced his flesh. Drew blood. He bit his lip to avoid crying out in pain.

He lay there until he was sure no-one had heard him, and until next door's hound had lost interest in the intruder.

Ryan peered out across a garden tended with care. The garden was overlooked by a large conservatory which ran the length of the building. One of its doors stood open, slid back behind its twin.

He could hear voices, but not words.

Ryan inched along the wall, silent as death, until he could make out what was being said.

The voice he heard was male. Slurred. Filled with fury.

'You made a pact with the devil!'

Ryan's hackles raised. There was something unearthly about the voice.

He couldn't make out the reply, but he was sure the voice belonged to Amelia.

This was the house.

'You'll pay!' the man slurred.

Ryan heard Amelia yelp in pain.

The conservatory door slid shut, and Ryan could hear no more. Whoever was in there didn't want the neighbours to know.

Ryan dropped to his knees. A partly drawn venetian blind hid him from view. He raised his head and risked a peek inside.

His view was limited to what he could see reflected in the glossy finish of the kitchen units, the vision distorted like a House of Mirrors.

He made out the back of a man, pacing around, gesticulating wildly. The man's arm extended as if he were reaching for something.

The man's right arm came up.

There came a flash of metal. A blade of some kind.

Ryan leapt up and slid open the conservatory door.

**

Stephen Danskin drove like a madman. He approached from the A19 through Boldon Colliery, ignoring the flash of a speed camera and three red lights.

He flicked on the radio.

'Anything on Curry yet?' he asked, urgently.

'It's a negative, Stephen. A complete blank. Having said that, the Customs vetting procedure is pretty much the same as ours. She wouldn't have got through if she had a record.'

'The sister?'

'Nothing of note. Ravi's checked Amelia's social media and there's a few old images of her with another girl. They aren't labelled, but it could be the sister. I'll get Ravi to send them through to your phone although I doubt they'll be much help.'

'What about the boyfriend? Either boyfriend, for that matter.'

'Another dead end.'

Danskin flashed headlights at an old biddy driving slower than a kerb-crawler. She didn't notice the signal. He hammered on his horn and the woman jumped like a high hurdler before pulling into the roadside.

'Isn't that a bit odd? That she hasn't shown off her fella?'

'Amelia Curry hasn't posted anything for over nine months. Quite possibly, since she got the Customs job. I guess one of the in-house rules is to keep a low social media profile.'

'Trust her to be a fecking goody-two shoes.'

'What is it you say, Stephen? You'll need to do some *'proper coppering'* when you get there.'

A tractor pulled out in front of him hauling enough of a harvest to keep the population of South Sudan fed for a year.

'Fuckity-fuck-fuck!'

'It was only a joke, Stephen.'

'Not you, ma'am.' He drummed his fingers on the steering wheel as the tractor wound its way along the country road at a steady twelve mph. 'Have you anything else for me?'

'I've called Nigel Trebilcock back in.'

'That solves all wor problems, then,' Danskin groaned.

Maynard ignored him. 'He's checking up on Stuart Hetton's info. I'll let you know what he comes up with. How far out are you, Stephen?'

He wasn't familiar with the area. He hoped the satnav woman was.

'GPS says nine minutes.'

'Report back asap.'

'Will do, ma'am.'

He cursed again.

'Don't wait up. It could be midnight if this bastarding tractor doesn't pull over.'

He tooted his horn like a native Sicilian.

CHAPTER TWENTY-SEVEN

Ryan had the element of surprise on his side. It was about the only advantage in his armoury.

The man held a knife aloft. The best way to disarm him was to grab it. Ryan grasped the man by his right wrist and kicked him, hard, between the legs; five, six, seven times.

Some missed their mark, but Ryan kept on kicking.

He levered the knifeman's arm back towards the man's face, and thrust his head forward into the man's nose. The man grunted but kept struggling back, twisting the knife towards Ryan. Jarrod butted him again. The man's nose erupted over his face.

It didn't stop the assailant. In fact, he lifted Ryan from the floor with the hand Ryan gripped and swung him around until Jarrod's knees slammed into a kitchen unit.

'Right, you bastard,' Ryan swore. He hammered his foot into the man's own knee, but he barely flinched despite the sickening crunch.

The blade slashed at Ryan, ripping open the scar tissue on his left hand, puncturing the flesh of his forearm.

Ryan's eyes teared and he bit down hard on his lip. This time, he kicked out at the man's hand. He heard the satisfying clang of knife against tiled floor.

In a blur, Ryan saw a woman's foot appear on the periphery of his vision. The foot kicked the knife out of reach of both men.

Ryan let go of the man's wrists and rained blow after blow into his midriff. The knifeman doubled over. Ryan brought both fists down onto the man's head, the nape of his neck and, as the man curled up, the top of his spine.

The man lay still.

Ryan stood over him, his breath rasping.

The knifeman turned his face towards Ryan and leered up at him through a blood-matted face.

'Shit.' Ryan didn't give the man time to react. He grabbed one of the remaining kitchen knives from the block and held it in his right hand.

'My turn, now,' Ryan said. 'Who are you?'

Amelia's voice, child-like and pathetic, warbled 'His name's Bryn.'

The man smiled again. Nodded his head. Then began to rise from the floor.

Ryan jumped on Bryn's damaged leg, landing with both feet on his shinbone. He stamped down again. Bone splintered like dry sticks.

Still the man smiled.

'HE did this,' Bryn said. 'No-one can stop him. He'll find me. He'll make me eat my own testicles, then he'll kill me. He kills us all.'

The man's eyes - wide, wild, vacant and unblinking – seemed to creep across the floor. They fell still, and he scrambled his fingers towards a swamp of congealed blood.

Bryn raised the hand. He held something between his fingers.

'This is how he does it.' The man stared at his fingers in wonderment. 'My precious.' He laughed until he started coughing. He spat out blood. 'My precious,' he repeated in a whisper.

The lunatic crawled through blood lake and propped himself against the wall. He tried to stand up.

Ryan had seen enough chemically induced psychosis before to realise the man was doped, not mad; but he'd never seen anyone as out of it as this.

He knew Bryn would stop at nothing, and nothing could stop Bryn.

Except, a kick to the head.

219

Ryan delivered it to perfection. Bryn's head thundered against the wall and flopped to his chest.

'We're going. Now.' He grabbed Amelia by the hand.

'I can't leave them.'

'Can't leave who?'

Alice dipped her head timidly. Ryan followed the direction of tilt.

'Jesus Christ!'

Two sets of legs protruded from a doorway; the tiles brushed red with blood where Bryn had dragged them along the floor.

Ryan poked his head into the tiny utility area.

'Fuck.' He inhaled deeply through his nose. 'It's too late. We can't help them. We need to get out of here.'

'I can't leave them here. Not like this. Not with him. I need to look after them.'

He held Amelia's shoulder. 'Listen to me. Bryn's not finished yet. He's not feeling anything. That stuff he held up? Drugs. He's away with the fairies and, as long as he is, he won't feel any pain. As soon as he comes round, he'll be as dangerous as fuck.'

'Drugs? Oh God, no. This is my fault. It's all my fault.' Amelia wept behind her hands.

Ryan glanced at Bryn. He'd started muttering. Attempted to prop himself up on his elbows.

'Now!' Ryan shouted. 'Go, go.'

'I'll come back for you. Both of you. I love you, and I'm so, so, sorry,' she whispered to her fiancé and her sister.

Ryan dragged Amelia Curry out the front door, up the driveway, and along the road to his Honda.

**

Stephen Danskin all but forced the tractor off the road and gave the farmer the finger as he sped by, pedal to the metal.

He took the entrance into Amelia Curry's driveway on two wheels and skidded to a halt next to an abandoned car. It wasn't a Mini Cooper, and it wasn't a Honda.

Danskin strode to the front of the house and knocked purposefully.

'Police. Open up.'

He stood back and took in the frontage. With no footsteps approaching the door, he edged to the left and peered through the window. He looked into a large, tastefully furnished lounge. Wall-mounted TV, tropical fish tank, spotlights built into the ceiling, and Turkish rugs scattered over solid wood flooring.

But no people.

He returned to the door, banged again, and turned the handle. The door was locked.

He waited a few more moments then slipped down the side of the bungalow.

The back garden was empty. Danskin noticed a flattened rose bush, as if someone had been thrown into it, but no-one was in it now. He could see the width of the conservatory, enough for him to see it was unoccupied.

He kept low, pressed himself against the glass, and edged along it, quiet as a mouse.

Danskin was conscious that his blood sang at his temples, a sure sign he was adrenaline-fuelled. He hoped he didn't need it.

The conservatory doors, closed though they were, afforded a view through into the kitchen. At first, all he saw was his own reflection. He cupped his hands around his eyes and looked again.

He saw blood. On the floor, smeared on the units: thick and crimson on the tiles, bright scarlet against the units.

'Aw, shit, man.'

He peered in one last time.

A man lay on the floor, spittle drooling from his mouth, vacant glassy eyes, and a leg bent at a crazy angle.

Danskin saw the man's lips move. The man held up a hand and stared at the gore clinging to his fingers like glue. Fascinated, the man wiped the filth across his cheeks.

Suddenly, the man head-butted the wall. Blood poured from the open wound, yet he laughed.

Danskin stood and tried the conservatory doors. To his surprise, they slid open without protest.

The man inside had turned his head and was staring at him.

'You're hurt! Stay still. I'll get help!' Stephen urged. 'What's your name?' he added, fumbling for his phone.

The man smiled at him through bloodied teeth and dragged himself out of sight.

Danskin stepped inside.

The man, still on all fours, reappeared. He crawled towards the DCI. His hand slipped back into view. He had straw clutched between his fingers. The man yanked at something, hard.

It wasn't straw.

It was hair.

With a head attached to it.

'Fuck.'

Danskin recoiled backwards, his foot slipping away from him on the blood-soaked floor as if he were Bambi on ice. Something snapped in his groin. 'Ah. Fuck.'

He struggled to his feet. The man held the woman's head towards Danskin like it was an offering to the Gods.

The man's lips opened, and he displayed his teeth in a blood-curdling smile. 'Beelzebub has a devil put aside for me,' the man croaked.

Danskin looked around him. Settled his eyes on a glass coffee table in the conservatory. He raised it above his head and brought it crashing down.

He weighed a nine-inch shard of broken glass in his hand and stepped towards the man of nightmares.

The man was stroking the girl's hair, cooing into her ear, when Danskin thrust the shard downwards.

The man rolled away at the last moment, the glass pierced the man's upper thigh. The spear missed his femoral artery but punctured a major vein.

A dark stain spread across the man's trousers as blood flowed from the wound.

'I'm the devil. He is the devil. We are all the devil's children.'

Incredibly, the man began to stand, one leg twisted behind him, Dawn Curry's head in one hand – and a kitchen knife in the other.

The madman screeched in false tongues, more noises than actual words. Inexorably, he edged towards Danskin.

The DCI inched backwards; eyes fixed on the crazy who swept a kitchen stool aside as if swatting a fly.

Out the corner of his eye, Danskin saw another body. A man. He daren't look away from the assailant but a voice kept telling him, '*Check it's not Ryan. Check it's not Ryan.*'

He checked.

It wasn't.

In that instant, the man was upon him; the woman's head held up against Danskin's face.

'I saved her,' the man slurred. 'Salvation is hers. I am the saviour!'

'You're fucking crazy.'

'Crazy?' the man cackled. 'I'm not the crazy one. HE is crazy. He who brings this upon us. But he won't take me.'

The man raised the knife. Brought it down.

Danskin yelled 'No!' as he ducked away.

When he looked up, the man was on the floor; a kitchen knife wedged in his chest up to the hilt.

The man opened his lips. A bubble of air-filled saliva appeared in his open maw.

The viscous bubble turned cherry red.

Peace descended on the bungalow and its victims.

CHAPTER TWENTY-EIGHT

'He's not picking up, ma'am.'

'Keep trying, Ravi.'

'Radio signal's definitely A-Okay. It's the DCI who's not responding.'

'I'll see if I can get him on his phone,' Maynard said, concern apparent in her voice.

'Do we know where he was going?'

'No, not the exact address. Easy enough to get. Sorry, ma'am. It should've been the first thing I did.'

Ravi Sangar tapped on the keyboard. 'Got it. We could get DCI Kinnear's mob out straight away,' he suggested.

Maynard shook her head. 'They're fully engaged on the case as it is. Now, shut up a minute while I give Stephen a call.'

A golden sun, low in the sky, peeked from behind cloud cover – a last hurrah before night fell. Danskin sat propped against the outside of the bungalow's closed front door, sucking in oxygen as a baby suckles milk.

He felt the phone vibrate in his pocket. Didn't respond at first. Couldn't. Too many horrors invaded his senses.

The vibration stopped. Started again.

Danskin delved in his pocket. Reluctantly, he swiped to accept the call.

'Yeah?' was all he managed to muster.

He heard a relieved sigh.

'We've been trying to get hold of you. Why aren't you answering your radio?'

'Cos it's in me car, and I'm not.'

'Are you okay, Stephen? You sound, I dunno…'

'*Okay?* I'm not sure I know what okay really is.'

Maynard took a deep breath. 'Right. Ravi's got news for you. First, I want an update. Where the hell are you?'

Danskin gave a humourless chuckle. 'Right first time, ma'am. Hell just about sums it up.'

'Cut the crap. What the fuck are you up to?'

Danskin sighed. Ran a hand down his face. Struggled to his feet and stared into the last rays of sunlight.

'I'm at Amelia Curry's. I ballsed up. I should have called it in earlier. I thought I could deal with it myself, what with the stakes being so high and all, and only having Rick's mob for back up.' He let slip a moan. 'Sorry, ma'am. I should have called it in,' he repeated.

'What's happened?'

'We've three dead here.'

'What? Are you sure?'

He snickered. 'Trust me, I'm sure.'

Maynard gasped. 'Please God, tell me Ryan's not one of them.'

'Ryan's not one of them, ma'am.'

The Super exhaled. 'Now, tell me he didn't do it.'

'He didn't do it.'

Another exhale. 'Okay. I'll get a full uniform presence there straight away. Forensics and SOCO, too. Do we know who the victims are? Is Amelia Curry one of them?'

'No, she isn't. Her sister is, though.'

'You have a positive ID? I mean, the photo Ravi sent was fairly old.'

Danskin let out another empty laugh. 'It's her, alright. Trust me, I got a pretty close-up view.'

'The others?'

'The two boyfriends, I reckon: one victim, one perp. The abuser – Bryn – was high as a kite. I mean, like, out of it. Possessed, almost. And, terrified all at the same time. I've never seen owt like it.'

'So, no leads? Nothing linking any of it directly to Op Sage?'

'There will be. I'm pretty sure a toxicology report will show this Bryn character was doped up to the eyes, and I reckon it was a heroin hybrid.'

'Sounds more than heroin to me, Stephen.'

'Hybrid was my key word. I believe it was mixed with Pervitin or fentanyl, or both.'

'Fentanyl? The stuff Hetton spoke about? How can you be sure?'

Danskin closed his eyes, but the horrors of the bungalow stayed with him. 'If you'd seen the state of him, you'd know. His injuries, some self-inflicted, were horrific, but he kept coming. He felt no pain.'

'Jesus.'

'He killed himself. Kitchen knife to the heart. One of the last things he said was something about the devil will get us all. That he wouldn't let the devil take him. I'm positive the devil he was talking about was Benny Yu.'

'Right. As soon as the first back-up arrives on the scene, you tell them what you want from them, let them liaise with forensics, and you head back here for a full debrief. Pronto.'

'Yes, ma'am.'

'Have you any idea where Curry is now?'

'I might have, aye.'

'Tell me.'

'I think she's with Jarrod. I think he's taking her to meet Benny Yu. Ma'am, I reckon I was right. He's trading in Amelia Curry for his folks.'

**

Ryan left the bungalow with Amelia in the Civic's passenger seat alongside him. She'd sunk into herself; morose, bereft and, for the most part, silent except for the occasional mournful sob.

Ryan left her to her thoughts as he piloted the Honda along country roads and side streets, ignoring highways and major routes. He wasn't familiar with the territory, but the expensive homes of Cleadon soon gave way to more subdued housing as he toyed with the outskirts of South Shields.

He headed roughly northwest with no specific destination in mind. He kept glancing at Amelia, assessing her mental state, wondering if she'd ever return to the young, carefree woman she'd been only a couple of hours ago.

'He killed them both,' she muttered. 'He took my Dawn. My Andrew. It's my fault. It's all my fault.'

Her voice became more strained, more sorrowful with each mile they travelled. As it did so, the more it grated on Ryan. He had his own issues to deal with, his own solutions to find, and Amelia suddenly finding a voice full of self-pity didn't help.

Finally, Ryan reached an area he knew. He spotted a track leading into a patch of industrial wasteland close to Wardley Welfare. He braked hard and fishtailed the Honda onto a surface of broken concrete and scattered bricks.

'What are you doing?' Amelia screeched, clutching the seat for support. The car hopped over a brick. Amelia's head bounced against the roof. 'Where are we going?'

Ryan remained silent and only pulled up when he was sure they were concealed from view.

'Stop whining!' he yelled at Amelia. He shocked her enough for her to stop repeating the same phrases over and over again.

'You don't understand. It's my fault. I did this.'

'It's okay,' he said, knowing it wasn't. 'It's over with.' Another over-simplification.

Amelia leant into him and buried her face into his chest.

'Ssshh. We'll sort this. You're safe now, and we can sort it.'

He felt her convulse against him, her tears dampening his shirt. Her voice came out muffled against his body. 'It was me he was there for. Not them. It's my fault.'

Ryan held her for a full minute before he felt her relax.

'There was nothing you could do to stop him, Amelia. Nothing.'

Her fingers gripped his shirt sleeves. Pulled at them. She started to wail again, so he let her hang onto him for as long as she needed.

With one final, huge sniff, Amelia sat up and rubbed the heels of her hands into her eyes. She tucked her hair behind her ears and attempted a reassuring smile.

It didn't kid Ryan, but time was pressing. He needed answers, so he dove straight in. 'Tell me what happened.'

'Bryn hadn't come for Dawn. He was there to see me.'

'Why? What's going on, Amelia?'

She turned to face him. She looked a mess. Flushed face, mascara-smudged cheeks, bloodied forehead from the cuts to Ryan's arms.

'When this poxy virus hit,' she began, 'My company made me redundant before there even was such a thing as furlough. I needed a job. Didn't want Andrew to think I was sponging off him. I barely knew Bryn. Only met him once, I think, but he found out I'd lost my job. He rang me. He said he knew people, and he'd fix me up with something.'

Ryan waited until Amelia gathered herself again.

'Next thing I know, I'm working in Customs Intelligence without even trying. I'd been there, what, a couple of months, possibly less, when Bryn rang me again at home.'

She became silent once more. Ryan resisted the temptation to glance at his watch. Instead, he said, 'Take your time.' Time was one thing he didn't have.

'So,' she continued after wiping her eyes, 'He tells me stuff about certain lorries. What they'd have on them. He tells me I need to make sure they get stopped.'

'And you did?'

'Mostly, yeah. I missed a couple 'cos I didn't want it to seem obvious, and I stopped a few which I hadn't been tipped off about because I knew they'd be clear. It wouldn't look right if I was right every time, you know?'

Ryan said he did know.

'Anyway, it turns out Bryn thought I should be right every time. When he found out I'd let some slip through, he got really mad. I mean, furious, yeah? He said if I didn't do exactly what he wanted, he'd make sure Dawn suffered. I already knew he was a mean bastard so I couldn't possibly think what he'd be like if I did something to upset him.'

Ryan stared out the windscreen. 'He asked you to do more.'

'Oh yeah. Lots more. He said I couldn't see Dawn. He might let her out if I was a good girl. So, I was a good girl. Every time he texted me, I'd flag up whatever he wanted.'

'Including *Tulpen Uit Amsterdam*?'

She shrugged. 'Yeah.'

Ryan began to see daylight in the darkness.

'Bryn went mad when Hannah told me to let it through.'

'So mad he came to yours to kill you?'

Amelia shook her head. 'No, I don't think so. He took it out on Dawn, like he said he would. Something else happened to him, Dawn thinks.' She let out a sob. 'Dawn thought,' she corrected.

'Such as?'

'Something scared him. Or somebody. Dawn said he'd taken something that night. I think he was into drugs, himself. Trading, or dealing, or whatever. He wanted to be a big shot, and I think he must have upset someone along the way.'

Ryan resisted the temptation to smile as the pieces began to fall into place. Bryn had been trying to interrupt the YuTube supply line, that's what he'd been doing. Double-crossing them with some other outfit, probably. He'd been using Amelia for it, which is why Benny Yu had ordered Ryan to bring him her head on a platter.

Amelia sighed. 'Andrew and Dawn – they were just in the wrong place at the wrong time. They didn't stand a chance.'

'No, Amelia. They didn't.'

'He stabbed her right in front of me, Ryan. Right in front of my eyes. Again, and again. Then, he turned the knife on me, and that's when I saw it in his eyes – he was scared shitless. He kept asking me if I'd told anyone about the lorries, if anyone knew he was involved. He wouldn't believe me. He was going to kill me like he…'

She flung open the door and dashed for the shelter of a part-demolished wall. Ryan heard her retch for England and wished he could join her.

But he couldn't. He had a call to make. He'd help Amelia if he could, but he had more important people to help.

His father and his brother.

He pulled the burner phone from his pocket and called Benny Yu.

CHAPTER TWENTY-NINE

A hushed silence fell over the Forth Street briefing room. Even the air conditioning system seemed to hold its breath as Stephen Danskin described the scene he'd stumbled across at Amelia Curry's residence.

In the room with him were Sam Maynard, Rick Kinnear and the ever-present Ravi Sangar. Danskin had noticed Nigel Trebilcock back on duty in the bullpen and he and Gavin O'Hara were picking up the reins as half of Kinnear's crew finished their shift.

Superintendent Maynard was first to gather her thoughts. 'Okay. We need to join the dots here. Stephen, we've made some progress while you've been away. No silver bullets, but progress nonetheless.'

Danskin admired how she put his emotional debrief into a mental drawer marked 'Over and Done With' and got straight down to business.

'Firstly,' she reported, 'We've had news that the Op Kop approach is beginning to pay dividends. They've managed to trace back three stages in the Merseyside chain. I felt we should adopt a similar approach, so I hauled Stuart Hetton in for further questioning.'

'Ma'am, I gave him my word we wouldn't do that.'

'Hush, Stephen. Needs must. He's the lowest tier we have, so I'm starting with him. At the very least, it prevents YuTube involving him further and it also makes sure he doesn't give Yu and his cronies the nod we're onto him. With us also holding Maric, Benny Yu is denied access to any of our key sources.'

Danskin conceded it made sense but voiced his one concern. 'I'm not sure we've time to start at the bottom up, ma'am.'

'It's all we've got unless DS Jarrod pops his head over the parapet.'

Danskin looked aghast. Glanced at Sangar and Kinnear. 'You told them?'

'Yes, I did. They're sworn to secrecy, but they needed to know what's at stake.'

'We've all got Ryan's back, sir,' Ravi reassured. 'I can't even imagine what he's going through.'

'Aye,' DCI Kinnear agreed. 'I don't approve, mind. It's against everything we stand for.'

Danskin pushed his seat back. Rose to his feet. 'And you think I don't fucking know that?'

'Hey, Stephen. I'm still on your side...'

'Then behave as if you are. Keep your shitey inquest until we've got Yu - and Jarrod's got his family.'

'Gentlemen,' Maynard said calmly, 'We've got work to do. We need to put differences behind us and get on with the operation.'

Danskin flopped back down in his chair and tried to focus on the streetlights of Gateshead twinkling into life on the south bank of the Tyne. How he wished a light would spring to life in his head and illuminate the way forward.

Sam Maynard read his thoughts. 'Things aren't as bleak as you might think. Ravi, tell DCI Danskin what you've discovered.'

Danskin shifted in his seat and through the fog of exhaustion concentrated on Sangar's words.

'Okay. I started at the beginning like the Merseybeat lot did and went back to the *Tulpen Uit Amsterdam* lorry and its convoy. As you know, at least one of the vans travelling with it travelled both north and south. It displayed false garage plates, and we feared they'd have been ditched. Well, the OCG isn't fool proof. They made a mistake. The van's using the same garage plates.'

'We know that for a fact?' Danskin asked.

'Aye, we do. It's had three hits on ANPR. All at different locations. All random. Doesn't seem to be any pattern to where it's turning up, so we can't second guess its next location.'

'Interesting. Where's it been? Any knowledge of drug activity around its locations?'

Ravi snickered. 'There's drugs everywhere, man, but nothing major.' He referred to notes on a tablet he had with him. 'Wallsend, down near the old shipyard site. Denton Burn, near the Royal Mail depot, and at a scrapyard in Swalwell.'

Gavin O'Hara interrupted apologetically. He came bearing gifts, a tray laden with coffee and energy bars. Danskin downed a black coffee as if it were beer. Once O'Hara was out of earshot, he spoke again.

'No pattern there, as far as I can tell; you're reet.'

Ravi was about to speak again when Danskin held up a hand.

'Just a minute, Sangar. Let's think this through. We've no sign of them travelling any major route, am I right?'

'Correct, sir.'

Danskin scratched the back of his head. 'Look, you all know I hate going off anything that isn't hard facts, but let's speculate for a minute. What if they ARE changing the plates on the van when they're travelling? That's why we don't pick it up on the road.'

Sam Maynard sat back. 'What are you thinking, Stephen?'

'Aw, I don't know, really. What if they use the garage plates as a signal of some kind? Stick them on so anyone from the OCG seeing it knows all's good?'

His voice picked up pace and volume as he became more confident in his theory. 'What if there's a third vehicle in convoy? The other van, perhaps, or – I don't knw…just another vehicle. Checking up on 'em, possibly. The YuTube mob don't want to run the risk of us intercepting phone calls or radio signals, so they go for something visual?'

The room stilled while the occupants considered the idea. Maynard, Sangar, and Kinnear took in coffee, while Danskin's face disappeared into his mug as he drained the last drops.

'Where does that get us?' Kinnear asked.

'It gets me back in front of the cameras looking for another vehicle, for starters,' Ravi said, rising to his feet.

'You can have DCs Anderson and Mowbray from me,' Kinnear offered. 'We'll need more than just you on this if we're to find the other vehicle quickly.'

'Cheers, Rick. Appreciated,' Danskin said.

'Right. That's something to work on, at least. Ravi, you're excused. I want the three of you on this non-stop until you find the invisible man.'

'Ma'am.' Ravi sprinted out the room.

'I've one other question, Stephen, before I let Rick update you with what he's uncovered. Why is this van turning up at these random locations?'

'Just another theory, ma'am, but I reckon they don't want to risk staying in one place. And, I'm thinking, that's because they've got Norman and James Jarrod hidden away in the back.'

**

Ryan abandoned the Civic right where Benny Yu had ordered, in a parking bay off the secluded Pottery Lane, an industrial road half a mile southwest of Newcastle City Centre. Once again, Yu's planning proved meticulous. There's no way Ryan would have found a vacant spot during daytime hours. Yu had time it to perfection.

Ryan climbed out the Honda and surveyed his surroundings. A warehouse, dark and forbidding, loomed behind the spot Yu had chosen for him to park. Ryan looked ahead to the blackened brick struts of a familiar edifice rising as threatening as Mount Doom: the King Edward Railway Bridge.

Ryan glanced back to the car. Amelia remained in the passenger seat, silent, lost, and haunted. She stared straight ahead, her face blank but, finally, dry. She was flat out of tears.

He'd told her he was taking her to the Forth Street station. She hadn't asked any questions, and she was vaguely aware Ryan had pulled up near where she remembered the station was. She saw nothing strange, nothing unusual, in the location.

When he stepped from the car, Ryan said he had a call to make. His words were stolen by the wind, and he repeated himself to ensure Amelia heard him. She had. Amelia Curry had given him a silent nod.

Now, out in a dark, windswept Tyneside night, Ryan Jarrod prepared for the first of two urgent calls.

He pulled out his personal mobile. The screen was dark as the night, the phone flat as a witch's tit. Which left him with the burner phone.

If it was rigged or bugged or tapped in any shape or form, his whole plan was blown. More importantly, with it went the slim chance of recovering his family alive.

Ryan knew he had to get this right.

He closed his eyes, said a prayer to a God he'd long since espoused, and long-dialled the only number engrained in his memory.

**

The HMRC lead, Dave Needham, stood alongside Hannah Graves' desk. 'Who's covering for Amelia Curry?' he asked.

'How many times do I have to tell you? I oversee the function of the port, not its personnel. The only people I have responsibility for are my uniformed officers. The other rotas are up to you and the Border Agency folk.'

'You mean you haven't any intel working on this port?'

'Correction, Mr Needham: YOU don't have any intel working the port.'

Needham looked around. Led Hannah away from prying eyes and eavesdropping ears.

'I know we've had our differences,' Needham said, 'But please don't undermine me like that in front of my staff.'

Hannah leant back against the black mirror which was the window of the lookout tower. 'Sorry to be blunt, but you – or at least someone who works for you – need to understand your priorities.' She chose her words carefully, mindful of betraying Amelia and her sister's situation. 'I'm hopeful Amelia will be back tomorrow. That's something else you should be checking, not me.'

Hannah got a glimpse of her mobile phone screen illuminate and fade, illuminate and fade. Her phone was on her desk, and its rhythmic pulse told her someone was calling.

'It might be Amelia, it might be Stephen Danskin, or it might be Ryan. Please God, let it be Ryan.'

Needham caught her wrist as she tried to manoeuvre by him.

'So, what do we do in the meantime?' he asked.

Illuminate and fade.

Illuminate and fade.

'How many dockings are expected tonight?' she asked, eyes on her phone.

Illuminate and fade.

Illuminate and fade.

Needham had no idea. He made something up on the spot. 'Err, another two on this tide.'

'Is it really so urgent you need cover for two more berths? I mean, the system-generated checks will still go ahead as normal. You'll lose what…four, five part-stops at most?'

Illuminate and fade.

Illuminate and fade.

'Sounds like I don't have a choice, do I?'

'No. You don't. Now, if you'll excuse me, I've work to do.'
Illuminate and
Fade.

'Bloody sodding hell,' Hannah swore.

**

It was Rick Kinnear's turn to provide his brief and, it irked Danskin to admit, he'd done impressive work.

'We've tried to track down Curry's sister's fella. Fortunately for us, Bryn isn't the most common name in the world so, when we cross checked the name against recently known drug offenders in our region, we had four hits.'

'Any one of them leap out and kick you in the nuts?' Danskin asked.

'Hell, yeah. A Bryn Calderwood. He worked for a short while at the Port of Tyne on the forklifts. Even had a couple of trips up north to Blyth, an' all.'

Maynard and Danskin exchanged glances. 'He knows Hetton?' Maynard asked.

'That's one for you to ask Hetton himself, ma'am. It's possible, for sure.'

'Anything else?'

'That's not even the half of it. Turns out his file is part-classified.'

'What the fuck…'

'That's what I thought, Stephen. He's being watched by the Met as a Level Two concern. That's why we've been kept out the loop.'

Danskin whistled. 'Level Two? He's a big player, then.'

'Not exactly, no. But the gang he works for are.'

'Let's guess. YouTube?'

Kinnear shook his head. 'Nope. A rival gang. Calderwood was about to be pulled in by undercover Met officers as part of Operation Tower because of his connections, but it never happened. Calderwood went off-grid.'

'Why disappear if he knew nowt about the Met investigation?'

'I think I can guess,' Sam Maynard suggested. 'In fact, you mentioned the possibility earlier, Stephen. We're into *'what if'* territory again, but supposing Calderwood had inside info about YuTube's movements through his connections with the other gang. It's not beyond the realms of possibility he was using his connection with Amelia to stop Yu's drugs getting through. Maximising the profits of the other gang.'

Danskin stood. Prowled the room. 'It fits. He'd sure be scared out of his shit if he thought Yu was onto him. If it is him, it means Maric wasn't involved – let's face it, he's stuck to his guns throughout – and it stands to reason Yu would come for Calderwood at some point.'

He clicked his fingers. 'The Devil he was babbling on about is Benny Yu, after all. I was right!'

The conversation was interrupted by Danskin's phone ringing.

'Bad time, Stephen. Cut the call,' Maynard ordered.

The DCI looked at the screen. 'It's DS Graves, ma'am.'

Kinnear rolled his eyes.

Danskin slid to accept her call. 'I'm tied up, Hannah. I'll ring you back, okay?'

Maynard waited impatiently for him to hang up. Saw his mouth drop open. Heard him say, 'His exact words, Hannah. I need you to tell me the exact words.'

He hung up.

'Hannah's had a voicemail. Ryan's been in touch.'

CHAPTER THIRTY

Ryan shivered as he prepared to make his second call. He raised the burner phone to his ear, then lowered it again. Swallowed hard.

His position brought back memories. He was close to where he'd scrambled onto the King Edward Bridge, through the gap in the igriddled fence, and walked out towards Geordie Amos.

It seemed a lifetime ago. To Geordie Amos, that's exactly what it was. Ryan's nostrils flared as he drew in oxygen. He made the call.

'I'm where you told me to be. Let's get this over with.'

Benny Yu's calm measured voice came back at him.

'Good timing, Mr Jarrod. Now, firstly, you need to find a spot to ditch the wire. You won't need it again. All you need to finish the job is this phone. Oh, you'll need the gloves and the masking tape, too. How could I forget?'

'Why do I need them? Why divvent you drive down here, give me Dad and James, and take Amelia with you?'

'Because it's not your decision to make, that's why not. Besides, I'm not finished with you yet.'

Ryan felt his knees wobble. The hubbub of traffic from the city centre streets, the howl of the wind; they evaporated at Yu's words.

'Please. I've done everything you asked of me, on time, and to the letter. Give me my family back and go fuck over somebody else.' Ryan knew he was losing the battle with his emotions. He had to get a grip. Had to see this through, and hope others would understand.

'Ryan, my friend. You've done me proud, and you're so, so close. That doesn't mean you've earned the right to piss me off, though.'

Ryan's eyes searched the surrounding streets, sought out any signs of Norman and James, or anyone who might put their lives in danger. He found nothing and no-one.

'You need to put the gloves on first,' Yu's voice instructed. 'Next, wipe down the wire with the cloth and dispose of both.'

Ryan lay down the phone and pulled open the boot of the Civic. As he went to don the gloves, his hands trembled. He made a ham-fisted effort to pull them on, his little finger missing its socket at the first attempt. The gloves felt different to the ones he normally wore; these had a gritty, powdery feel to them rather than the smooth latex of the City and County standard issue.

He tried again and wiggled his fingers into place. As he did so, he sensed Amelia watching him from inside the car, imagined the scowl on her face as she wondered what he was doing.

Ryan picked up the phone. 'Done.'

'Next, you need the tape. That's for your friend. You need to cover her mouth. Remember, if she screams and draws attention, this is over. I needn't tell you what consequence that will have.'

Ryan looked back towards the car. Amelia's face was all he expected it to be, and more. He took a few steps further away and lowered his voice.

'No. She's been through enough. I'm going to walk away, leave her in the car, and she'll be yours.'

'The tape is for her,' Yu repeated.

'No.'

'Yes. You need her to understand that she must do as you tell her. We wouldn't want her to fuck this up for you at the last moment, would you?'

Ryan remained silent.

'Would you, Ryan?'

'No,' he whispered.

'That's the boy. After you've got her nicely taped up, you're going to walk her onto that bridge, and only stop when you're at the spot where you had your meeting with Mr Amos.'

Ryan glanced around him, watching for any activity out of the normal, anyone lurking in the shadows. His heart skipped at movement to his left.

A tortoise-shell cat snuck away, only the mouse's tail visible from its mouth.

'Fucking hell,' he gasped.

'Are you ready to do as I asked?' Yu continued.

'Why would I do that? HOW can I do that? It's hard enough for me to squeeze onto there, let alone drag someone with me. Amelia's hardly going to assume we're going for an evening stroll, is she? She'll struggle, man.'

'Mr Jarrod,' Yu snapped. 'You are starting to seriously irritate me. I don't care how you do it but do it you will.'

'Jesus, man. Why up there?'

'Because you get a nice view, Ryan. The city is all lit up, sparkling like Blackpool illuminations. The bridges, too, and the headlights of the cars crossing them, oblivious to what you are doing. It'll look lovely, I promise.'

'Fuck the view.'

'Very well, then; if you want the truth, I'll give you the truth. Because I will be watching, that's why you're going there. Just like I watched you with Mr Amos. I could be in any building, any vehicle, any shadowy lane. And I can disappear in the blink of an eye. You must know, if I do, your father and brother shall disappear with me.'

'Who ARE you?'

Benny Yu chuckled. 'I doubt you shall ever know. Besides, it is time. You need to do as I ordered. Just in case you don't believe I'm watching you, I shall call again when I can see you're where I want you.'

'How long have I got?'

'You've very little time, Ryan. Very little indeed. Remember I am close, Mr Jarrod, and I have those precious to you even closer.'

The line died.

**

'What did he tell her, Stephen?'

Danskin paced the room, slapped his shaven pate as if switching on his brain, and held his hand out to hush the room.

Maynard and Kinnear followed him with their eyes, back and forth like they were watching a tennis match. The Super saw Kinnear open his mouth to speak but she held a finger upright in front of her lips. Rick Kinnear nodded his understanding.

Finally, Danskin spoke.

'Okay, he told Hannah he loved her, which is fair enough, but it also indicates he fears it might be the last chance he has to tell her. Then came the complicated bit, and why I asked for Jarrod's exact words.'

'Which were?'

He kept treading the same path in the carpet. 'Hannah says his actual words were, *'Tell Stevie I've gone back to where I started. Ask him to look out for Brenda-May White for me.'*

Sam Maynard pinched her nose. Rick Kinnear's brow creased.

'What's that all supposed to mean?' Kinnear asked.

'I've nee idea, man. That's what I'm trying to work out. One thing's for sure, he's never, ever called me *Stevie*. That tells me he's warning us summat isn't right. Getting our attention.'

'Right,' Maynard said, 'Let's break this down. *Back where he started* – where's that?'

243

Danskin wrinkled his brow. Pulled at an earlobe. 'Whickham, possibly. That's where he's from; where he started, where he still lives, and where his folks were taken. If he means where his career started, as a Special he'll mean Pudding Chare. That's where he handled his first case, I believe. Or the old University site where the Tyneside Tyrant started his reign of terror, which was Jarrod's first involvement with us.'

Kinnear shook his head. 'I don't think so. That's too obscure. Not relevant.'

Danskin tisked. 'What do YOU think he meant, then?'

'If he's trying to tell us something about this case, I'd guess he's where all this began for him.'

'The bridge!' Danskin made for the door.

'Stephen: wait! Let's work through the rest of it. Who's Brenda-May White?'

'Never heard of her. I have absolutely no clue.'

It was Maynard's turn to scrutinise what Ryan had said. 'You know, it's a funny way to put it.'

'Put what?'

'He said, *'Look out for Brenda-May White for me'*. Why not say, look after Brenda-May White, or take care of Brenda-May White?'

Danskin screwed his eyes tight, steepled his fingers. 'I don't know...wait a minute – *'look out for'*: I think he's telling us we need to find this Brenda-May White.'

'But we don't know who she is.'

'Get O'Hara to run the name through our files.'

Kinnear and Maynard followed DCI Danskin out the briefing room.

**

'Sir, ma'am: there's no Brenda-May White on our records.'

'Check again, O'Hara.'

'It's pointless. We can't waste time running it again. I've checked 192.com as well and there's only nine people called Brenda-May White in the UK. The closest is Penrith.'

Danskin wiped sweat from his brow. Flicked it onto the bullpen floor. 'It's got to mean something.' He walked away from the others while he gathered his thoughts. For a moment, he felt something register, then it disappeared like a dream on waking.

'How are you getting on identifying other vehicles, Ravi?' Sam Maynard asked.

'Sorry, ma'am. It's taking longer than I thought. I've got three or four possibilities but, really, I'm clutching at straws if I'm honest.'

In the background, they heard Danskin chuntering away, *'Back to the beginning, Brenda-May White, back to the beginning, Brenda-May White.'*

Rick Kinnear shouted across to one of his lads. 'Check with Op Kop. See if the name Brenda-May White means anything to them. It's possibly an alias.'

Danskin stopped chuntering. He stood still as a statue. His face contorted as a whirlwind of thoughts raced through his brain.

'I wonder,' he said to himself. Then, louder, 'Bugger me – of course! Oh, Ryan – you're brilliant!'

Ravi Sangar, Gavin O'Hara, Rick Kinnear and Sam Maynard all stared at him, expectantly.

'Well?' the Super urged.

Danskin composed himself. 'It'll sound ridiculous, but I think I'm right. I bloody-well hope I am. Sangar – you said there were a few possible vehicles linked to the van.'

'Yes, but…'

'Shut up! Just listen. You mentioned Operation Kop, Rick, and we know that stands for *knowledge of possession*, right?'

'It's an acronym, yes,' Sam Maynard confirmed.

'What if Brenda-May White is an acronym of sorts, too?'

Maynard gave it a second's thought. 'It depends on what you think it stands for.'

Danskin smiled. 'How about if it's a reverse acronym? Was Ryan telling us to look out for a BMW? What if Brenda-May White is a BMW? Sangar, is one of the vehicles you've flagged up a Beamer?'

Ravi's mouth fell open. 'It is. A bloody white one, at that.'

Danskin punched air. 'Can you pick out the reg?'

Ravi called up the still images of the four potential cars. 'Aye, clear as day.'

'What are you waiting for? Feed it into ANPR.'

'Do you want a silent marker again?'

'No way. I want a noisy as fuck marker. I want everyone out looking for that car. No, every UNMARKED patrol out looking for it. Ma'am, can you mobilise firearms?'

'Whatever you need, you've got it, Stephen.'

'Okay. This is important. We do not intercept that vehicle until we know Jarrod's family are safe. Stalk the life out of it, but don't move in. Not until either me or the Super give the okay. Okay?'

'You do realise we're putting all our eggs in one basket, don't you?' Kinnear cautioned.

'Yes, thank you. I'm fully aware of that,' Stephen Danskin snapped. 'But it's the only bloody basket we've got.'

'Sir!' O'Hara's voice. Urgent. 'We haven't got time for firearms. The Beamers pinged already. Twice, in fact. Once leaving the Sage car park, then again heading down Bottle Bank towards the Swing Bridge.'

'This is it!' Danskin whispered. 'All units to the Quayside. Now! Any sign of the van?'

'Negative, sir.'

'It'll be there. It has to be, for all our sakes – especially Jarrod's.'

Sam Maynard's eyes shone with admiration. 'It's looking good, Stephen. Well done. Excellent, in fact.'

'Cheers, ma'am, but I don't think this is finished yet. Can I leave you and Rick to run things from this end? Remember, no blues and twos, no choppers, no dogs – just good old fashioned proper coppering.'

'You can, Stephen, but - I'd like to know what you'll be up to.'

He stared out the bullpen windows. Apart from his reflection, he picked out the lights of the Sage building on the far bank of the Tyne. Turned to face upriver. Put his hands on his hips.

'You know that bridge you cross when you come to it? It's right there. That's where I'll be.'

CHAPTER THIRTY-ONE

Ryan turned full circle. He surveyed the scrubland the Honda sat on, watched for movement inside the few cars parked nearby, and listened to his heartbeat drown out all other sound.

To his right, he could make out light reflecting from the green roof of the Utilita Arena, behind him the glow from the Centre for Life. To his left, the bustling bars of the Quayside shone with neon and, directly in front of him, Forth Tower was ablaze with light from the windows of its apartments.

Benny Yu was right. With the correct equipment, once Ryan was on top of the railway bridge, he could be seen from just about anywhere.

Ryan wanted to play for time, but he had none. Neither did his father nor brother. He had to hope against hope Yu would free them, just as he had Maddi and Lance, once he was finished with Amelia Curry.

The thought of Amelia brought him back to his task. His hands were sweating under gloves which had already turned transparent because of it. Through the back window of the car, he saw Amelia's head. She sat still as a mannequin, staring forward. He wanted to throw open the door and set her free.

Instead, he threw open the door and, in one swift movement, bound her mouth with tape.

Amelia's eyes opened wide with shock. Her hands shot to the gag. Tried to rip it off, only for Ryan to grab her wrists and bind them together, too.

Muffled noises came from beneath the tape. An attempted scream, Ryan had no doubt. To be sure she didn't succeed, he wound two more layers around her face.

He pulled her from the Civic. 'I'm sorry,' he told her. 'I've done everything I could. We've hope yet but, if it goes wrong, I want you to know I'm sorry.' He looked at the steps to the bridge. 'We're going this way.'

Ryan felt light-headed. Assumed the lack of food and sleep had finally overpowered his adrenalin. He kept shoving Amelia from behind, cajoling her forward whenever she stumbled - which was often - until they came across the gap in the fence.

Ryan pushed her and she rolled down the scree on the embankment until she came to a stop, face-down in a growth of thistles.

He scrambled down after her.

Ryan felt sick. Memories of Geordie Amos came to him, like a slideshow flickering in front of his eyes. Over the bridge's wall, he saw life as it should be: lights dancing in the river; cars, buses, vans – all moving far beneath him, lit up as if they were automatons in a Fenwick's window Christmas display.

Ryan felt his stomach knot as he cajoled Amelia along the grey shale of the bridge.

They came across a spot where floral tributes lay, he presumed put there by the British Transport Police on behalf of Maddi and Lance. The bouquets were already dead; ragged and blackened by turbulence and diesel fumes spewed out by outdated InterCity 125s as they thundered across the bridge.

He wondered if Amelia Curry had anyone left to lay tributes to her.

When they reached the spot Ryan knew so well, he shoved Amelia to the ground, though she went down as if she was already half-way there.

She lay against the blackened wall, legs splayed wide, head to one side. To Ryan, she appeared calmer, more tranquil, her breathing less laboured than before.

His phone rang.

'I told you I'd be watching, didn't I?' Benny Yu said without introduction. 'You can trust me, you see.'

'You'll keep your word, then, yeah? Dad and James?' Ryan thought his own voice sounded drunk. He put it down to the strength of the wind.

'I will. When it's done.'

Ryan felt confused. The words took an age to register. He blinked four times.

'So, what now?' he said, utterly exhausted. He coughed. Turned his head away from Amelia and retched. Nothing came up.

'I think you know. This has to end.'

'My…my family.'

He could hardly breath. *Is this what a heart attack feels like?* he thought. But he had no pain. He felt nothing at all.

'Your family are safe, Mr Jarrod. That's all you need know. Take comfort from it, won't you?'

Ryan turned to face the shoulder-high, striated wall. He peered through it, down far below him, with eyes which were losing their focus.

He saw a vehicle flash its headlights from a partly concealed parking bay somewhere around Skinnerburn Road. Was it a white BMW? He had no way of knowing.

The voice on the phone, dim and distant, spoke to him once more.

'Goodbye, Ryan. Thanks for everything.'

Ryan lost the feeling in his legs. His hands. He heard the phone hit the gravel alongside him. He struggled to peel away the tape around Amelia's mouth with fingers which refused to function as they should.

Her face was a deathly white, lips purple, eyes flitting behind closed lids. He felt for a pulse. Panicked when he couldn't find one, then realised he still wore the gloves.

Ryan fumbled around until a glove peeled from one of his hands. A white clump of something, congealed by his sweat, fell from it.

'Amelia,' he thought he'd said, yet no words came. 'He's a bastard, isn't he?' were the next words he tried but failed to utter.

His head pulsed noisily, like a rumble of thunder in his ears, and the sound seemed to become louder and ever closer.

Ryan felt himself tip forward. His head hit something cold and metallic. His vision swam. He blinked, and his sight cleared enough for him to recognise the outline of something next to him, its opening stretched and warped like a used condom.

For a split second, he wondered about him and Amelia, then sighed in relief when he recognised it as the mouth of his discarded glove, congealed powder clinging to its maw.

Powder.

Before his world faded to grey, and between bursts of manic, insane laughter, he managed to mumble two words.

'Fucking fentanyl.'

**

At the top of a black stone parapet, Stephen Danskin fought for breath after the exertion of the climb.

He stood alongside a diamond-patterned wire fence. The hole in it invited him through. He could see little in the darkness, and he needed a closer view. Danskin accepted the fence's invitation.

Once through, he spread his arms wide for balance and surfed down the embankment on a wave of shale.

Oddly, there was more light trackside than from above, a downward sliver of faint moonlight cast ghostly speckles off the pearlite steel track and refracted back up from the fuggy halo threatening to envelope the Quayside.

In the half-light, Danskin saw something up ahead. It looked like a bin-liner lying next to the rail. His stomach told him this was no bin-liner.

It only needed a few strides for him to realise it had to be Ryan. Danskin found walking on gravel awkward. He stepped between the rails, discovered more purchase on the sleepers, and increased his pace.

He quickly knew he'd been right. It was Ryan. He lay on his stomach, head turned to one side, almost against the rail.

'Ryan!' Stephen yelled into the gale.

Ryan remained still.

'Ryan! It's me – Stephen Danskin.'

No movement.

'It's Stevie,' he tried, hoping the codename would provoke a response.

When it didn't, he bent almost double against the wind and broke into a sprint. He tripped on a sleeper, sprawled on the gravel, his hands grazed and bleeding from the sharp stone. He scrambled to his feet and resumed at a jog, hopscotching from sleeper to sleeper.

As he did so, it dawned on him how little room there was for manoeuvre. The bridge, which had appeared so wide from below, was almost entirely taken up by track. Sure, there was room for trains to pass, but they must come damn close to the wall.

Danskin wiped grit and dirt from his palms.

'Ryan!' he called again. 'Jarrod, are you okay?'

Stupid question.

Danskin pulled the mic on his lapel close to his mouth. 'Control, this is Sierra Victor Two. I need paramedics to the King Edward Bridge. Urgent.'

'Received. They'll be on their way as soon as.'

'Not good enough. I need them now.'

Danskin switched off the radio. Didn't want the distraction of listening to updates.

He was half-way to Ryan when he saw something behind the prone detective. It was a pair of legs, feet upturned against the track. They belonged to a young woman, presumably Amelia Curry.

Her impossibly wide eyes stared into space. The woman sat propped against the bridge wall, motionless, her head slightly turned, a mortal incarnation of Bride of Chucky.

There wasn't a flicker from either Ryan or Amelia.

'Bollocks.'

Danskin sensed a frisson in the air, like the moments before a lightning storm. His hair stood erect from his scalp as a crackle and burst of static appeared above his head. A bright flash grabbed his attention. Then, a spark. And another.

Danskin heard it: a sound like a hurricane, building and strengthening. The gravel beneath his feet began to agitate and shift. Two beams of brilliant white light illuminated the curve of the track at the south end of the bridge.

He couldn't see the metallic beast, but he knew it was there; knew it was coming.

'Oh shit, shit, shit!'

CHAPTER THIRTY-TWO

'What the hell's happening on that bridge, Rick?'

'I dunno, ma'am. Control say Danskin cut the radio after requesting medical assistance.'

'Who for? Is he hurt?'

'That's all I know, ma'am. Medics are furious they've got nowt to go on.'

'Goddamit!' Sam Maynard flung her pen against the bullpen wall. 'This is all going to shit and back.'

DCI Kinnear couldn't argue with her assessment. It was, indeed, going to shit and back.

The atmosphere in the bullpen was both frantic and frenetic. Ravi Sangar adapted the SAGE technique in order to track the location of all units. He also kept an eye on ANPR alongside Gavin O'Hara, who wore a set of headphones at a jaunty angle as if were mixing tracks in a nightclub.

Nigel Trebilcock had dashed down to the Quayside area with a couple of DCI Kinnear's mob while the rest of Rick's crew co-ordinated activity and monitored radio traffic.

Gavin O'Hara's voice cut through the din. 'Ma'am! Over here. Quick!'

'What is it, Gavin?'

'The van's just pinged. It's got its garage plates on again.'

'Where?'

'We've spotted it heading down Bottle Bank. Looks like it could be meeting up with the BMW.'

Maynard looked at Kinnear. 'Perhaps all's not lost, Rick. This could be it.'

She grabbed control of the radio. 'All quayside units – we've got action. I want all access to the quayside denied from Dean Street, the Ouseburn and the City Road areas. No more traffic permitted into the area.'

She moved the radio from her lips. Brought it back to her face.

'As for the BMW and the van, softly, softly does it. Do not intervene until I signal. Repeat: hold your position until I give the word.'

Superintendent Maynard looked at Kinnear who nodded his approval.

'All units confirm this message is understood,' she concluded.

**

On the bridge, Stephen Danskin ran towards the two figures lying prone against the railway track.

The Azuma let out a predatory growl as it waited at the red signal on the southern approach to the bridge. Danskin knew he had little time. As soon as its designated platform was vacated, it would be on the move again.

He got to Ryan just as the noise built once more.

The beast had begun its charge.

The DCI grabbed Ryan around the shoulders and tried to drag him away from the track. Jarrod was so heavy. Heavy, and greasy from track oil and the blood which still leaked from his arm wound.

Ryan Jarrod was going nowhere.

Danskin reached over Ryan and wrapped both arms around Jarrod's legs. He gave a mighty heave, and Ryan's face slipped from the track and fell into Amelia's lap.

Amelia herself remained upright; her only movement a slight shift of her head as it listed further to one side with Ryan's weight.

Danskin seized her ankles and swivelled them away from the track just as the approaching wind became a gale, and the gale became a tornado. Even at less than half-speed, he felt the force of it rip hair from his scalp.

As he rolled Amelia against the bridge wall, a horn blared so loudly Danskin thought his chest would explode. He threw himself over the pair of them, so close to the fence his arm poked through and dangled down towards the Tyne far below.

The train forced a tsunami of air in front of it which hit Danskin with the intensity of a thunderbolt. The momentum slammed his face against the bridge wall, drove the unconscious girl against his chest. All air bellowed from Danskin's lungs.

In a split-second, the wind direction reversed as the train's cab passed the trio. Now, it pulled and sucked at them, inviting them to sample the irresistible force of the Azuma.

Danskin felt the laws of physics drag him inexorably towards the beast's gigantic metal wheels.

**

The van turned left at the Newcastle side of the Swing Bridge, away from the Quayside and a gathering of unmarked City and County Police vehicles.

Instead, it travelled along The Close, so steadily it was almost invisible to the throng of partygoers on the streets.

Outside The Copthorne Hotel, a handful of domiciliary staff wheeled out trolleys laden with laundry. Again, no-one noticed the van.

Where most traffic would continue uphill, the van turned left; onto the narrow, sheltered Skinnerburn Road. A couple of hundred yards in, it flashed its lights and received a response from a parked-up white car.

Half a mile further on, the van turned right at the entry of Shot Factory Lane, stopped, reversed out onto Skinnerburn Road again, and retraced its steps back towards the BMW.

**

The noise of the train was terrific; the heavy bass *whoomph* as each carriage passed instantly replaced by the high-pitched shriek of metal gripping metal.

Danskin scrunched his eyes tightly shut. Sensed the Azuma thunder inches from his head. He felt the heat of friction as the wheels bit. Heard electricity pulse through the overhead cabling; and his nostrils filled with the stench of fumes and scorched metal.

Then, almost as frightening, came an absolute silence.

Danskin raised his head and watched the rear of the last carriage disappear into nothingness as the train took the bend into the Central Station.

The beast was gone.

He lay still for a moment, revelling in peace and the realisation he was alive.

He was alive, but were the others?

Danskin turned to Alice. Felt for a pulse. There wasn't one. 'Fuck.'

He put his cheek to her lips. A light breath. He sighed with relief, before wondering if it was just his imagination. He leant in again. The wind atop the bridge meant it was impossible for him to be sure.

Danskin rolled her off Ryan and checked him, too, with the same inconclusive result. He slapped Jarrod's cheeks.

'Come on, Ryan. Come on, son.'

Danskin's police radio slipped from its holder. Settled beneath Ryan's head. The DCI clawed it out from beneath him and felt for the panic button standing proud from the radio's surface.

With fingers numb from shock and effort, he depressed the button. He now had ten seconds of airtime which allowed him to cut across all channels.

Danskin opened his mouth to raise the alarm. Instead of words, he spewed vomit into the speaker.

He hoped they'd get the message.

**

'What was that?' Sam Maynard asked.

'A panic alert.'

'Was it Stephen's signal? It was, wasn't it?'

Abi Leigh – one of Kinnear's least experienced detectives – confirmed the alert came from the radio of Sierra Victor Two: Stephen Danskin's issue radio.

'I didn't catch what he said, ma'am', Abi reported.

'I don't need any words to interpret that. Ravi – any update on the ETA of the paramedics?'

Sangar tapped at his keyboard. 'Around three minutes away, ma'am.'

'Can they access the bridge?' Maynard queried.

'Never get an ambulance along it, but they can access on foot. Subject to trains, of course.'

Sam Maynard and Rick Kinnear froze like statues.

'Jesus Christ!' they said, together. 'Gavin, has anybody told Transport what's going on?'

The look on O'Hara's face told Maynard all she needed to know.

'Do it. Now. Stop all traffic. It's the bloody east coast mainline. There'll be trains right, left and centre.'

Kinnear checked his watch. 'London train is due in on the half hour, ma'am. It's now thirty-five.'

'It went through before Stephen's alert?'

'We can't be sure the train was on time but, if it was...' He left the sentence hanging. The shake of his head indicated there was nothing left to say.

Maynard felt her legs wobble. She rested against a chair. Plonked herself down in it.

'Ma'am,' Kinnear picked up again, 'I'm no expert but I'm pretty sure the London to Edinburgh train is usually followed into the Central by a Cross-Country. If Stephen and co evaded the Azuma, they'll be lucky to do it again. We either need the electrification cut before the next one comes or pray it makes its approach via the High Level and not the King Edward.'

'Get a shift on with the Transport Police,' the Super bellowed at O'Hara. 'I need that power off ten minutes ago.'

**

The van crawled down Skinnerburn Road and came to a halt alongside the parking bay which housed the white BMW of Benny Yu.

The bays were too slim to accommodate the van. It stayed on the narrow road, hazard lights flashing, the route to the quayside blocked by its presence.

A Skoda drove by in the opposite direction. Its driver didn't give the van a second glance. Nor did the woman behind the wheel of a Fiesta which followed moments later.

Still the van lingered. The darkened rear window of the BMW slid down to reveal a muscle-bound man sat behind the driver. Next to him, a man of Oriental appearance sat impassively, staring ahead.

The passenger-side door of the van opened. Words were exchanged between the two heavies in each vehicle before the BMW window glided shut.

The horn of an ancient Ford Escort blared as its driver braked hard to avoid a Ka which pulled out from behind the van. The driver of the Ka pointed at the van, apportioning blame to it. The occupants of the Escort waved an upraised middle finger at the Ka owner.

The BMW and the van remained stationary throughout the altercation. Several moments later, a newly resprayed Mini Cooper made its way uphill. As it drove by the van, the BMW engine fired up. The gleaming vehicle pulled out, and the van driver engaged gear noisily.

The two vehicles rolled along Skinnerburn Road in caravan until they reached the junction with The Close. The BMW indicated right. The van followed its lead.

And the tiny light beneath the adjacent Forth Towers CCTV equipment glowed red.

**

'Ma'am! Sir! We've got them!'

Sam Maynard and Rick Kinnear raced towards the voice, scattering sandwich packaging and spent coffee mugs in their haste.

'Where?'

Gavin O'Hara slipped off his headset. 'BMW and the van spotted by one of Rick's mob monitoring live camera feeds. They've just passed Forth Towers seconds ago.'

'It's definitely them?'

Ravi Sangar joined the discussion. 'ANPR just pinged. It's confirmed. It's them, all right.'

Maynard grabbed the mic. 'All units – we have a positive sighting. Repeat: a positive sighting. BMW and van heading to quayside. Hold for my word.'

Sam Maynard took a second to gather herself. Looked towards Rick Kinnear. 'This is it, Rick. I hope to high heaven Stephen's been right about this.'

'Aye, me too. This is shit or bust for Operation Sage.'

Maynard's face set grim. 'It's worse than that for Ryan Jarrod and his people. Christ, if we're wrong…'

The radio crackled into life. The familiar Cornish burr of Nigel Trebilcock filtered through the static. 'Ma'am, I have visual on them. They've just passed The Cooperage and are continuing along Sandhill. Wait! They've gone straight on at The Guildhall. They're going right along the waterside, so they's are. I've lost visual.'

Another voice picked up the story. Rick recognised it as one of his squad. 'I see them. Suspects still on visual. They're passing beneath Tyne Bridge now.'

Back in Forth Street, Sam Maynard moistened dry and cracked lips. 'Hold your positions,' she whispered. Feeling foolish, she repeated the order louder.

The BMW crawled along the Quayside, stopping as drunken revellers stepped from the footpath onto the road.

A hen party – a dozen or more girls dressed in pink tutus and wearing inflated condoms tied to wire haloes on their heads – sauntered along the centre of the road. The bride, complete with L-plates taped to each breast, sucked a vividly coloured cocktail from a penis-shaped straw. One of her friends lifted her from the road and sat her on the bonnet of the white BMW.

'Shit!' the voice spat from the radio. 'We have potential interference. Suspect engaging with members of the public.'

'Oh, for fuck's sake!' Maynard swore. 'Not now.'

The bride stood. Turned her back to the windscreen, bent over, and mooned at the driver. Then, she stumbled from the bonnet, allowing Yu's BMW to continue.

'Latest status?' Maynard urged.

'All clear, ma'am. BMW on the move again. Van still following.'

Maynard felt herself relax. 'Jesus, this is hard work.'

The convoy crawled past Trinity Chambers. More folk poured from The Hooch, dancing, singing, and laughing.

A white car passed them; a van close behind. No-one gave the vehicles a second thought.

Until the rear door of the van flung open and a body, trussed like a roll of carpet, slipped from the rear of the van.

A girl screamed.

The crowd turned to look. Saw a second object fall to the road. People fumbled for their phones, eager to capture the scenes on camera.

But the van was already gone, accelerating after the speeding BMW.

'Ma'am, two objects have been jettisoned from the rear of the van. Looks like bodies. Convoy on the move, at speed.'

Maynard screamed into the radio. 'All units: go, go, go!!'

CHAPTER THIRTY-THREE

Oblivious to the activity on the roads beneath him, Stephen Danskin saw the revolving lights of the paramedic first response vehicle flash on the road nearest to the King Edward Bridge.

He saw a flashlight roam over the railway track as the paramedic searched for Stephen, Ryan, and Amelia. Danskin ran towards the beam, waving and crossing his arms above his head. The light settled on him, and he beckoned the paramedic towards him with frantic gestures.

The medic shook his head. Pointed at something. Seemed to shout but the wind was in the wrong direction and carried his words away. Danskin saw an ambulance pull up close to the medic.

'You haven't time to wait for your mates, man. Get down here, now!'

Again, the medic pointed towards something above Danskin's head.

Shit!

The power was still live. Which meant another train may arrive any second.

Double shit.

The DCI glanced back and forth between Ryan and the paramedic, paralysed by indecision.

Something changed. Danskin wasn't sure what it was, at first. Then he noticed the absence of white noise; the hum which had been a constant companion since setting foot on the bridge.

The power had been cut, and the paramedic and ambulance crew were scrambling down the embankment.

Danskin raced back to Ryan.

'They're here, son. Just stay with me, yeah? We'll get you fixed in no time.'

One of the ambulance crew was first on the scene. He was the youngest, fittest, but most inexperienced of the three attendants. When he saw the blood seeping through Ryan's shirt, his first reaction was to tend the wound on his arm.

'Forget his bloody arm, man.'

The medic turned his head towards Danskin in a *'Don't tell me how to do my job'* way, staring up at him through his ppe visor.

'It's not his arm that's the problem,' Danskin explained. 'I'm pretty sure he's been drugged.'

The medic opened his equipment bag. 'Do you know what he's taken?'

Danskin was pretty sure he did know.

'Pervitin, possibly…

'Thanks.'

'…but I think it's more likely to be fentanyl.'

The paramedic shot backwards as if he'd been poked by a cattle prod.

'Have you touched him?' the medic asked from as safe a distance as he could get.

A female paramedic arrived at scene. 'I'm Marianne,' she said. 'What have we got?'

'I'm almost certain it's fentanyl.'

Marianne sucked air between her teeth but didn't retreat like her colleague. 'Both of them?' she asked as she pulled on a second layer of gloves.

'Probably, yeah.'

Marianne jabbed Amelia in the thigh with a Naloxone pen as she quickly updated the third medic. He responded by grabbing another pen and injecting Ryan with the same adrenalin concentrate.

'Have you touched either of them?' Marianne asked.

'I asked him that,' the first man on the scene said, keen to show his worth.

'I checked for a pulse and any breathing,' Danskin confirmed.

'No CPR? No mouth-to-mouth?'

Danskin shook his head. Realised the woman's concentration was on her patient. 'No,' he vocalised.

'How are you feeling?' Marianne's colleague asked.

'Like I've been hit by a train. No, seriously, I'm okay.'

'We'll need to check you out.'

'I'm not going anywhere,' Danskin replied.

Through the shrieking wind, the DCI heard a faint noise. A groan. He looked at Ryan. Saw his eyelids flutter open, then close again.

'Thank fuck for that. Aboot bloody time, lad,' Danskin whispered.

'He's not out the woods yet. Marianne, how's the lassie?'

'She's not responding. I'll administer a second dose. They'll both need oxygen.' She reeled off a list of other items. 'Robert, go got them.'

The youngest of the three disappeared back to the ambulance, relieved to abort the scene. And the fentanyl.

'You're Danskin, I presume?' Marianne belatedly asked. When he confirmed, she told him he really should get himself checked out, pointedly adding 'Although, if it is fentanyl, it's fast acting. I'd think you'd experience some effects by now. No dizziness? Nausea?'

Danskin looked at the pool of vomit around his radio. Considered it for a moment. 'None,' he concluded.

'He's coming round,' the male paramedic said. 'Early days, mind.'

Stephen looked at Ryan. Saw his protégé offer a weak smile. Danskin winked back.

'Assuming it is fentanyl, any idea how they were exposed to it?'

'Not a clue,' Danskin said.

'Gloves,' Ryan whispered.

All three stared at him.

'What did you say?'

'Through my pores. From the gloves.' He waved a limp hand in the direction of the gloves Yu had given him. 'And the tape for her.'

Ryan's eyes closed. Fluttered open. Rolled back in his head. His body stiffened. Jerked.

'He's fitting,' the paramedic said. He reached for his bag. 'Administering diazepam.' He stripped off his hi-vis vest and used it as a cushion for Ryan's head. 'We need Robert back here with the rest of the kit.'

Marianne looked towards him. 'We need more than that. We need the air ambulance. She's slipping into respiratory arrest.'

**

'Urgent update required,' Sam Maynard yelled into the radio.

A muddled chatter of voices, all speaking over one another, replied.

'Tango India Three. You go first.'

'Vehicles still together, ma'am. Picking up speed. All other traffic barred from entry.'

'Are both vehicles still on Quayside?'

'Yes, ma'am. They've just passed exit to City Road without taking it.'

'Yankee Delta One – any news on the condition of the hostages?'

'Ma'am, I can confirm I've seen one sitting upright,' Trebilcock's voice replied. 'I don't have visual on second.'

Maynard puffed out her cheeks.

Another voice came over the radio.

'I think we've spooked them. They've spun three-sixty. Heading back the way they came. Repeat – suspects retracing their route.'

'Aw fuck,' Maynard swore without cutting the mic.

Ravi Sangar looked up from his monitor. 'If they continue, we have a stinger unit deployed at the junction with Broad Chare.'

'This is our chance.'

Rick Kinnear tisked. 'There could be a lot of collateral damage. It's busy around there. If they lose control, they could wipe out a dozen or more bystanders.'

'Do you want these fuckers caught or not, Rick?'

He sighed. 'Let's do it.'

Maynard ordered the stinger unit to prepare.

A cop in plain clothes positioned himself in the shadows of the Cat Café. He could see the BMW approaching at speed, the van close up behind. Although the officer could see them, he was hidden from the drivers lines of sight.

The cop flicked his wrists as if he was fly fishing. The stinger snaked across the road with perfect timing.

The wheels of the BMW hit the steel spikes. Three pops confirmed a clean hit. The stinger was designed to bring its target to a slow, controlled halt, but there was always a risk it could go wrong.

This time, the stinger did its job. The BMW skidded, but the skid was in a straight line. What none of the City and County force had considered was the proximity of the van to the car.

The BMW decelerated. The van didn't – and it was right up the arse of the white car.

The van shunted into the rear of the stricken car with the effect of a flipper on a pinball machine. Flattened tyres or not, the BMW spun in a series of circular movements, somehow evading the bollards separating the road from the cycle path.

Like a waltzer car, the BMW continued to spiral. It crossed the cycle route, skidded onto Hadrian Wall's Path, and only began to slow as it approached the riverside.

In super slo-mo, the car edged towards the riverbank. It brushed aside a steel rail. It teetered on the brink of the quay but held its position. Slowly, tantalisingly, it rocked. Once. Twice.

And disappeared over the quay into the Tyne.

The stinger operative raced towards the fence. Nigel Trebilcock joined him. Only the light from the Sage building illuminated the murky water, but it was enough for them to see the BMW float fifteen, maybe twenty, yards from the quayside.

The car bobbed on the shifting surface. Its nose dipped.

And the river swallowed it whole.

With it went its occupants, much as the North Sea had taken Silvia Maric.

**

Ryan and Amelia had oxygen masks strapped to their faces. Ryan was sitting upright, but his eyes were glazed as if he were drunk. Amelia remained flat and unconscious.

Danskin had heard the commotion via his radio. The vomit spillage meant it worked intermittently, so it sounded like a Norman Collier comedy routine.

Still, he'd heard enough to know it was over; that Benny Yu and his YouTube operation were, quite literally, dead in the water.

More importantly, he knew both Norman and James Jarrod were alive.

'Can I talk to him?' Danskin asked.

'Five minutes max. You won't get much out of him,' the paramedic warned.

'I don't want anything out of him. I just need him to understand something. Will he be able to hear me?'

The medic nodded. 'Sure. He's going to be okay, you know. We got to him in time.' He glanced towards Amelia and his colleague. 'Not sure about the other one. We'll do all we can for her.' He looked to the skies just as the floodlights from the air ambulance picked them out in a shaft of blinding white light. 'Hopefully, cavalry's here just in time.'

The paramedic knelt next to Marianne and helped her care for Amelia.

Danskin spoke to Ryan. 'I know you can hear me, Ryan. Your dad and brother – they're going to be fine. Do you hear? We got them back for you. Sam, me, everyone – we all did it for you, Ryan.'

He held Ryan's hand as he spoke. Imagined he felt Ryan squeeze it in acknowledgement. And nearly fainted when Ryan spoke.

'Thanks, Stephen.'

'You can talk?'

Ryan offered a faint smile. 'Unless you just dreamt it, aye – I can talk.'

'Good. But don't. Rest. You're going to be fine in a couple of days, but you need to rest.'

'Amelia?'

'She's alive.' It wasn't a lie. She was. For now.

'I'm gonna be shot with shit for this, aren't I?' He slipped the oxygen mask back over his face. Inhaled deeply several times before removing it. 'I've risked lives. People have died. All because of me. I fucked up, didn't I?'

'No, man. Howay, think about it. The YuTube line's gone; Yu's gone. How many lives do you think that's saved? You did nowt to Maric. Well, apart from give the Superintendent kittens and shoot a few holes in a hotel wall.'

'Amelia and her people, though.'

'That would have happened anyway, man. No, I reckon you've got a commendation coming your way. There'll be an investigation, an enquiry, for sure. But I bet you'll come up smelling of roses.'

He squeezed Ryan's hand again. 'Now, get some rest, and I'll see you in a couple of days, yeah?'

'Dad and James – you're not kidding me, are you? They really are okay, yeah?'

'Watch my lips. They are fine. Comprendez?'

Ryan nodded. 'Will you do one more thing for me? Tell Hannah I love her. And I'm sorry.'

'She already knows you love her, kidda.'

'Tell her though, won't you?'

A paramedic arrived to attach the helicopter winch to Ryan's stretcher.

Above the roar of the rotor blades, Danskin said, 'I'll tell her on one condition.'

'What's that?'

'You promise me you'll never, ever call me Stevie again.'

CHAPTER THIRTY-FOUR

FOUR DAYS LATER

It was good to be home. Well, not home, exactly, but good as.

Ryan feared the village he'd spent his entire life in would never feel the same, not after everything that had happened.

His fears were unfounded. Even in a silence which could have been uncomfortable, he felt calm, relaxed, and at peace. Norman Jarrod sat one side of him, James the other. Just like old times. Almost.

Doris Jarrod broke the silence. 'It's lovely to see you all,' she said for the third time. 'It's a pity Ernest isn't here. It's ages since I've seen him.'

Ryan cast an anxious glance towards James. Ever since 'it' happened, James had withdrawn into himself, became the sullen teenager of yesteryear. Ryan worried about him. Right now, he worried his brother would say, *'He's been deed twenty years, man.'* But his fears were groundless. James stayed silent.

'It's lovely to see you all,' Doris said again. 'Norman, what have you been up to today?'

Ryan knew his dad would dine out on his stories of the last week for years to come and was relieved when Norman satisfied himself with a 'Not much, really.'

'And Ryan, I see you've brought a friend with you. What's your name, dear?'

'It's James, Gran,' Ryan replied before his brother could speak.

'Well, it's lovely to meet you, James.'

James Jarrod slunk in his seat with a Gary Numan sneer etched on his face.

Ryan didn't correct his grandmother. Instead, he picked a photograph from her bedside table and placed it gently in her hands. It was a photograph of all four of them – Doris, Norman, Ryan, and James. Ryan had no idea whether Doris would recognise James from it, but he thought it was worth a try.

He was about to say something when his phone rang. He took the call by the bay-window of her room.

'You're joking me? Seriously? Is this a wind-up?' Ryan was laughing for the first time in a week. 'No, of course. I'll pay, and I'll be there soon. Thank you.'

Norman raised an eyebrow.

'You'll never guess what? That was the kennels. They said I was overdue collecting Spud. They need the pen for another dog. Can I collect him today, they asked?'

'But I thought you said…' Norman glanced towards Doris. Changed his words. 'But you said they'd sent you a photograph on your phone, didn't you?'

'Aye, they did. It must have been some other poor bugger's dog. I mean, I'm sorry and all that, but old Spud's there and waiting for us! He's absolutely fine!'

'I don't think I remember Spud,' Doris said. 'Was he Maureen's cousin?'

'Don't worry about it, Gran. It's not important.'

A light tap on the door interrupted them. Gordon poked his head into the room. 'Sorry to interrupt,' he smiled. 'I just wanted to say ta-ra to my favourite girl before I go.'

'Hello, Gordon. Ernest,' she said to Ryan's dad, 'This is my good friend. Gordon, his name is.'

For Doris's sake, they all behaved as if they'd never met before.

'Your shift over with then?' Ryan asked.

The man looked sad. 'Yeah. For good, I'm afraid.'

'What? No way, man.'

Gordon shrugged. 'That's the way it is with Agency work. Here today, gone tomorrow. I'll miss the old girl.'

Ryan appeared anxious. 'Not as much as she'll miss you.'

'Don't worry. She might feel something's not right for a couple of days, but she won't know what. After that, she'll have forgotten I ever existed, bless her. Anyway, I just wanted to say goodbye.'

Norman stood. Went to shake Gordon's hand. Remembered the protocols, and satisfied himself with a 'Cheers, mate. For everything.'

'No problem,' Gordon smiled. I'll be off. Take care, my darling,' he said to Doris. 'Be a good girl.' He turned to the others. 'You should be proud of her. Make sure you look after her.'

With that, he was gone. Ryan asked Gran what she'd had for lunch. Doris swore blind she hadn't had any, and the silence which should have been uncomfortable but was anything but, descended again.

'Bloody hell. What now?' Ryan's phone again.

He walked to the window to take the call. Watched Gordon drive off into the Whickham sunset.

'Jarrod,' Ryan said.

'Hello again, Ryan.'

Ryan's spine turned to solid ice.

'You really have been a silly boy. I thought better of you, Mr Jarrod. I really did. And now, I am especially angry with you. I'm not nice when I get angry.'

Ryan's mouth flapped open and shut. No sound emerged.

'You didn't seriously think I, Benny Yu, would be so foolish as to be in that BMW when I knew your people would be fixated on it, did you?'

'But you were in it,' Ryan whispered.

'Then how come I'm speaking to you now? No, no. That was just a poor waiter who my people found working in some abominable Stowell Street restaurant. A few false documents, and you all jumped to the obvious, but incorrect, assumption.'

Ryan lay his head against the cool glass of the windowpane to prevent himself from collapse.

'Now, down to the purpose of my call. As you know, my friend, I like retribution to be swift and painful. In your case, I am making an exception. While it will be painful, it may not be swift. It may be next week, it may be next month, it may be next year. You will never know when I am coming for you but take my word: come for you I shall.'

Ryan swallowed hard. He wanted to speak but knew the terror in his voice would show. He didn't want to give Yu the satisfaction. Instead, he listened.

'You see, Ryan, I want you to be so terrified you'll wish you wore nappies. Every time a car cuts you up, every time someone steps out in front of you, and every time your phone rings and nobody's there, I want you to think of me, and I want you to shit your pants very loudly and very messily.'

'You bastard,' Ryan whispered.

'Yes, I am rather, aren't I?' Yu laughed.

'You won't get away with this.'

'Oh, I will. But I'm not finished yet. You need to listen and listen well. It's not only your good self you need worry about. I've already taken your father and brother once. I can do so again. And then there's that pretty girlfriend of yours. Think what fun I could have with her.'

'Don't you dare!'

'And what about your dear old grandmother?'

'No chance. You wouldn't get an opportunity to get anywhere near her.'

'Wouldn't I?'

'No. You wouldn't.'

'I think I would, you know. After all, you've just seen how easy it is for me to get someone inside that institution you call a home?'

Ryan froze, his thoughts scrambled. 'You mean Gordon?'

'No, I mean Goran. But remember - never contradict so, when Mrs Jarrod named him Gordon, Gordon he became.'

'He's one of yours.' It wasn't a question.

'One of many, yes.'

Ryan was aware he'd sunk to the floor. He vaguely heard Norman ask if he was alright, even James seemed concerned. Doris told them to leave him if he needed his beauty sleep.

'Mr Jarrod, it's time for me to go. You need to understand we shall meet again. I already know when. You, of course, never will. Until it's too late.'

Yu chuckled, devilishly.

'Sooner or later, I'll see you for one final time, my friend. *Yi hui jian.*'

Yu stopped speaking. In its place, music played.

Ryan knew the tune well. He felt tears crawl down his cheeks, even before the strained vocals arrived to haunt his soul.

'Every breath you take
Every move you make
Every step you take
I'll be watching you.'

******

Acknowledgement:

To you - for taking the time to read Operation Sage. Your interest and support mean the world to me.

If you enjoyed this, the fifth Ryan Jarrod novel, please tell your family, friends, and colleagues. Word of mouth is an author's best friend so the more people who know, the greater my appreciation.

I welcome reviews of your experience, either on Amazon or Goodreads. Alternatively, you can 'Rate' the book after you finish reading on most Kindle devices, if you'd prefer.

If you'd like to be among the first to hear news about the next book in the series, or to discover release dates in advance, the best way is to follow me by:

Clicking the 'Follow' button on my Amazon book's page
https://www.amazon.co.uk/Colin-Youngman/e/B01H9CNHQK

OR

Liking/ following me on:
Facebook: @colin.youngman.author

Thanks again for your interest in my work.

Colin

About the author:

Colin had his first written work published at the age of 9 when a contribution to children's comic *Sparky* brought him the rich rewards of a 10/- Postal Order and a transistor radio.

He was smitten by the writing bug and has gone on to have his work feature in publications for young adults, sports magazines, national newspapers, and travel guides before he moved to his first love: fiction.

Colin previously worked as a senior executive in the public sector. He lives in Northumberland, north-east England, and is an avid supporter of Newcastle United (don't laugh), a keen follower of Durham County Cricket Club, and has a family interest in the City of Newcastle Gymnastics Academy.

You can read his other work (e-book and paperback) exclusive to Amazon:

High Level *(Ryan Jarrod Book Four)*
The Lighthouse Keeper *(Ryan Jarrod Book Three)*
The Girl On The Quay *(Ryan Jarrod Book Two)*
The Angel Falls *(Ryan Jarrod Book One)*

The Doom Brae Witch
Alley Rat
DEAD Heat

Twists *(An anthology of novelettes)*
****

Printed in Great Britain
by Amazon

38221585R00157